Battl

From _____ nced out,
piercin_____ y struck,
then _____ citors re-
charge_____ ng, spar-
kling, glittering, deadly, over the waiting
world of Acheron.

Beams burst forth, straight-line lances containing hundreds of trillions of watt-seconds of
energy. The targets moved, and the speed of
light actually began to seem slow. A beam
struck a ship squarely on an armor plate. Three
meters of plastic-ceramic-titanium honeycomb
was chiseled out of the plate. Engines produced
multiple trillions of watts of power, which was
hungrily consumed by drives, guns, support
systems. Every ship tried to avoid being where
the next beam would pass.

Hours passed. People died. And on the minds of
every combatant, on both sides, one question
outweighed all others. *Where are the Missiles?*

NOT IN OUR STARS

JEFFERSON P. SWYCAFFER

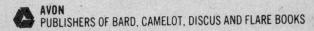

AVON
PUBLISHERS OF BARD, CAMELOT, DISCUS AND FLARE BOOKS

NOT IN OUR STARS is an original publication of Avon
Books. This work has never before appeared in book form.
This work is a novel. Any similarity to actual persons or
events is purely coincidental.

AVON BOOKS
A division of
The Hearst Corporation
1790 Broadway
New York, New York 10019

First Avon Printing, September, 1984

AVON TRADEMARK REG. U. S. PAT. OFF. AND IN
OTHER COUNTRIES, MARCA REGISTRADA, HECHO EN
U. S. A.

Printed in the U. S. A.

WFH 10 9 8 7 6 5 4 3 2 1

Several of the concepts and nomenclatures used in this story are from the games Imperium™ and Traveller®, published by Game Designers' Workshop and designed by Marc W. Miller, to whom all my thanks for his kind permission regarding this use.

—*J.P.S.*

Dedication:

This book is dedicated to
Irene Williams, because of whom,
Glover Davis, in spite of whom,
and the crew of the *Fair Phyllis:*
Susan, Atanielle, and Karyn,
for the joy of whom,
I have written this book.

The fault, dear Brutus, is not in our stars,
But in ourselves. . .
                              —*Julius Caesar*

Though Philomela lost her love,
Fresh notes she warbleth, yes again.
                              —*Thomas Morley*

Chapter One

In her large office deep inside the Spaceport complex at the naval base on Tikhvin, Grand Admiral de la Noue shivered. Outside, through the large plate window, the deep night arched, flecked with countless bright stars, shining coldly through the thin atmosphere of the desert world. Inside, even with the lights blazing, the chill and the darkness managed to invade.

"What do you know of Admiral Michael Devon?" she asked of Captain Athalos Steldan, her chief of intelligence records.

"Devon?" Steldan smiled. "The hero of more battles than I can name? The fighting man's fighting man? The best strategist and fleet commander we've got?" His smile grew lopsided. "I know that he's the most dangerous man in space."

De la Noue nodded. Her blond hair drifted in the never-ending draft from the air-circulation vents. Pacing, her long legs propelling her from end to end of the room in search of warmth, she struggled for composure. Her skin, stretched over high cheekbones, was pale beneath her deep hazel eyes; she breathed on her hands, and returned to her desk.

"He earned his Admiral's stripes at the age of forty-one," she said at last. "He was given command of the Second Squadron of the First Fleet. That year, the Sonallans declared war; he was given full freedom to act."

Steldan looked up. "He's never needed to be given freedom to act; he merely acts. Guiding that man's actions is like guiding a hurricane: impossible."

"He's a hurricane in our service."

"True. He's done miracles for us in the battles he's won.

And I won't say that I don't trust him; that isn't the issue. He is a law unto himself, however, and won't brook supervision."

De la Noue looked away. "Athalos, I may be in danger of losing my Praesidium post."

"Things have come to that?"

"Read this," she muttered, and handed him a one-page document.

He took it gingerly. It had the feel and the very formal look of an international statement of position. Reading it, his face grew grave.

We of the seventy sovereign worlds of the region known as the Philomela Outreach declare ourselves and our worlds independent, free, and beyond the control of the parent body known as the Concordat of Archive.

The paper continued, expressing at some length the Outreach's intentions.

Steldan looked up and met de la Noue's gaze. Her face, youthful for her forty-one years, took on a concerned, slightly confused expression.

"A military solution?" he asked, as gently as possible. She nodded.

"Admiral Devon, better than anyone else, could suppress the rebellion," he said hesitantly.

"It would put him in the field again. He's been chafing at the bit since the Sonallan war ended. Isn't it better to have him at the head of a fleet than idling at headquarters?"

"Perhaps. Probably. I can't help remembering that he was a chosen friend of your predecessor."

"They came to a difference of opinion," de la Noue said unhappily.

"When your predecessor murdered the fleet at First Binary." Steldan thought for a minute. "Admiral Devon has never forgotten nor forgiven that, and never will. He also resented that you were named Grand Admiral and that he wasn't."

"Would you question his loyalty?"

"Strangely enough, no. He may not like you, but he's no mutineer."

"He disobeyed orders at First Binary," she reminded

him. "He stayed behind when he'd been ordered to retreat. Isn't that an indication of a mutinous personality?"

Steldan spread his hands. "He was acquitted at the investigation. He saved eighty-two ships, including his own. He's always been a man to walk the tightrope between mutiny and heroism; he's always come down on the right side."

De la Noue leaned forward in her chair. "I'm giving him a fleet—a somewhat oversized one—and sending him out into the Outreach to pacify it. Do you think he can handle that? To defeat a rebellion without destroying the people and the planets?"

"I think that he'll do very well, as he always has," Steldan said. Shrugging, he rose to take his leave. There was much that needed seeing to in preparation for Admiral Devon's upcoming military adventure.

A knock sounded at the door. Without waiting for a response, Admiral Michael Devon strode in. De la Noue perforce stood to receive him.

Michael, tall, blond, square-jawed, and wide-shouldered, stepped briskly forth and took a seat in one of the chairs facing the desk. His clean-shaven appearance reinforced his decisive air, while his bright blue eyes reflected the lights of the room and mirrored his sky-blue uniform tunic. His gaze flicked across the document on the desk. Without asking permission, he reached forward and snagged it, proceeding to speed-scan its major points.

"So. It's come to that," he said, dropping the paper back onto the desk.

For some reason, the air in the room seemed colder now. De la Noue grasped her elbows and searched for calm.

"Yes. The Praesidium voted unanimously to respond with force."

"And I'm to lead it?"

De la Noue considered descending to sarcasm and quickly discarded the thought. To deliberately antagonize this man would be worse than foolish.

"Yes."

"I can do what you require." He leaned back and relaxed. "How familiar are you with my combat record?"

"I've read the abstracts."

He smiled. "The key word, of course, is 'abstract.' You weren't there; you haven't seen it. Have you ever seen battle? Have you ever had to deal with the problems of making a decision under fire? At the Third Battle of Closse, my beam battery accounted for two and one-half kills. I watched the Captain receive the commendation. At the Frozen Rock, a spinning hell of a battle, I waited while the commander held the ship in ready reserve. We never went in, and men died in our absence.

"My first command was a missile-slinging Escort Destroyer. In the radar-blanking radiation over Tar's World, I showed anew what tactical-use surprise can be. I stood by while another got credit."

He raised a hand to forestall de la Noue's objection. "My sin, in each of these cases, was a minor infraction of the rules. I tended to ignore the exact wishes of my superiors in order to fight a better battle.

"At the First Battle of Binary, I committed a major infraction of the rules. I was ordered out, and I stayed. Do you know what it feels like to be forced to make that kind of decision?"

He smiled, a wide grin beneath eyes that remained serious. "Of course you do. Anyone who has ever had both responsibility and been under the command of a superior officer has faced that choice. My case was unusual only in the drastic nature of the dilemma. I was lucky; I chose correctly."

His smile faded; he became businesslike. "So I'm to be sent off into the Outreach to put down this rebellion."

"Yes."

"With what strength?"

"I've ordered all Sectors to donate toward the fleet that will accompany you. The Line Worlds Sector sent a full-strength Battleship, fresh out of the construction yards. They named it the *Philomela;* it will be your flagship."

"I see. What else?"

"Four Heavy Cruisers; two Motherships full of Fighters; several Shock Cruisers . . . We're still forming up."

"It seems a lot like a wolf trying to clear out a room full of flies." He turned it over in his mind, gazing just over de la Noue's head. "I don't see any real difficulty."

"Your orders will be along soon. I've given you three years."

Michael snorted. "Against that pack of insurrectionists? I'll have them back in line in three months." He leaned forward. "There's more, isn't there?"

De la Noue felt the malice behind the words. Michael grinned mirthlessly, his clear blue eyes boring into hers. She nervously brushed her long hair back from her face. "We'll want you to normalize the situation as fully as possible. The rebellion centers primarily in a twelve-world industrial zone, which should be your first target. Obviously you're not out to punish the Outreach, only to pacify it, and restore loyalty."

He continued to stare at her. "All right," he said at last. "I've some plans. I'll check them out with my staff, of course, but . . . To start with, I'll make the most of counter-revolt. There will be loyalists out there, and I'll take advantage of that."

As always, de la Noue felt unsure of what the man truly thought. Even while speaking to her, he tended to dismiss her, as if she weren't really important to his view of the world.

But if he was opinionated, conceited, stubborn to an intolerable degree, he was also the most capable military strategist the Concordat had.

"It won't be easy—" de la Noue began, and stopped short at the sharp look he threw her.

"Since when is it supposed to be?"

"Admiral Devon . . ." she began, frowning.

"I'll say this once," he ground out. "This is going to be my operation. I'm fighting this one my way. Once and for all, I, and I alone, shall make the decisions that affect my command."

He stood to leave. Before he turned away, however, he favored de la Noue with a friendly, self-mocking expression, a little smile that admitted, gently, that he'd perhaps overstated his case. De la Noue, her anger disarmed before it had fully formed, stood also.

"I'd better see to my staff," he said finally. "I'll see you in three months."

De la Noue searched for an overtone of menace in those

words, so enigmatically had he said them. When he was gone, the room felt no warmer.

In an officers' lounge, Captain Lisa Engel, leader of Michael's Scout and Fighter fleets, met with Captain Edwards of the *Philomela*, with Commander Joan Rogers, the fleet's intelligence chief, and with Commander Arbela Sh'in, the operations and planning chief.

Engel got straight to the point. She was a tall woman, with green eyes in a stiff face flanked by wings of lustrous brown hair, and a strong figure whose outlines were discernible through her flight-brown jacket.

"What do people see in him?" she asked. "Most of his officers tumble over themselves like puppies to gain his favor."

Edwards, older, darker, his face sharper yet faintly worried, answered sourly, "He's strong, imposing, and can command loyalty. While younger men envy him and try to emulate him, the old Admirals stand in the corners and eye him with grudging approval. He's got all it takes."

"One word from him," Sh'in snapped, "one word, one out-of-place action, and I'll deck him." She slouched down in her chair, folding her thin arms before her.

"He'd snap you in two," Edwards sighed. "He could probably whip all four of us."

"Have you seen him in the chart room?" Sh'in continued impatiently. "Does he care where he rests his hands?" She shook her head, brushing wisps of her long black hair out of her brown eyes. Her high cheekbones made a mocking mask of her face. "He doesn't do that when a *man* is on the board." Her black uniform hugged her narrow hips.

"He's like that," agreed Captain Engel. "But we didn't meet here to revile him. We met to agree to support each other when one of us disagrees with him on a course of action."

"What's the use?" Sh'in sulked. "He'll just say, 'Bring it up at the next election,' and stop listening." She turned her sour gaze on Edwards. "And why are you here? You're not a woman. You and Michael should get along fine, sharing 'masculine camaraderie' and the 'healthy respect between two strong men.' " She looked as if she wanted to spit.

"Admiral Devon has the impression that I'm a coward. After the First Battle of Binary—" He stopped, unable to continue.

"That's all right," Engel said quietly to him, resting her hand on his arm. "It doesn't matter now. We—"

"It does matter," Edwards forced out. "Admiral Devon petitioned to have me removed from command. He points to my court-martial . . ."

"You were acquitted," soothed Engel, her eyes worried.

"On a technicality. I'll admit that. And, knowing that, Admiral Devon has assumed that I was truly guilty of cowardice when I led the retreat from Binary. He's determined to have nothing to do with me. He'll only speak to me to give direct orders, or to deliver mild sarcasms that are meant to hurt."

"What do we do, then?"

"All that we can do," put in Joan Rogers. "We serve him as best we can, regardless of what we may feel toward him personally." She was unable to meet the gazes of the other three, who looked at her sharply. Her red hair, in a short pageboy cut, complemented her pink face and her red and white operations uniform, which she pulled tightly about her. Hunched into herself, she stretched her hand out hesitantly to lift a cup of coffee.

Sh'in grimaced. Engel nodded resignedly.

"It's true," Edwards seconded. "This operation is more important to the future of the Concordat than it might seem."

"Idealistic, aren't you?" Sh'in muttered. Engel motioned for her to hush.

"In a way, I guess I am," Edwards agreed. "The events on this frontier will determine the Concordat's destiny for several centuries."

"Funny," Sh'in quipped, "how that doesn't matter to me as much as whether or not we all come through it alive."

Joan Rogers stirred herself. "That would depend upon how well we can work together. And that means working with the Admiral."

"Working with Devon?" Sh'in spoke for Edwards and Engel when, too flippantly, she snapped, "He's the most unpleasant man I've ever been cold-shouldered by. This isn't going to be a campaign of battles; this is going to be a war."

At the party that was thrown to celebrate the fleet's upcoming departure, Michael found himself very much the center of attention. For a while he enjoyed himself, playing the part of the hero-to-be with a savage joy.

Overhearing a remark concerning him, he carefully turned to confront a young officer standing nearby, unaware.

"Fourteenth," Michael corrected him. "I'm the fourteenth in the Devon family line."

The young man was nonplussed; he hadn't realized that Michael had heard him speak.

"And none of these justly famed ancestors ever held rank of less than Captain." Returning to the conversation he'd just turned from, he continued his exposition on the campaigns he'd been in.

"The Sonallans, being five-decimal humanoids, are too damned much like us. There's no trusting them."

Joan Rogers, his companion, nodded solemnly, nursing her one drink of the evening. She started to speak, but Michael, oblivious, overrode her.

"Actually, my father died in the First Battle of Binary," he continued, without anger. "There the fleet was taken out with ridiculous ease. The Sonallans, however, were unable to follow through with the victory. That brought my grandfather out of retirement, and he and I fought together in the Second Battle. He commanded a two-Dreadnought reserve squadron, while I commanded the declined flank. My formation pierced the Sonallan battle line and decimated their support fleet."

"Do you still hate them?" Joan asked innocently.

Michael eyed her sharply, and found an excuse not to answer when two men in Marine officers' uniforms attempted to gain his attention.

"Whom will we be fighting?" one asked. The other, whom Michael recognized as a Colonel Sheffield, stood by, carefully gauging Michael's response.

"They started out as small bands of raiders, hitting our shipping and raiding small settlements," Michael answered, trying not to appear condescending in the eyes of the more alert of the two. "After a while they combined, merged themselves with local planetary governments, and began to absorb functions of those local economies." His answer came automatically, easily; most of his mind was focused on finding a way to get rid of the far-too-observant Sheffield. Hadn't the man ever learned not to stare at people that way?

"Out here on the Trailing frontier, the Philomela Outreach is our best hope for an orderly expansion. If it pulls away and claims independence, it will hurt us more than we can afford."

"And all six members of the Praesidium voted to slap them down, correct?" The question sounded innocent, and Michael treated it as such. Possibly Sheffield was just curious. *I'm more tired than I've been for a long time,* Michael admitted to himself. *I may be imagining trouble.* Nevertheless, Sheffield's attitude irked him. Sheffield, chief of staff for that brilliant General Vai . . . Michael looked carefully at the man. Thick, quick, too clever by half, without letting it show, Sheffield was what Michael rather wished his own staff looked like, with a manly stance and commonplace, dark features.

"The Praesidium of the Concordat can't do anything more than coordinate central responses," he said clearly, answering Sheffield's question a bit too thoroughly. "Grand Admiral de la Noue didn't need their backing, perhaps, but with it, she's got a blank check. The problem is, she hasn't been on the Praesidium long enough to know her way around." *And that's a hell of a lie,* he thought. *De la Noue's danger isn't from her inexperience. I still don't know whose side she's on.*

"Doesn't the Outreach have legitimate grievances?" Sheffield asked. Michael looked long and hard at him, seeing him for the first time as he really was. This man would bear watching.

"Maybe they do," Michael responded, forcing himself to a calmness he didn't feel. "But there are channels for that sort of thing. No planet that condones piracy can expect to benefit from Concordat protection." He realized with a start that a sizable crowd had formed around them, a rough circle with Sheffield and him at its center. The other

Marine, the younger one who had asked the first question, was nowhere to be seen.

"It's going to be a long voyage, folks," Michael called out as he raised his empty glass. "Let's use the evening for something other than talking business." Striding purposefully, he led a small rush to the bar.

All the rest of the evening, Michael felt slightly ill at ease. It irked him that he couldn't pin down exactly what annoyed him.

As officers' parties go, he decided, it wasn't all that bad.

Two days later the fleet departed for the Outreach.

Chapter Two

The *Philomela* hung in orbit, an eighteen-hundred-meter Battleship, a cold, thin shaft against the stars. Seventy meters thick for most of her length, with a hexagonal cross section, her outer surface was sectioned into large plates along her length: armored slabs of thick chainplastic. Between them were the crevices housing missile bays, clusters of laser turrets, and her antimissile screens. Toward the front of the ship, six fifty-meter pods spread, pointed at either end, forming a hexagonal cluster. The rear of the great ship widened into a hundred-meter engine complex, terminating in six thirty-meter engine vents.

The ship's size was deceptive; approaching it on a carefully matched course, an observer would see it as a smallish thing, scarcely worthy of the name "Battleship." Soon, however, as it continued to swell in the viewscreens, other ships would become visible: the tenders, Scouts, Fighter screen, and the two Motherships, themselves huge, that accompanied the monster in their midst. Finally the ship's flank would fill the screen as the ferry ship eased into a crevice between two of the *Philomela*'s armor plates. Engulfed in one of her eighteen hangar bays, the small ship with the observer would settle as the bay control room initiated the smooth transition to artificial gravity. Stepping out of the boat onto the solid deck-grid, the observer would be scarcely aware that he was aboard a ship at all.

The ship's crew was just above one thousand; the elite assault division of Marines aboard numbered twenty thousand, in standard triangular organization. The full fleet had a complement of a little less than 120,000 men and women, and 140 Jump-worthy spacecraft.

The *Philomela* carried 200 short-range Fighters in the

six clustered carrying pods; the two transports *Tegula* and *Later* each carried 450 Fighters. Although each Fighter had armament roughly equivalent to a standard Scout ship, they were not Jump-capable, and were thus dependent upon their Motherships. Often in the past, fleets that were superior in firepower had been defeated before the Fighters had had time to deploy. High-speed launch tubes tended to offset the advantage of place, as well as the standard tactic of dropping out of Jumpspace as far as feasible from the enemy.

Michael wouldn't hear of such a cowardly tactic.

"Do you want to give them warning?" he demanded of Captain Engel, giving Captain Edwards a sidelong glance to sharpen the point. "Refused. You'll have surprise working for you, and that should damned well be enough."

"Sir," Engel persisted coldly, "not all of my pilots have been in combat. I'm not going to risk them by—" She bit back the words, aware that Michael had ceased to listen. *Amazing how well he does that,* she thought bitterly, looking helplessly to Edwards. He spread his hands uselessly. Michael could meet her gaze, face alert, while the little doors behind his eyes simply swung shut. Engel spun and left. Both she and Michael were aware of what it had looked like to the bridge officers present.

Those fools see me as an hysterical amazon, Engel fumed. *Other than Edwards, of course, and what can he do? The rest of them, damn them, see me as having been put in my proper place, without a word, by that strong, silent bastard!* She wished, for the thousandth time, that she was still a pilot, sublimating her hatreds in the heady experience of battle, where when you hit something, it died, dammit!

"Admiral Devon." Captain Edwards spoke hesitantly. "She's right." To everyone else in the fleet, he was "Michael"; to Edwards he was "Admiral Devon." But he had promised to support Engel, and so . . .

"I won't accuse you of being a coward, Captain." That, as far as Michael was concerned, closed the discussion.

If there were much more of that, Edwards knew he'd lose his crew. He'd be unable to give an order without having it okayed by the Admiral.

He didn't expect to enjoy this operation at all.

* * *

Trouble struck in the middle of Jumpspace, the one place, if place it could be called, that ships ordinarily enjoyed perfect immunity from annoyance.

While undertaking Jump, the fleet seemed to move in formation through a ghostly void, all a rich red-orange, oven-hot, where the stars were visible as black dots much like those on a photographic negative. Nothing here could ever be said to change, and only ship's routine kept people from killing each other to relieve their boredom.

Until all thoughts of boredom were dispelled harshly as, aboard the Heavy Cruiser *Vostigée,* the main engines borderlined themselves catastrophically. Despite the best efforts of the ship's computer, the Cruiser folded itself into normal space as its Jump-field ripped apart in spirals, collapsing abnormally.

Damage-control computers worked frantically to stabilize the twisting fields, to damp the engines, to seal the several gashes in the hull. Soon the ship settled into a skewed spin, and the artificial gravity slowly returned. By that time, however, the engine baffles had begun to denature more and more rapidly, their damping force fields fading unevenly.

Aboard the *Philomela,* Michael was the first to understand what had happened, after the fleet-formation compensators automatically dropped the entire fleet out of Jumpspace, with first the *Philomela,* followed by the rest of the fleet, falling into normal space. Michael took instant command, leaping to the control boards without hesitation. Captain Edwards noted that the Admiral's orders were obeyed without any help from him. Although this was as it should have been, it irked him to be treated like a supernumerary on his own bridge.

The fleet was now strung out in an uneven line along the direction of its travel, the ships too far apart to support each other. Captain Engel wasted no time launching the *Philomela*'s Fighters, and word was sent to the other ships to close to a rough battle formation. At the end of the line the *Vostigée* spun into place, visible only through ships' telescopes.

"No enemy in sight," Commander Sh'in reported, her customary casualness no longer in evidence.

"Stay on alert," Michael responded.

What does he think? I'm going to take a nap? Sh'in watched her board with more than usual readiness.

To the first officer of the *Philomela,* Commander Beamish, Michael gave instructions for hailing the *Vostigée.*

"*Vostigée* ejecting life-pods," Sh'in called. Along with everyone else among the bridge crew, she had noticed Michael giving orders to Beamish rather than to Edwards. If that kept up, Edwards wouldn't have a chance of making an order stick.

"Launch cargo shuttles in four minutes. Have two medics aboard each. Half the shuttles are to retrieve life-pods. The other half, under my command, will attempt to board the *Vostigée.* All clear?"

"Perfectly, sir," Beamish snapped. Tonight, in his quarters, his friends would gather to congratulate him on his having been given the de facto command of the *Philomela.*

The rescue effort, set in motion to Michael's commands, proceeded swiftly, almost automatically. Michael himself was the last man off the *Vostigée.* Carrying two downed crewmen and dragging another, he squeezed into the escape pod with only a few seconds to spare. When Commander Rogers, by his side, saw that the corridor held only dead men, she turned to Michael; receiving a high sign, she sealed the double door and hit the jettison key. She had not yet begun to tremble by the time the pod was retrieved.

Shortly afterward, the level of radiation on the dying Cruiser became unlivable, spreading throughout the ship from its disintegrating engine room. The last act of the ship's chief engineer, after he had ordered his men out, was to stay behind to flush the drives. The ship wouldn't explode, at least not on its own, but it would be a radioactive hulk, hanging motionless between the stars.

Within twenty minutes the pod was unsealed aboard a cargo bay on the larger *Philomela.* Room was found for the walking wounded, while the more serious cases of radiation poisoning were treated in one of the Battleship's four sick bays. The hallways and corridors were covered with the injured for a distance outside each sick bay. Periodically a medic would cycle through, making chalk marks on the patients' uniforms to indicate severity of poisoning. Occasionally he would mark a double cross in black. Someone would be found to remove the corpse to storage for later examination.

"What in hell happened?" asked Captain Edwards when a spare moment left him alone with Michael.

Michael turned and stared at him in mild reproof. "Wasn't it you that said this operation was going to be 'a piece of cake'?"

Edwards paled. "Yes, sir. I said that."

"First cake I've ever seen that bites back."

Edwards watched his superior turn and leave. With a start, he let Beamish nudge him aside in an attempt to catch Michael's attention.

"Sir?"

Michael turned back and raised an eyebrow inquiringly.

"What do we do with the wreck of the *Vostigée?*" Beamish gave no indication of acknowledging Edwards's presence.

"Scan it. Try to recover the contents of its computer. Then put three standard missiles into the engine room." Once again he moved down the hallway.

Beamish spun, and passed Edwards by without a glance. To a fire-control officer, he snapped, "You heard the Admiral?"

The officer nodded.

"Well, then, see to it."

Four minutes later the hulk of the *Vostigée* received three missiles near its stern. From the viewscreens of the *Philomela,* the Heavy Cruiser could be seen for a long moment as a bright spark, brighter than the background stars. Then nothing. The three thermonuclear warheads had done their job, and all that remained of the Cruiser was an expanding, thousand-kilometer sphere of radioactive gas.

"It had to be sabotage," Joan Rogers said quietly to the assembled chiefs in the large conference room amidships. The fleet was again under way, no enemy ships having been found in the vicinity of the disaster. Michael regarded her alertly.

"Why?"

She looked down at the files on the table before her, fighting not to blush under the man's intent gaze. He so totally overawed her; she could not meet his eyes. "The ship had had its annual maintenance shortly before our departure; all was five-point normal. The ship's records, pulled by your order, gave no warning, no indication of anything wrong until the drive fields shredded."

Commander Sh'in spoke up in agreement, muttering with unwarranted seriousness, "I helped her examine the records. Whatever happened, happened so fast that even the computers couldn't compensate. That doesn't sound like anything normal, or even something you could do from the main control panel in the engine room. It's more like there was a bomb, or someone cut a control cable."

"I see." Michael looked stiffly at the two younger women. "Commander Rogers, take the stories of every man that escaped the wreck. If there was a saboteur, he likely was the first into a life-pod. You may use the ship's auto-log to see if you can discern which pod ejected first." He looked about. "Beamish, give her any assistance she needs."

And that, silently snarled Sh'in, her wide eyes blazing, *is all that Beamish needs by way of permission to smother Joan with "assistance." He'll end up making the report to Michael himself, upstaging Joan and cementing Michael's favor. If only the kid were a bit more assertive . . .*

Captain Edwards grimaced at Sh'in in an encouraging, comradely fashion, to which she responded by looking at the ceiling and breathing out. *No damned help he'll be, of course.*

Joan was engaged in furious note taking in her file, still fighting away a tendency to blush.

"Then if there's no other business . . ." Michael began.

"There is." Heads swiveled toward Captain Engel, sitting sternly by Captain Edwards's side. "In the future, I'd like better than a fifty-second warning to recall my Fighters."

"In battle," Michael reminded her, "Fighters are often taken aboard with only a fifteen-second warning."

Engel flared, leaning forward over the table. "This was no battle. Furthermore, in a battle around an inhabitable world, stranded Fighters have somewhere to go to surrender. Here . . ." She trailed off. Once again he wasn't listening.

Letting the silence settle for a few moments, he asked gently, "Did we lose any Fighters, Captain Engel?"

"No, but we literally did not have a second to spare. And if we'd failed to pick up even one, I'd have ordered the Mothership *Tegula* to stay behind to retrieve it."

"I recommend that you reconsider that judgment if the opportunity arises again." He let his heavy expression melt into a forgiving smile; the argument was moot. He stood, surveyed the room for a long moment, and left.

Captain Edwards was the next to leave; to avoid appearing as if he were following Michael, he left by another door. The effect was almost as bad. Joan Rogers and Commander Beamish left together, soon followed by most of the remaining officers.

"Engel," Sh'in asked when only they were left, "how do you hold on to your temper when he does that to you?"

"I like to imagine myself beating the hell out of him in single Fighter-to-Fighter combat."

"I know how you feel. As far as he's concerned, I might as well not be on this ship. If there's an operations or planning problem, he'll handle it himself. I seem to be preparing battle plans just for the practice." She slouched back in her chair and drew up her knees, knotting her long fingers around them.

"Why don't we tell him what we think?"

"I'd rather go down to the laundry and pepper his underwear."

Engel frowned and shook her head. Sh'in's flippancy was so out of place here. She regarded the woman carefully, wondering how much she could be depended upon.

"I don't like to think what Michael would say if he knew you'd said that," she said at last, trying for seriousness.

"He might know. Allow me to suggest that this conference room might be bugged."

Engel considered that realistically. It was the sort of thing Michael might do. No doubt the idea that there was a saboteur aboard had occurred to him before the meeting began, and places where enemies might gather to plot had been ordered watched.

"You know something?" Sh'in said in a loud stage whisper.

"What?" Engel hesitantly replied.

In a normal speaking voice, Sh'in answered her. "I think our commanding officer is a screwing loony."

They would never learn whether or not Michael had heard them.

Chapter Three

For years John Burt had been known to his crew as "Two-Pistol John." Aboard a small, stolen spacecraft upgunned into a raiding vessel, they had hovered about the fringes of interstellar commerce lines, picking off occasional ripe merchant ships. It was said of Burt that he could drop eight men in the time most marksmen would take to kill five; the stories told about his many raids, hijackings, and boarding actions were repeated through the Sector, despite his stoutly maintaining that most of the tales were exaggerated.

Not long into his career he had put together a small fleet, with financial backing from unscrupulous benefactors and a good sense of management on his part. Soon, certain planets decided to cooperate with him and pay monetary tribute rather than lose far more money to his raids. Instead of wasting the money, he plowed it back into his fleet, or returned it to his backers in order to finance yet larger loans.

The planets complained to the Concordat, and some of them banded together to raise clean-up fleets. It seemed, however, that the Concordat was too intent upon the war out on the Sonallan rim, while the small, local fleets were unable to clear the raiders from their strongholds. Instead, working both openly and secretly, the raiders edged their way into local control. The planets that aided them thrived, while their foes withered. Within two years there was a substantial raider faction in every planetary government in the Outreach; within three years the raiders were the core of the unified drive for independence.

John Burt was a rare type of person—a man of great tal-

ent who nevertheless devoted himself to theft. When the
raider leaders of the Sector gathered at Graysend, he
emerged their unquestioned leader. When the last Sector
Navy fleet caught his fleet in ambush, he fought clear,
only to turn around and demolish them.

A black-haired bear of a man, preternaturally dexter-
ous, he had risen to the challenge of administering a Sector. Now he was in effect the only government present, and
it surprised many how good a job he did. His justice was
rough, sometimes brutal, but it was justice; he made no
exceptions for his crewmen or for his allies. The planets
were run quite smoothly, and it was he alone that kept
it so.

At times he yearned to return to the spaceways. He
missed the old thrill of the many battles he'd been through.
He had commanded many a ship, had had two blown out
from beneath him, and he had fighting in his blood.
While not a bad pilot, his particular joy had been in
manning the ship's lasers, in lining up the perfect shot
that disabled a foe's engines without ruining the target
for salvage.

He was no fool, however. He knew that he'd never again
be what he once was. The days of the lone wolf were over,
at least in this Sector. Now he was an administrator, and
an Admiral. He knew, without doubt, that sooner or later
the Concordat would respond.

He stood in the middle of a small group of subordinates
and reviewed his plans for defending the Sector.

The fleet?

"Rotten shape, sir. Finding qualified maintenance
personnel is impossible. We have seven hundred combat-
ready ships, in readiness conditions from twenty to ninety-
five percent. Multiplied average is three hundred first-line
ships, mostly small ships, Scout equivalent."

The planets?

"Fortification plan moving slowly. We've got defense
satellites in good spreads around the dozen most important targets. On the ground, we've got high-intensity
missile and antimissile projectors emplaced according to
schedule. We're still short on the missiles themselves,
though."

The economy?

"Sir, we're doing the best we can. The locals no longer resent our presence the way they did. I've given your fleet chief some breakdowns. . . . Once we removed the load of the Concordat's taxing and regulatory machinery, things started picking up. If we haven't seen any real improvements, it's just that an economy of this size can't reverse itself measurably in less than five years."

"Gentlemen," Burt said slowly. Not a man there didn't feel awe at his personal strength. "They're going to come in here soon, and try to take this away from us. Can we stop them?"

His chief of the fleet, Andrew North, thin, nervous, quick, a man who knew when to answer and when to shut the hell up, looked nervously at the planetary defense chief, Robert Bishop. North answered Burt's question. "It depends upon what they send. We could hold off a lot . . . a hell of a lot, really. But if they send an armada, we'll lose."

Bishop, dark hair piled high over his severe face, gave a sour, unsupportive grimace, although he didn't disagree strongly enough to say so.

Burt looked to Harold Court, his ground troops commander. Court met his gaze. To put the question to him would be unnecessary and to answer it pointless. Burt had taken the most personal care with the ground forces, knowing that the fleet was a brittle shield. There was the equivalent of one reinforced division on each of the twelve core planets; although not by any means a match for the elite Concordat Marines, these defenders would have the advantage of place. One of Burt's highest priorities had been the building of positional defenses for these ground troops. Court had not disappointed him.

A far cry from my first crew, Burt thought. *Gone are the old hell-raisers, the intense and witty bastards who'd drink themselves blind, and fight the next day. And gone, too, is "Two-Pistol John." I haven't fired a shot in anger for— gods! Has it been two years?*

He'd tried to be a good governor, a good leader, a bright example for his followers. That meant not staggering out of a drug bar at dawn with an unconscious friend under each arm, as had happened quite a few times in the old days. It meant instead keeping clean, and well-dressed (but he'd be damned if he'd shave off his beard!), and staying sober at all times. He'd learned how to keep control over a larger domain than merely his one, two, or five ships.

If a plebiscite were held tomorrow, how would he do? Sometimes he felt he'd win. Other times, it was only his firm control, rigid but not brutal, that forestalled counter-rebellion. And worse by far than any loyalist troublemakers were the radicals, ostensibly on his side, whose ideals, if adopted, would lead to the bankruptcy and collapse of his would-be free state.

Against these and other obstacles he'd maintained production, distribution, commerce. The people weren't starving—they were actually doing slightly better now than under the immoral treatment of the Concordat—and they were free from raiders. That thought always amused Burt. No would-be rivals had lasted very long at all, and their victims were recompensed from the new government's treasury. Burt did all he could to preserve goodwill.

Would it survive an intervention by the Concordat?

He'd damned well find out.

After the meeting Burt conferred privately with North. The young fleet chief had the most education of any of Burt's direct staff, and therefore served as intelligence and planning chief also. He was one of the few people alive that Burt would defer to, but only in the most abstract of political matters.

"Andrew."

"John. Don't look so glum. We're getting stronger all the time."

"I just don't like it. From the very first, I've had no choice. If I had, I'd never have occupied the planets at all. It's too much like playing into their hands."

"I know. 'If you show them a wall, they'll know how to break it down.' You'd be happier scattering, resorting to hit-and-run tactics. The only thing is, where would you get your supplies?"

"I thought maybe a secret base somewhere that we could retreat to, as well as be supplied from."

"And secret bases have never stayed secret long. How do you put a stockpile of missiles on an asteroid somewhere without anyone knowing about it?"

Burt looked searchingly at his fleet commander. He'd never had any reason to question North's loyalty, yet why was the boy always vetoing his best ideas? *No, that's not fair,* he corrected himself; North simply knew more about such trivial details.

"What we're running here," North continued, "is an older trick. We put our installations on top of the cities so that they'd have to kill their own people to knock our defenses down."

"How do you feel about possible Concordat loyalists in our midst? Should we worry about fifth column activity?"

North grinned at his boss. "We don't, but they do. It's like this: here we suspect every citizen of harboring loyalist sentiments, and we're on guard at all times. But the spies and saboteurs I've placed with the Concordat Navy will be unexpected."

"How the—" Burt exploded. Reining in his temper, he asked, "How did you manage that?"

North was taken aback. "It . . . it was part of your orders to me years ago. You said . . . you said to set up a spy network on the planets we were capturing, and while I was at it, I . . ."

"And you never told me about it?"

"It didn't seem important. There are only a few of them, and I told them to simply infiltrate, and not to do anything unless it came to war."

"What kinds of things are they likely to do?"

"I . . . left that open. I said that if war erupted, they should aid us."

"War has erupted."

"I know that, sir." He straightened. "Can it do any harm to have some behind-the-scenes assassins and saboteurs?"

Burt laughed hugely by way of answer. "You astable, backwashing, pencil-snapping nitwit. Of course you did the right thing! But you sure as decay should have told me sooner! Carry on. For every capital ship you cost them, I'll give you a planet!" He thumbed North roughly in the shoulder and left, more proud of his staff than he'd have thought himself capable.

He already owed North one planet.

Chapter Four

In decades past, when large numbers of troops were transported across large interstellar distances aboard spacecraft, they had been frozen in stasis for the journey. It saved valuable tonnage that would be needed for life support and cut down on the huge amount of food and expendables needed.

The troops, on the other hand, viciously resented the notion of being helpless and unconscious during the trip, completely at the mercy of the ship's crew. The stasis freezing was far from safe, they argued. Demanding live passage, the troops, supported by their senior officers, had staged a ten-Sectors-wide one-hour mutiny.

Now the stasis generators were used for storing the troops' food, life-support allotments were increased, and shipboard boredom killed almost as many men as had faulty freezing. On the *Philomela*, the troops were elite Marines; this cut down drastically on the number of fatalities due to fights or suicides, while it increased the number of broken limbs and ribs from the men's bickering. They knew just how hard to hit a loudmouth to shut him up without badly injuring him.

They were also callous, scarred veterans, for the most part, resistant to the time-filling make-work that General Matthew Vai kept inventing. He knew how they felt; he agreed with them completely. But if they should become a nuisance to Michael, they'd be in for trouble they'd have difficulty imagining.

With Michael's permission, he'd scheduled a rotating system of drills, mostly simulated boarding actions or repulsion of boarders. Randomly selected battalions would spread through precisely defined areas of the ship, preparing assaults or defenses against their simulated foes. Toward the end of the month-long voyage, he'd planned a mock battle between the two highest-scoring battalions, using lasers powered down to centiwatt simulators. He also planned a couple of surprises, to test the officers more than the troops.

Aboard the other capital ships and the four transports, each carrying troops, Vai had ordered similar drills. One month wasn't long, actually, but troops needed something to occupy them. False combat was the next best thing to real fighting in such circumstances.

Vai was of average height, thin to the point of gauntness, and wore his thick black hair a little longer than regulations suggested. Although well into middle age, he would look as if he was thirty until he was eighty, from which point he would look no older than forty. It was said of him by his men that he was more machine than man, which was true; he'd lost a large portion of his body to an artillery duel in a battle some time ago. The prostheses he'd been given were almost as good, and in certain ways better. His men were also fond of pointing out that the part of him that mattered was human.

To his chief of staff, Colonel Sheffield, Vai was a not-so-minor miracle. He was the leader he'd dreamed of: a General with imagination and style. To him and to the men, Vai was like a god: his authority unquestionable yet profoundly just.

Vai himself looked to Michael Devon, if not with awe or worship, certainly with respect and solid loyalty.

"Matthew," Michael addressed Vai, entering the communications room that Vai used to coordinate the current drill.

"Sir."

"Come aside." Michael led Vai out into the corridor. "Can you spare two squads of troopers for each of our capital ships? I'd like to post an engine-room guard."

"Certainly, sir. I'll put them under Commander Rogers's authority."

"No. I'd like them to remain under your command."

Vai frowned. "Of course they still would be. I just meant . . ."

"I know. Matthew, we haven't caught our saboteur yet. Commander Rogers is inexperienced, lacking in fire. Give her a few years. . . . I want someone knowledgeable watching the engine rooms.

"For instance, suppose one of your sergeants noticed something—oh, trivial, but suspicious. He'd tell his lieutenant, who'd tell Sheffield, who'd tell you. What would you do?"

"I'd look into it, I guess."

"Right. I'm not sure I can depend on Rogers. She'd be too likely to shrug it off, not from carelessness, but . . . You see. This is as much for her protection as for the fleet's, as far as that goes. This early in her career, she doesn't need any oversights on her record. And we cannot afford to lose any more Cruisers."

"Agreed on that point, sir." Vai had lost half a regiment on the *Vostigée*.

"I thought you'd understand."

"Yes, sir."

"Another thing," Michael said. His attitude had subtly shifted from an almost guilty reserve to his normal, all-business outlook. Vai understood, suddenly, that it had cost Michael quite a bit to bypass Commander Rogers that way and that, despite appearances, it had indeed been for her protection.

"I've arranged for extra parcels of arms, ammunition, and such to be dropped to the target worlds, with your troops. These will be doled out to the volunteers I expect will rush to join us. You'll have to be careful to differentiate between opportunists and true freedom fighters, but I think the investment will be worthwhile."

"It will complicate things," Vai said crisply. "I'd prefer to pacify the worlds under a unified command."

"You might not have time. I can't leave the Marines behind when the fleet moves on. Time is of the utmost importance in this campaign." Michael lowered his voice. "We have another enemy than the one we've come to fight. I'm sure you'll understand if I say no more, but . . ."

Vai didn't know what this was supposed to mean, but he certainly knew enough to stay silent. Another enemy?

"I'll handle this myself—the armaments drops, that is. No mistakes will be made."

"Good." Michael clapped him on the shoulder and departed. Vai stood in the corridor for some time, considering the notion of a new enemy. It made no sense . . . and in some ways, it made too much.

He shook his head and returned to the small control room. The second battalion seemed to be doing well in the drill, controlling all access points and control rooms against their theoretical enemies. Vai pulled Sheffield aside and in a low voice told him of Michael's decisions. Sheffield nodded and left the room to arrange the engine-room guards.

The drill completed itself, the computer/referee awarding the battalion a definite victory. They had repelled hypothetical boarders by proper application of firepower at the (simulated) hull breaches. They'd had some problem with spectators from the ship's crew, who had tended to wander toward the "fighting." Vai dismissed this; in a real battle, they would stay the hell away from any fighting unless ordered in as a reserve.

The computer drew up the final evaluation: efficiency was over ninety-five percent, in the shady region just shy of perfection. The estimate looked good. Vai asked himself sardonically if he had truly expected anything else. These troops had seen it all; the second battalion had been first on the ground in the pitched battle for Tenh Sonallae, where more had been asked of them than could reasonably have been expected. It was delivered, and more, despite their seventy percent casualties.

He left to confer with the battalion's commander, to give the man a hearty congratulation. The second looked quite good. Soon they'd prove themselves in real combat, where Vai was sure they'd look even better.

The fleet, led by the *Philomela*, swept through the border areas of the Philomela Outreach, bypassing systems that could be considered raider-controlled. These systems, Michael explained, were of marginal interest, and would be cleaned up during the later portions of the campaign. On the bypassed planets, local bands of freedom fighters rose up to overthrow their captors, expecting aid from the fleet. When that aid failed to materialize, the counter-rebellions faded. They were not without effect, however;

the raider governments, seeing the fleet pass them closely by, knew that their time was short. On several worlds, the governments turned over control to local ad hoc formations and fled or went into hiding. And on some worlds, the resistance movements succeeded instead of losing spirit when the fleet gave no help.

Here, in these most conservative subsectors, conservative due to their proximity to the main strength of the Concordat, the worlds would stand or fall following events, not leading them.

When the fleet was one week away from the twelve industrialized worlds that held the Outreach's central power, Michael ordered two Destroyers to return to the border region to assist the locals in restoring order. Even that nearly insignificant detachment electrified the area—by showing that the eyes of the Concordat had not overlooked things there.

It also had the effect of cutting all links between the Outreach and the body of the Concordat. No news flowed; the blackout and blockade were airtight.

Michael operated alone.

Shortly before the fleet was to drop out of Jumpspace to assault Beremer, a minor planet of the dozen central worlds, Michael met with Captain Engel.

"You want me to do what?" Her voice echoed down the corridor. Crewmen grinned at each other, but knew enough to say nothing. In a lower voice she continued, "I will by no means split the Scout fleet into that many parcels."

Michael looked at her with amused interest. "It was not a request, Captain."

"The idea may be good," she said with obvious reluctance, "but single Scouts cannot blockade entire planets."

Michael looked down at her benignly. He had to admire her fire; if only she was as spirited when she agreed with him as when she didn't. "When we've smashed the twelve-world alliance, the survivors will scatter. Your fleet will scatter as well. All this should be perfectly clear to you. Your Scout ships can harass the remnants, trailing them, hitting their bases, and raiding the raiders, all with little or no danger to themselves."

"This fleet has only got forty Scouts along." Why, she wondered, was she explaining the obvious to him? He knew, and he didn't care. His condescending attitude, his listening to her so very patiently when his mind was already made up, angered her almost more than when he simply refused to listen. "In supporting pairs, they could perhaps . . ." She let the sentence die. There was no use.

"The pursuit is the most essential part of the battle," he explained, trying to be gentle. "There will be quite a few space-worthy survivors, who must not be permitted to trouble us again."

"Why don't you let the Scouts form a screen to prevent their escape in the first place?"

"Your Fighters will be deployed to that end."

"But . . ." She pulled in her temper. "Who, then, will convoy the transports down to the surface?"

"Captain Engel," Michael stated firmly, "in the computer, coded under your name, is a copy of the battle plan. Study it. Be prepared to implement it. Come to me if you have any legitimate objections." He turned and left.

Engel wasted no time getting to a computer outlet. The audacity of the plan exceeded her wildest dreams.

Chapter Five

The fleet, deployed for maximum effectiveness, folded itself out of Jumpspace with a precision and suddenness that even Michael had to admire. Within seconds, Engel's Fighter screen was launched, ending the most dangerous phase of the breakout: the brief period during which the fleet had been the least protected.

"Enemy flotilla on post." Data followed.

Michael heard Joan Rogers's voice and nodded approvingly. She was calm, although he heard in her voice the tension, the slight crispness. He was confident that she'd face what came at them without breaking.

Commander Sh'in, of course, sat as relaxed as one can sit and still face one's board. Her computers did most of her work for her, while she spent her time idly monitoring her screens. Michael imagined that her fertile mind was diverting itself in some way; maybe she was composing scurrilous couplets about him. That brought him a bit closer to her in his mind; he'd once sat a board and composed satiric rhymes about his superiors. Even Sh'in, he conceded, had her strengths.

Unaware of his scrutiny, she muttered, for Joan's hearing, "They're mutually supporting. However, we can get them while they're assembling."

Michael strolled forward. "Take us in."

It wasn't much of a battle, as far as elegance went. The fleet moved in, scorning the use of emergency acceleration, and hit the scattered enemy formations like an avalanche. From a distance, the points where the two fleets met were visible as sparkling areas, each twinkling flash of which was a thermonuclear warhead or multi-trillion-watt laser beam touching upon an enemy ship.

Captain Engel worked around the clock keeping her Fighter fleet coordinated. Virtually living on stimulants, she forced order out of the chaotic battle, spending long hours with the boards and with Sh'in. Commander Sh'in followed a less active path, setting up autonomous computer projections in advance and letting them run her post when she was too tired to remain awake. Even so, her sleep was interrupted twice by unforeseen shifts in the course of the battle.

Michael was at the center of the operation and seemed to be overseeing every facet personally. Continually he made the rounds of the large command bridge that controlled the operations of the Battleship, but as often as not he would be found elsewhere: usually in the small passageway that led out from the rear of the command bridge. This area was the fleet command bridge, and here, side by side, Joan Rogers and Arbela Sh'in coordinated the grand strategy of the entire armada. No move they made, no instruction they gave, was missed by Michael; they learned to live with him bending over their shoulders and double-checking their status boards.

Late on the fourth day of the battle, the raiders realized what should have been obvious from the beginning: this battle could not be won. At this point, as they began to withdraw piecemeal, Michael ordered Captain Engel to report to a sick bay. Although she showed the strain in every fiber of her being, she had the strength to tell him where to go. Michael had two Marines enforce the order. Engel was too exhausted to curse them properly and, with only the feeblest resistance, let herself be half carried away.

Michael took command of the Fighter screen, and ordered the fleet to drive the now-fleeing raiders into it. The Fighter strengths of the Motherships *Tegula* and *Later,* previously little harmed, were quickly battered, suffering attrition of almost forty percent. They managed to stop well over two-thirds of the raiders' remaining ships from leaving.

"He's trying to destroy my command," Engel raved when she heard. Captain Edwards stood by her side, where he seemed to be spending most of his hours. He held her gesticulating arms and tried to restrain her furious words.

"He couldn't stand the thought of someone else beside him controlling ships," she snapped.

"He's in command," Edwards said calmly, although his heart was wrenched to see her so.

She flailed the more strongly; Edwards held her. "It's no less than murder." The tears were slick upon her face. Many of the lost pilots were men and women she'd fought beside, and more were youths she'd helped train.

War is murder, too, Edwards thought, and said nothing as Engel's rage subsided into deep, exhausted sleep. He remained by her side as long as he was allowed.

At four o'clock—fleet time—the crippled remnant of the defeated raider fleet surrendered. Michael supervised while the few remaining enemy ships jettisoned their last missiles, their turrets, and their fuel. Michael's Destroyers matched courses and took aboard the living and wounded crewmen. The dead were incinerated with their ships, blown into dust by small missiles shot at the unresisting targets.

Two days later the transports and shuttles began to land, carrying troops down to conquer the planet. Aiming for blasted areas near the largest cities, their way cleared by an intense missile bombardment from the *Philomela*, the troops landed in precise formations and deployed.

They had barely begun to fight when Michael ordered them recalled.

Amazed, Vai read the orders again. They called for the immediate evacuation of all troops from the planet's surface. The local volunteer formations, which had been hastily armed as per Michael's orders, were to be abandoned, left to fight by themselves. Vai gazed awestruck at Sheffield. The Colonel returned his glare, suppressed fury showing in his every feature.

"It's . . . monstrous!" Vai snarled.

Sheffield shrugged. Michael had gone from an ideal warrior-hero to something less than a traitor in his eyes, and all in the past few minutes. He was hurt and puzzled; he felt utterly betrayed. How would the men feel, he wondered?

Vai wondered the same thing. How could he order this withdrawal without looking like a damned fool? The orders were clear, however, and he intended to obey them. His men, even his junior officers, would never forgive him for the decision.

"Follow Michael's orders, then," Vai said to Sheffield, who wordlessly turned and stalked out. Vai arranged for his support forces to give a sustained disengaging bombardment, shifting the missile fire from above to where it would most help the partisan forces. It was the last gift he could leave them.

For the next few hours he supervised the confused withdrawal, fuming as he watched hard-earned ground being returned uncontested. In some places he was able to arrange for the partisan forces to take the field, but more often the best that could be done was to help cover their retreat.

The long day rolled toward its end. Streams of men and equipment flowed into their assembly points, and cargo shuttles, landing vehicles, and the massive transports themselves lifted the divisions into storage orbit. From a low hillside where the evening breeze whistled through a discarded twenty-meter radio tower, Vai watched the orange sun sink diagonally behind the far city. He'd hoped to be inside that city in two days, its master in three.

As darkness settled, Sheffield silently approached. "Sir?"

"Yes?" Vai shook himself. "Are the troops aboard?"

"Yes, sir."

"Let's be off, then."

Aboard the *Philomela,* as the dejected troops off-loaded, their wounds already seen to, Captain Edwards confronted Michael.

"Admiral Devon," he asked quietly during one of the few moments that Michael wasn't engaged. "I was hoping that you would give me an explanation."

"What? No threats? No fits of histrionics?" His fatigue showed, in his eyes, around his mouth. Otherwise he was straight, his blond hair neat, his uniform fresh and sharp, blue and white against the greens of the corridor.

"I'll leave that to Commander Sh'in," Edwards said simply.

Michael breathed deeply. "You know, that's the first time anyone has bothered to ask first before making a judgment."

"It may be the last. Vai's transmissions, and those of his officers, have not been kind to you."

"What was Vai's casualty rate? It averaged two-tenths of a percent per day. Not much—except that we have several more centrally defended planets to take. And our time is limited."

"And after those worlds, there are who knows how many strongholds and secret bases. I know. But why . . . ?"

"I timed it to the hour. The partisan ground forces have an eighty-five percent chance of taking their own planet back, and holding it."

Edwards thought it over. "It sounds good, I will admit. Couldn't you have told them, and your own troops too, ahead of time? They *hate* you."

Michael winced. "I know. But damn it, look at how they fought. Do you think they'll be that inspired on the next world, when I'll have to do the same thing? Will they fight like the demons they were here, knowing that they'll never be allowed to triumph?"

"It didn't make all that much difference," Edwards said, frowning. It amazed him that Michael bothered to talk to him at all; he didn't know to what to attribute his temporary success.

"Damned if it didn't! They were glorious this time. That's what I counted on. Their reputation will fly ahead of us, until we hit our third or fourth planet, when the raiders will trip over themselves to surrender. The respect of my troops is not too great a price to pay."

"Rot! You set yourself up as infallible! That's the greatest way to maintain high morale, high efficiency . . . until you make a mistake. It's a damned balloon: big and impressive, but fragile. You've just punctured your damned reputation, and it's going to be hell rebuilding it."

Astonished by the tirade, Michael was forced to agree. "What do you recommend, then?"

"Blame it on me."

Michael stared.

Edwards continued. "I'll offer you my resignation, which you can magnanimously refuse. You gain stature, and I've none to lose." For some reason he was unable to feel for Michael the hatred that should have filled him. As it was, his crew felt little personal loyalty to him; if his plan succeeded, it was not too much to imagine that his life could be imperiled. But without the intense, irrational loyalty that Michael could command, the mission, more important to Edwards than all else, could never be completed. His life was a small price to pay to put an end to a rebellion that could set the Concordat back a century.

Furthermore, it might, just might, prove to Michael that Edwards was not the coward he'd been branded.

"No," Michael said after some thought. "I'll pull through without such deceit."

Edwards searched for either gratitude or condemnation in the pronouncement, and could find neither. He waited.

"I'll go before the men and explain just why I lied to them." Gaining strength from this decision, Michael thanked Edwards abstractedly for his support, and left.

Edwards stood uncertainly for a short while. What, then, was his status?

Michael, flanked by Vai and Sheffield, addressed the troops. Tall in his blue and white dress uniform, the double-breasted tunic tight across his chest, the pleats hanging razor-edged, his hair shining beneath the floodlights, he spoke to the larger roomful of Marine officers and noncoms. He spoke also to the closed-circuit cameras that carried his words and his presence to the rest of the fleet's troops.

The men that he saw were hostile. Slitted eyes and flared nostrils made masks of many faces. Other men and women sat with cold impassivity, deferring their harsh judgments until later.

"All right, guys, listen up!" The surprisingly tough, no-nonsense tone startled those that had expected contrition.

"I'll take it for granted that you all want to get home to your families before our three-year orders expire.

"I'll pass briefly over the fact that we haven't got any battalion-level replacements available.

"And there's no point in dwelling overlong on your com-

bat record—the 44th is over fifty years old—or your history—fifty years without a major defeat.

"You obeyed your orders then, and you obeyed them today. Good. Because if you hadn't, if you'd participated in
the Concordat's first *real* mutiny in over a hundred years,
if you'd decided you'd rather have me as an enemy than as
a supreme commander . . . you'd quickly have found out
what kind of enemy I can be!"

Never apologize. Take the fight forward.

"What was your goddamned gripe?" Despite the bitter
words and the harsh tone, his face was uncontorted, his
bearing smooth, imperial. "Were you so engrossed in killing half-trained planetary militia—with substantial help
from the fleet—that you lost track of time? Were you so determined to revenge yourselves forty times over for your
losses that you didn't want to come back?

"This isn't a grudge match, or a combat of honor. We're
here to do our job. We're here to pacify this Sector.
Pacify, not beat them into the dirt. You don't get loyal citizens from a wrecked city; you don't treat your *own people*
like rapine-bent invaders.

"Gentlemen, I yanked you because there are eleven
more worlds out there that need to be persuaded, one way
or the other, that their interests lie with us. Pounding
their capitals into scrap with heavy artillery is not the best
way to do it. Maybe we won't need to fight on each of these
eleven worlds. Maybe we will. I hope not. I hope that, by
showing them what we are capable of, we can make them
realize the futility of their position.

"If they don't, we hit them. Hard."

Speaking now to the cameras, now to the troops present,
he worked on the major points: time, space, and force. Precisely, on some unseen cue, a large projection map of the
region appeared behind him, to which he referred without
looking. Motionless by his side, General Vai and Colonel
Sheffield watched the troops, and by their very presence
lent Michael a vital air of legitimacy.

"Quille next, and after that . . . who knows what
damned world?" he went on. "One by one we'll hit them
until they surrender. And they will surrender, because
they have no choice.

"Neither do we.

"Time for us is at a premium. This fleet may not be large by the standards of a full war—in fact, it's rather small—but we're tying up personnel and material that the Concordat may need elsewhere, and soon."

Sheffield maintained his neutral expression. Vai blinked, and resumed his stance. What was Michael talking about? What did these hints of other, unsuspected foes mean? Michael hadn't prepared him for any such revelation.

"Danger exists all around us," Michael continued. "We have enemies that we know of, and enemies that we don't know of. Our preparedness is absolutely vital.

"I'll do my duty, Marines. You do yours.

"That's all."

With a final lingering glance over the assembled officers, he turned and stalked from the room.

He had patched up his credit with them at a wise time. Only later would it be clear whether or not he had regained their respect.

Chapter Six

The fleet moved away from the planet, accelerating outward toward a point where the gravitational gradient declined enough to permit the drop into Jumpspace. The Fighters were recalled, this time with enough warning to fully satisfy Captain Engel, and the fleet folded itself into the orange richness in perfect order.

After the several days that even a short interstellar Jump consumes, the fleet broke out high above Quille, the second planet on the schedule. In the harsh glare of another strange sun, the Fighters scrambled, coordinated by Engel and her staff. While the Fighters swept into defense patterns, Commander Rogers searched the space around the distant blue planet, looking for enemy formations and hoping any foes were not already lining up on the fleet.

She scanned the radar computers' reduced returns and raised an eyebrow in disbelief. Aloud she spoke into her throat microphone, knowing how silly her words would sound at the various battle stations throughout the ship. "No enemies in orbit. None hanging in space. None on any transfer course. There's no one here but us."

"Keep looking, and vary your search frequency." This was from Michael. Damned foolish he'd look if they had burst into an empty system. He waited with a terrible patience.

The final word came back; this world had been abandoned to the loyalists below, who quickly radioed to affirm their control.

"Do we secure from battle stations?" asked Commander Beamish.

"Yes," Michael said softly.

Beamish leaped to obey.

Captain Edwards felt completely out of place on his own command bridge. It probably wouldn't be long until Beamish began to take liberties, delivering slights, little cuts at Edwards's expense. There would be damned little that could be done to stop this. Any confrontation would work to Edwards's final undoing, and a showdown in private would be completely pointless.

It occurred to Edwards then that there was one level below that of verbal infighting. If this was to be an elemental struggle, one chattering ape against another, fighting for the leadership of the tribe, he could be as apish as his first officer, and maybe more so.

The air of self-assurance came back to him as he resolved not to be intimidated by Beamish. *I'm in command of this damned ship, and no one is going to say otherwise.* He banished from his mind the crushing cost of failure.

Neither Beamish nor Michael had been watching him as his resolution returned to him; Engel had been, and while she didn't know what he had been thinking, she felt better for the strength he was plainly feeling.

The troops, aggressive as always, felt disappointed again, having been cheated out of a good fight.

Grand Admiral de la Noue sought out her chief of intelligence records, Captain Athalos Steldan, to get more information on Michael's progress. In the officers' lounge in the central naval base on the desert planet Tikhvin, they discussed the problem.

"Michael has closed the frontier," Steldan complained. "It wasn't covered in his authorization, but he's shut off the Courier route at every location."

"Why would he have done that?"

"I don't know. No messages can get in or out. The pilots are sent back, on Michael's orders." His wide face was serious, his green eyes narrowed in deep thought.

"What about his supply lines?"

"His support flotilla should keep him supplied for some time. Even if he's wiped out, he will have damaged the raiders severely. What worries me is that without accurate reports we can't prepare proper plans. How can we know how best to help those planets?"

De la Noue considered this. "Take the Sector reserve fleet, then. I'll put it in your command, and you'll follow Michael and find out what the heck he's up to. Congratulations, Commodore."

"Um. Two objections. My command experience is, hm, spotty at best, and I don't like leaving the Sector without a reserve."

"Overcome with ambition, aren't you? I'll give you a good exec, someone who can cope with the details, while you merely run things. As for the Sector, what are you afraid of? There's no way the raiders are going to boil out of the Outreach in a massive invasion fleet, and all our other borders are secure. And who's in charge here, anyway?"

Steldan grinned crookedly. "You are, Grand Admiral. I'll be ready when the orders come through."

They spoke for another hour on unimportant topics, refilling their mugs with the excellent officers'-lounge coffee. De la Noue left first, to arrange the release of the reserve fleet.

Steldan sat, quietly pondering the situation. With his tall frame folded comfortably into the lounge chair and his open face thoughtful, his dark hair contrasting quietly with his gray and black duty uniform, he presented a convincing picture of reflection. The room slowly darkened as the blazing sun of Tikhvin settled behind the Spaceport Fighter hangars, visible through the floor-to-ceiling windows in the lounge. Rising, Steldan strode to the window and looked down over the small Fighters' boost-grid. Dust from the black desert blew in gritty wisps over the larger landing field, where at the moment three large tankers sat shimmering in the late-afternoon heat.

Life had never evolved here. The Concordat of Archive, reluctant to let the strategically located world be wasted, had begun seeding its atmosphere with trillion-ton batches of oxygen-fixing microorganisms that would, given another seventy years, produce a livable, if hot, garden-world. The process had already liberated enough oxygen for breathing and had cooled the desert's surface temperature some three degrees.

First, of course, the naval base had been built. Centrally

located, strategically critical, the world was needed to core a new Sector.

The Tikhvin Sector, it was already being called; this world was destined to become its capital. And de la Noue had ordered its reserve fleet mobilized, to be sent out into the Philomela Outreach in pursuit of a perhaps over-zealous crusader.

Steldan shook his head. She had been right, of course. There was no way the raiders could get this far. Nevertheless, it went against the grain to strip any region of its last protection.

The sun, a dazzling pinhead when visible, a bright blue glow when obscured, cast ink-black shadows over the Fighter grid as it sank further below the titanic hangars. Steldan turned the lights on and tapped inquiries into the lounge computer. The reserve fleet for Tikhvin was composed of an Attack Cruiser, three Heavy Cruisers, and a battle-scarred Dreadnought. Supporting these were several Light Cruisers, fifteen crumbling Destroyers, an almost respectable Scout fleet, and a Fighter squadron that could be launched from the Dreadnought. He'd seen worse.

He next checked the list of free officers, trying to guess whom de la Noue would assign to him as exec. The list was too long, he finally decided, to determine this, but two or three looked to be more than just average, two-mission Captains. He looked more carefully at their unclassified records and decided he liked what was there. One Captain Douglas seemed most likely. Having missed assignment to Michael's fleet because of a conflicting assignment with a maintenance division, he had expressed a desire to lead a flotilla to the Outreach in a supporting role.

It was no surprise, therefore, when Captain Douglas presented himself to Steldan at the latter's office early the next day.

"Commodore Steldan?"

"Come in. Have a drink." Outside, the temperature was soaring toward the mid-forties centigrade, with the worst yet to come; inside the Spaceport office building, the air-cooling system whispered cool drafts through hidden vents, refrigerating the offices.

Captain Douglas at first glance was straight Navy issue, appearing as if stamped from a die as one of thousands.

Tall, slim, with short dark hair, a stiff military bearing, and unremarkable features, he was, at best, nondescript. Steldan noted with inner amusement that this impression remained at second glance. The man seemed to have no handles, nothing the mind could grip on as individual. And yet his file had mentioned—Steldan groped mentally for a moment, recalling what he'd read yesterday—two campaigns against the Reynid, and some mop-up work against the Sonallans, themselves damnably tough enemies.

"I've examined the reserve fleet," Douglas said quietly. Steldan recognized the soft Line Worlds accent. "We can have it manned and ready inside a week." Disapproval gave an edge to his words. Steldan felt like defending himself, protesting that stripping the Sector wasn't his idea. Instead he tried to smile.

"I'm sure that both the fleet and you will satisfy me. We'll be primarily on a recon mission, to see how Admiral Devon is doing."

"Will we be joining our fleet to his?"

"The orders leave that to me. It would depend upon how he's progressing."

"If I know Admiral Devon, we'll meet him on his way home, having completed his mission." Douglas didn't seem at all happy about that prospect.

Steldan felt doubt, but said nothing. Why had Michael closed off communication?

What was happening out there?

The raider leaders met in a small room on the outskirts of the planet Acheron's one significant city. John Burt sat motionless, his face set, while North and Bishop took turns shouting at each other and at him.

"I can't fight them head on!" This was from North, who should well know what his fleet was capable of.

"But I can hold them!" Bishop growled. "John, you've seen the defenses." He was now almost pleading. "I can hold this planet—"

"Robert Bishop, you're a damned fool." Bishop paled at the sharp reprimand from Burt. "And you weren't one two years ago." He leaned forward. "Think, you nitwit. They've got Concordat Marines. Do you think your damned irregulars can hold out against those?" He sat back carefully. Both men watched him, waiting.

"It's hit and run. If it pleases them to bowl in here like herd animals, that's fine; they'll find we've set them a snare.

"Andrew, we'll fight . . . our way. I want the space around this planet seeded with mines as thick as fleas. Nothing fancy, just passive nuclear warheads.

"Robert, organize some companies of snipers. When they land here, I want them made miserable."

"There will be loyalists who will rise against us when the Marines land," North said uneasily.

"Let 'em," Burt snarled. "This planet is going to be a demonstration. They'll know that if we can't win, we can make them pay for it." He looked at each of them appraisingly. "You know I've never ruled by fear. There'll be no reprisals against misguided Concordat loyalists. They're going to take this planet; we've as good as lost already.

"But they're going to learn that it'll cost 'em.

"Have Court prepare evacuation plans so that after we've stung them as badly as we can, we can run. Round up as many volunteers to stay behind as you can find. We can make Acheron unlivable for their damned occupation forces; we can maybe even take the planet back from them once they've gone."

"We haven't got too much time," North suggested. Seeing the expression on Burt's face, he hurried on. "I'll go and put together an underground, then."

"No. Bishop, that's your job. With or without the populace's help, make this planet unlivable for the Concordat."

"Yes, sir." Bishop left, determined to forge a partisan/terrorist team Burt would be proud of.

After he'd left, Burt asked of North, "What about our secret weapon? The saboteurs with the enemy fleet?"

"I can't be sure, of course. They have no way of getting in touch with us. If they're able to strike again, it'll be during the battle, when things are most hectic."

"Good," Burt murmured, although he knew it was both good and bad. It couldn't be planned on ahead of time. That, he'd always known, was a fine way to lose a battle.

Michael stood on the spacious bridge of the *Philomela*. Through the illusory window to the outside provided by the main viewscreens, the bright blood-red of Jumpspace pulsed with its subtle hues. Black dots stood out in place of stars; small discs where the viewscreens blocked out what would be a dangerously energetic ultraviolet.

He mused darkly. Someone had murdered the *Vostigée*. He'd find the man, and when he did . . .

The battle was upcoming, as the fleet prepared to leave Jumpspace above the world of Acheron, chosen by both sides to be the site of the showdown.

Chapter Seven

Aboard the *Tegula*, Lieutenant Jaquish was unable to sleep. Knowing he'd pay for it tomorrow, he rose and dressed, intending to give his Fighter a last inspection. He was tall, slim, blond; his reflexes were in the top three-tenths of a percent, and his coordination and dexterity matched this. Graduating from flight school at the top of his class, he had been immediately assigned to a Fighter wing and shipped off with the *Tegula*. The fact that he'd never flown a combat mission gave his superiors little concern. There was only one way to learn, and that was to get out there and do it.

He passed the sentry at the intersection of the ship's corridors without comment; the sentry looked at him without interest and waved him along. During the last battle, Lieutenant Jaquish had been in the reserve formation. He'd gotten to know his little ship, even to trust it. But tomorrow he'd be fighting for his life, and the day after that would bring more of the same. With two-hour-on, three-hour-off shifts, he and all of the other pilots aboard the *Tegula*, *Later*, and *Philomela* would be pushed to their limits during the expected two-day run of the space phase of the battle. He didn't look forward to it.

When he arrived at the entrance to hangar deck 5-C, he bumped into sentries who were more inflexible. Lacking clearance, he was turned back. As he left, he heard one of the sentries muttering into his radio, reporting the sleepless pilot.

Lieutenant Jaquish strolled to the nearest elevator and ascended three levels, searching for the observation room overlooking his hangar deck. Soon he found it. Through the oversize windows he could see the huge multi-platformed hangar deck, with Fighters arranged by sections, ready for launch. Around the Fighters technicians scurried, inspecting the craft and running last-minute systems checks. By one of the launching tubes, Jaquish's Fighter waited, unattended, already fueled up. Although the small ship was streamlined and thus could make a planetfall, its true capabilities were best showcased in vacuum. No ship could be perfectly tailored for all atmospheres, and thus the Fighter's combat abilities were designed around interplanetary battle. Once he got into the soup around the world ahead, he'd be outclassed by the aircraft designed specifically for that world.

For now, he was content to stand and watch his little ship gleam under the hangar's spotlights. A fine little needle-formed instrument of death, with weapons surgically precise . . . After a time, perhaps, he'd return to his cabin and catch some sleep. Perhaps.

He looked up. The many-leveled hangar bay was more impressive than he'd remembered. To the right were the special-purpose craft: the missile-boats, decoy-drones, and electronic-countermeasure ships. And above those, in a corner . . .

What *was* that? It was about as large as a ground-car, and was placed so as to be invisible from most places in the hangar. Lieutenant Jaquish remembered the destruction of the *Vostigée*. Could this be a bomb of some kind? Whatever it was, it certainly didn't belong where it was. Anyone could see that it wasn't anchored. If the ship should rock, the object would fall, probably damaging several Fighters.

He stepped out of the room and soon found a sentry. "Ho, fella. Something isn't quite right."

The sentry made perplexed motions. "What's wrong?"

Jaquish led him to the doorway. "You want to tell me what the heck that thing is?" the pilot asked, pointing to the misplaced and hidden object.

"Can't tell, sir. Pardon me while I report it." He unclipped his radio and spoke into it. Jaquish couldn't hear the reply.

"I'm told to keep you here, sir," the sentry said, and stepped back to watch the pilot more carefully. Jaquish shrugged. He wasn't responsible, at least.

Soon he saw armored guardsmen from the bomb-disposal crew approach the hidden device. Three more guardsmen, wearing chainplastic battle armor and carrying laser carbines, entered the observation room. Two covered Jaquish, while one directed the men below by radio. One of the bomb-disposal team finally floated up toward the device, riding a gravitic lifter. Jaquish wryly thought of the mess he could be in if this turned out to be a false alarm.

The man examined the device, while Jaquish and the first sentry watched. The other two, ship's Marines, no doubt, closely watched Jaquish. The bomb-disposal technician seemed to be probing the bulky object with a sensing device. The distance was too great for anyone in the observation room to be certain.

With a great lurch, the ship threw itself to starboard. Artificial gravity flickered off, then came up again, and anti-concussion fields snapped on throughout the vital areas of the ship. Jaquish didn't understand. The device, and the man examining it, were still there. What had exploded? Abruptly, lights and reserve power failed. Painfully, awkwardly, the *Tegula* twisted itself back into normal space, dragging curdled wisps of Jumpspace fields through the bucking gap. At the moment that the ship looked most as if it might pull through, the hole in space wrenched, spinning clumsily, and sheared through the already punctured hull, sawing the Mothership into two unequal parts. The bomb had been only one of several.

The rear third of the *Tegula,* heavier by far than the nearly hollow front portion, managed finally to collide with the rest, producing a final jarring shock before the hulk settled into normal space, rotating lifelessly. Secondary explosions flared for a while, subsequent chains of destruction that were visible from outside the disaster. Aboard, a sleet of radiation from the dead engines showered all but the few protected areas; fire-extinguishing compounds filled the hallways, extinguishing people as well.

Andrew North had just earned another planet.

The Concordat of Archive was like a large crystal, unevenly cut, in its region of the galaxy. Fault planes ran through it, a lattice of instability. Any one of those planes, given enough pressure, could separate, shattering the whole.

The Philomela Outreach, with its justified resentments, provided such a weakness. Taxed heavily, and depleted of its manpower by conscription, the Outreach still suffered from the effects of the Sonallan invasion of 1103, all the way across the Concordat from the Outreach. It didn't matter that there were no other sources of troops and ships; it didn't matter that the Concordat was seriously threatened. The invasion didn't threaten the Outreach, and thus the Outreach's citizens felt unjustly exploited. After the costly war, few of the ships and personnel returned.

The raiders offered a quick fix to the economic stagnation that followed. Governments began subtly to shift in their makeup. Against stout, if minority, opposition, the tariff policies, Port Authority procedures, and planetary court rulings turned against the Concordat.

Perhaps the suppression of the loyalists was a mistake. The common confiscations and crimes against persons did not eliminate loyalist sentiment; they stiffened it.

On Acheron, several loyalist groups still struggled with the popular organizations that supported the raiders.

The nearing presence of Michael's fleet electrified them.

"You and your 'prudence' can be blasted," hissed Losse Merent, his patience with his lieutenants dissolving. "When the Marines land, it's going to take more than just scouting for them to make us the new government. We'll have to take over the city." He went on quickly, overriding any objections. "The army, the reserve, and most of the police will be out losing to the Concordat troops. The city will be bare. We know the sensitive locations—power station, government office building, general staff headquarters— and we've got the manpower to take them."

Of the thirteen men and women in the small room, only Denise Voleur and a very few others fully disagreed. Denise was also quick enough to make the first response. "Crap." As much as she despised such language, she knew how effective the vulgarity would be. All eyes swung to her, some mildly surprised, some heartily and smilingly seconding the opinion. "We can take those locations, sure.

And two out of every three of us will be dead. Some new government.

"If the Concordat fleet is going to take over this planet, the best way for us to gain legitimacy is to work with them." She looked about the room. Casadesus, the elderly loyalist and spiritual adviser to the combine, seemed the most likely ally. Denise wished she'd had time to speak with him before this meeting. She was far from sure of him, and only in comparison with the other counter-rebels in the room did he appear promising.

"Casadesus"—she wondered, for the first time, what his real name could be— "has agreed to be our contact with the Concordat troops when they land. Fine. He'll present us to those troops as a government-in-exile, rather than as a batch of dissatisfied troublemakers." Her strong voice overrode a number of comments; she mentally noted exactly which of the members of the combine most disagreed. As she'd expected, Casadesus said nothing, watching her and the others carefully.

"We're armed—with assault rifles and grenades. Not bad. What do we do against PGMs, APLs . . ." She broke off. Some of the group didn't know the terms. "They have the heavy artillery. They have radios. And they have the defense!" What was she doing wrong? While she argued these points, the attitude of the group seemed to shift against her. Was she actually swaying them toward Merent's position?

Taking advantage of Denise's hesitation, Merent grabbed hold of the audience again. Leave it to Voleur, he chortled silently. If she tells people "X," they'll vote "Y" every time.

"Miss Voleur has some good points," he said, his face all seriousness. "However, our main advantages will be speed, surprise, and a detailed plan of action, hammered out in advance. Nothing will be left to chance. Nothing." Poor Voleur. Never tell an ex-military man that his troops are no good. Never. Nine of the people in this room had been in Acheron's armed forces when the last planetary elections were held. When the System Trade Party—better known as the Damned Pirate Sympathizers—had won, these men and women had been forced to retire. What wasn't obvious was how many enlisted men and women

had also quit—when their terms had expired, of course—
and had quietly aligned themselves with the combine.

The combine. A quiet group. It had to be, on a world
where Concordat loyalty was cause for losing one's property. Sometimes people's lives were lost as well. The System Trade Party, promising and delivering abundant and
cheap wealth, showed little mercy to those who wanted the
cornucopia dismantled. That the wealth was gained ille-
gally didn't seem to bother the Party.

"Casadesus will indeed contact the invading troops, if
he will accept the job." Merent looked at the old man, who
smiled and nodded slowly. "Miss Voleur was correct in
that point. We must appear to those troops, and to their
commander, as a legitimate government. But our military
role cannot be underplayed. If we can decapitate the Party,
then the battle for this world will be shortened, and we
need that. The longer they fight for its possession, the
more damage they'll inflict, damage our economy cannot
afford."

Although he'd never participated in any military action
on a larger scale than quelling riots, he knew enough
theory of war to be concerned. If a planet doesn't fall to an
orbiting invader in less than five weeks, it won't fall at all.
Beyond that point, the only way to win is to beat the
planet—industry, economy, and all—into powder. The Concordat, with its traditional missile superiority, would have
the stand-off destructive capability to do that with compar-
ative ease. Losse Merent had no particular love for the
Concordat, but since they would win eventually, it was vital that they win quickly.

Denise Voleur, listening with disgust, still disagreed,
and knew that many of the others in the room had reservations.

Casadesus rose. "I think that both of our friends are correct, and that the best of both their plans can be used." He
had once been a physically mighty man; now, well into his
hundredth year, he was still imposing. From a start in the
combine's lower ranks, he had worked his way up through
the secret organization cell by cell to stand among those at
the top. Tonight, thought Denise, he might well become
their leader. Again she wished she knew more about him.

"We will strike at the government and the military, as

Brother Merent proposes, striking not to kill but to capture. No Concordat troop commander will negotiate with assassins. Understand that." His white hair drifted from under his shapeless cap. Strangely colorless eyes darted about the room, fixing the members and remembering them.

"We will also work with the invaders, to guarantee that the combine is chosen as the caretaker government"—he emphasized the word "caretaker"—"instead of a coalition of Party members. I will accept the job of envoy, to coordinate our efforts with those of the Concordat."

That, as far as the remaining members seemed to be concerned, was the final word. Soon the meeting broke up into two parts, one to discuss technical aspects of the operation, one to discuss strategy and politics.

Chapter Eight

Delayed seven days by the wreck of the *Tegula*, Michael's fleet fell through the unreal barrier and into normal space in proper position above Acheron. From the *Later* and the *Philomela*, swarms of Fighters hurtled, flung one every three seconds from each of the fifteen launch tubes the two carriers had. While the *Later* continued discharging Fighters, the *Philomela*, with a numerically far smaller screen, moved to protect the Mothership from any attack.

The attack came, and soon. Within seconds of launch, the Fighters found themselves in furious combat with two clouds of mines. The Fighter pilots sprang into frenzied alertness, adrenaline racing through their systems . . . only to lapse back into an almost amused scorn. The mines were drift type, with no maneuverability. The high orbits crawled with them, and with high-velocity sand-shot as well. Unfortunately for the defenders on Acheron, nuclear warheads have a very limited effective blast radius in a vacuum, and no ship had come out of Jumpspace near enough to one to be bothered. For three hours the Fighter pilots enjoyed the job of clearing a lane through them with cinch shots at the virtually harmless devices.

Until it was discovered that one out of fifty was a live mine with full maneuverability. Appearing just like a drift mine, the first of the live mines burst into action with a precise, five-gravity thrust, heading on a collision course with the *Later*.

Lieutenant Jaquish stopped it with a lucky deflection shot, and had to stretch his luck to the utmost to avoid the angered robot bomb.

"It's not *luck*," he had been known to say. In flight school, when his oxygen tank had lasted five minutes longer than it should have, saving his life during an accident, he explained it away as a result of his not panicking and breathing slowly. When all but two of his graduating class had been forced to groan in dispensary during an outbreak of some nameless virus, he and his roommate enjoyed a seven-day pass, claiming it was clean living, no more, that had spared them.

And when the *Tegula* died, killing all but seventeen of its complement, he had automatically responded that it was because of his Fighter having been already fueled, and his knowledge of that vital fact, that he had escaped.

Anybody else would have called it luck.

"No damned smart bomb is going to chase *me,*" he muttered to himself, and flung his craft to the left so that the mine, chasing him, would be offered a better shot at the *Philomela.* The mine, sensing the larger, slower target before it, continued forward while Lieutenant Jaquish circled below it and put three laser shots into its drive. A somewhat belated high-energy beam from the *Philomela* completed the job, vaporizing the mine before it had a chance to detonate itself. Although it was well out of range of the *Philomela,* Jaquish, within its blast radius, was rather thankful.

"But it wasn't luck," he said to himself.

Joan Rogers had her hands full, managing the computers that displayed before her on her screen a full bank of red-lit warning lights, indicating a sky full of foes: mines, live mines, and ships. The ships were spread out in small groups, with random orbits, hiding with their power down. Did they know that she could see them? The red lights brought out reflected glints of rose in her red hair, and a flush to her cheeks. Her eyes were intent; she bent forward to her controls.

At the operations console, Arbela Sh'in lazily typed in instructions arranging the Fighter screen for maximum defense. In this endeavor she was soon interrupted by Michael.

"Commander Sh'in, if you hadn't noticed, we're attacking, not defending. Clear that board."

Sh'in mockingly docile, drawled, "Yes, *sir,*" and savagely wiped the operation. What would that madman be most likely to want? A frontal attack with no screen at all? As Michael turned to leave, she caught his attention. "What formation do you want the fleet in? Fighters on forescreen?"

He didn't answer for a moment. Then: "Attack formation. Close in, and send the Fighters ahead."

Sh'in stared at the man. Berserk. He must think he's on a longship, waving a sword, wearing a fur jacket. Fur on the inside. And there's no way anyone is going to tell him anything about the facts. *Oh, sir? Do you realize you're throwing away our missile superiority?* "Bah! Honorable men fight with axes, not with cowardly bows and arrows. Attack!"

Joan Rogers, with her overview of the battle, watched the Fighters fly forward, to be the first to contact the enemy. On her screen that matter became clear, then confused, and clear again. While the larger ships drove forward at speed, the Fighters herded the enemy into knots, strings. Ideal targets for salvos of missiles. Why was the Admiral withholding fire?

She watched the casualty figures tabulating themselves at the side of her screen. Too fast, they mounted.

Five minutes later, at Michael's order, the fleet made turnover, to fall toward the enemy in a decelerating curve that would end with the two fleets mingled. This would allow precise-beam firepower to annihilate the enemy, but at a drastically increased cost in friendly casualties. Joan shook her head in perplexity. It was as if Michael was in an intense hurry.

The fleets closed to beam range, the deadliest closeness allowed. Joan Rogers sat back in her chair and breathed deeply, shaking with nervous exhaustion.

Her part in the battle was over.

On the command bridge of the *Philomela*, Captain Edwards was too busy even to curse properly. Why did Admiral Devon need to stay here, running the Battleship, when his proper place was with Sh'in and Rogers, controlling the fleet? There he was, watching the ship's status board and calling out orders as if he were the Captain. Worse, he intended to stop the ship right in the midst of the enemy, there to slug it out at close range.

The only consolation Edwards felt was that Commander Beamish was just as eclipsed by Michael as he was. The bridge crew leaped to Michael's commands without the slightest need for either Edwards's or Beamish's approval, and to hell with tradition.

As he watched, Captain Engel approached and offered him a wry smile. He smiled back, and together they stood and watched. The Fighters were no longer hers, just as the *Philomela* was no longer his. Now, however, her pilots were dying, and at a rate she'd never experienced before. A pilot herself, the impact hurt her badly.

Having nothing to say, Edwards took her hand. She gripped back, the tension wrenching at her.

Across the bridge, almost experimentally, Beamish called out an order. "Prepare missiles for launch."

"Countermanded!" Michael snapped. "There will be no missile launch." Beamish glared at him. The bridge crew exchanged nervous glances.

"Excuse me," murmured Edwards to Engel. "It won't do any good, but I've got to talk to him." He started across the cramped room, aware of Engel following him.

Michael sensed his approach and turned to face him. From his expression it was plain that he had no patience to spare.

"Sir?" Edwards asked in his calmest voice. He squarely met Michael's gaze.

"You may have noticed that the planet below is fortified." He turned from Edwards. "That's all."

A chill crawled up Edwards's spine. Admiral Devon was saving an entire fleet's load of missiles to bombard the surface of one planet? Nothing, absolutely nothing, could survive such a devastation.

He spun and walked away. Captain Engel stood, fists balled at her sides, until with a weary slump she followed Edwards.

"He can't be serious. Can he?"

"I don't know," Edwards answered, "but I'm damned sure of one thing. He won't get away with it. I'm still Captain, and while I am, I have the command interlocks. The computer won't allow fire toward a planet without my order."

"What happens when Michael replaces you?"

Edwards allowed himself his first small smile of the day. "The computer is a better lawyer than he thinks if he tries that. And so am I. There are limits to the amount of bombardment that even Michael can order without invoking emergency powers. I'll play along with him until that point, and then blast his plans apart."

"How many civilians would that leave dead?"

"Millions. But if I refuse even the most extreme of legal orders, I have no chance to fight him on the illegal ones."

"And if the computer happens to suffer from an untimely hit?"

Captain Edwards thought that one over. "The backups are less discriminating. . . . We'll hope the computer survives. They're built to last."

That was all the conversation he had time for. The fleet, tail first, dropped into the middle of the enemy. At this range all electronic disguises became useless; the enemy consisted of forty craft of sizes from Scouts to two Light Cruisers, and a rapidly shrinking screen of some sixty Fighters. The Concordat Fighters, now numbering less than four hundred, darted among the enemy craft recklessly, inflicting damage beyond what was expected of them, and taking more serious losses as well.

From the *Philomela* heavy beams lanced out, piercing enemy ships wherever they struck, then blinking off while the capacitors recharged. The three Heavy Cruisers likewise opened fire, concentrating more on the enemy Fighters than on their jump-worthy craft. Behind the van, the *Later* hung back, relying on the other ships for protection.

Within minutes the enemy ships had the range on the *Philomela* and the Heavy Cruisers, and began methodically to work their beams over the best available targets. Using precision-fire tactics, they aimed for the Concordat ships' gunnery bays, trying to aim between the Battleship's segmented armor plates.

For long hours the battle hung, sparkling, glittering, deadly, over the waiting world of Acheron. It only remained to be determined whether exhaustion or weaponry defeated the raiders.

Beams burst forth, straight-line lances containing hundreds of trillions of watt-seconds of energy. The targets moved, and the speed of light actually began to seem slow. Most beams missed, but those that hit gouged away great portions of armor plate.

Despite air-conditioning and padded couches, the gunners sweated, their muscles cramping with tension. In a titanic weapons bay, twelve guns, mounted, fired in rotation, moaning loudly once every sixth of a second. Elsewhere, in a small turret, one woman ignored her computer targeting, the sweat dripping from her face, until she seemed to merge with her gun, firing it manually at a target she could only dimly see.

A beam struck a ship squarely on an armor plate. Three meters of plastic-ceramic-titanium honeycomb were chiseled out of the plate, which, being five meters thick, survived. The next shot might strike between the plates.

Engines produced multiple trillions of watts of power, which were hungrily consumed by drives, guns, support systems. Every ship tried to avoid being where the next beam would pass. Between them, small Fighters flitted, relying upon speed and maneuverability to dodge the questing lasers.

Hours passed. People died. And on the minds of every combatant, on both sides, one question outweighed all others.

Where are the missiles?

"We've done all we can, John." Andrew North spoke from the doorway to the radar room where John Burt stood watch. "We'll have to run. From here on, it's up to Court and Bishop."

Burt pulled off his headphones and walked to North. "Why haven't they been using missiles? We should have had to run hours ago. We're doing far better than we should."

"And you've noticed that they have one fewer Mothership now than they did at Quille."

The grin on Burt's face was genuine. "You've done well, Andrew.

"All right," he continued. "We'll have to run. What have you got in mind?"

"Well, I did manage to cook up a little scheme. . . ."

"Does it have anything to do with the two hundred drift mines you had us save?"

North smiled. "Damned straight. We run. They follow. We let 'em get close, then we dump the mines in their path."

"We'd have to let them get mighty close."

"Yeah, we will. But we never expected to win this one, just to make them pay for what they took." Anguish crossed his face. "I don't know why they're not using missiles. It doesn't make sense. I don't know, and that bothers me." He breathed heavily. "Anyway, my plan goes further. After we run, we jump out, right? Except that the jump is just a nanojump, so that we can give them a final attack run."

"Do you know—Of course you do. Is it worth it?"

"We'll lose from eight to fourteen ships. I know all about fractional jumps: distortions, gradients, and all. But the ships that live through it will be right where the enemy expects them the least."

It was actually worse than that, he knew. The complications were deadly in a fractional jump. The drives would be snapping space like a steel bar, rather than bending it like a bowstring. Death or explosion was all too possible.

"Do it," Burt said, and left to transmit final instructions to the ground forces, which were about to inherit the battle.

Soon the battered raider fleet began extricating itself from the fray, edging into a loose formation while avoiding predictable courses. In less than an hour it was plain that they intended running.

Far above the crescent glow of the planet Acheron, the remaining twenty-odd jump-capable ships of the raider fleet pulled slowly ahead of the massive Concordat fleet. The raider Fighters, system craft only and not capable of jump, headed back toward the planet. Only twenty survived.

Slowly, almost clumsily, the raiders increased the distance, while beams lanced and arced between the fleets. Concordat Fighters, energized by the development, darted in to fire at point-blank range, dashing away between the enemy formations.

As if crippled, the raider fleet yet pushed outward, their

rear gunners firing continuously, adding yet another series of beam-scars to the Concordat capital ships.

One of the Heavy Cruisers, touched upon by a critical beam shot, lost speed and fell back. No one knew how badly it had been damaged; no one cared. A brief cheer echoed over the intercom of John Burt's ship, as with a new strength the gunners carried on.

Two long hours later the Fighters were at last recalled, limping home to the *Later* or to the *Philomela*. The raiders were ready to jump, still only slightly ahead of the Concordat ships. Finally, at the designated moment, each raider ship released a load of drift mines and immediately began to scatter, preparing to drop into Jumpspace.

Michael had been ready for exactly that move. Within two minutes, all the mines had been picked off by precision-beam fire from the *Philomela* and from the remaining two Heavy Cruisers. Less than half of the mines had even been allowed to explode, and those explosions were without exception harmless.

After another minute, as the raiders separated from each other, the *Philomela* dropped a triple salvo of missiles. On tails of fire the deadly darts fled at highest acceleration directly toward their targets. Contacted by the weapons, ships either died pyrotechnic deaths or were heavily damaged. Beams from the Heavy Cruisers helped complete the devastation, cutting down the ships that had escaped the missiles.

Four raider ships made it into Jumpspace.

It was the first time during the entire operation that no one could fault Michael.

Chapter Nine

"Casualty lists, Admiral." Commander Joan Rogers entered the conference room quietly, a haunted look on her face. At arm's length she handed the report to the man next to Michael and turned away, walking to the end of the table before seating herself. Arbela Sh'in watched her, feeling an abstract sense of sympathy for the crushed Commander. For herself, Sh'in felt only anger, dulled now to a warm ache somewhere in her gut. The casualty figures were incredible, with over fifty percent losses in the Fighter screen, and no ship in the combat portion of the fleet undamaged. The Heavy Cruiser *Tödlich* had had its engines blown out and was now drifting farther and farther from the planet at a steady 110 kilometers per second. How had they managed to put a shot into its rear when it was pursuing the enemy? It was clearly not a case of sabotage, however, and radiation leakage was fortunately minimal.

Two hundred and sixty-eight Fighter pilots had died, with three recoverable, wounded pilots. And one who'd had his ship shot out from under him but who had escaped unscathed himself. How anyone could be that lucky, Sh'in was certain she'd never understand.

Joan looked physically sick, she decided, watching the younger woman at the end of the table. While Commander Beamish gave his damage report—an optimistic one, but who wanted to listen to that lizard?—Sh'in studied the intelligence chief. *Look at her. Is she going to vomit on the table? She'll be okay if she makes it through the conference. Afterward, I'll see what I can do to cheer her up.*

Commander Rogers didn't make it through the conference.

As Beamish sat, Joan stood. Her face was even paler than before. Sh'in knew what was about to happen, but could not stop it.

"Damn you, Admiral Devon! Damn you!" Joan's voice was firm and clear, without the filtering fringe of hysteria that Sh'in expected.

"You're in command now," she continued, "and I haven't got the support to change that. But when we get back, I'll by the gods have you canned."

Michael's response seemed cruel, although he didn't mean it to hurt. "Commander Beamish, will you have a medic step up here and escort Commander Rogers to a sick bay?" Beamish complied, speaking closely into the intercom before him to hide his grin. Joan was sufficiently in control to avoid making a protest, or to sit down. She stood, arms at her sides, eyes locked with Michael's until the medic arrived; she went with him without resistance, and did not look back.

"Anyone else?" Michael asked. There was pain behind his face, very little of which he let show. His gaze lingered longest on Sh'in. Sh'in smiled at him, a cruel, hungry grin.

"All right, then. Commander Rogers will not be reprimanded; she was tired, as are we all. I'll look in on her later." Beside him, Commander Beamish appeared slightly disappointed.

He wanted her sacked, thought Sh'in. *He's next in line to replace her.*

"As long as I am in command," Michael continued, "my orders are to be obeyed without question. The time for explanations is afterward. Here. Does anyone feel that I mishandled the battle?"

Sh'in stood, smiling tigerishly. "In my own personal opinion, sir, I think you did a crappy job." She sat down.

"Anyone else?"

Captains Edwards and Engel looked at each other, each wondering how the other felt, and if he or she had the courage to say it aloud. Michael caught the interplay, and nodded. "Some of the rest of you have reservations as well."

He stood and walked partway around the table to stand near Sh'in, while still addressing the room. Sh'in understood what this was supposed to do: contrast his massive height with her short frailness, intimidating her physically in front of the roomful of officers. Disgusted, she had to admit that the tactic was a well-chosen one.

"Every missile we drop comes from ships' magazines, and is irreplaceable. We're at the end of a long voyage into enemy territory, and there are no replacement missiles to be had. Since it was obvious that we could beat the enemy without this waste, I proceeded to do so.

"Missiles have always been the Concordat's main naval strength. But when there are other, more efficient means of winning, it makes the most sense to use them.

"This war is not over." The way he said this made it ominously evident that he meant more than the reduction of the world Acheron, more, perhaps, than the pacification of the Outreach. He stood silently for a while, surveying the room. Sh'in, looking up at him, was the only person in the room who dared meet his gaze, and her expression clearly announced how much she disagreed.

"General Vai?"

"Yes, Admiral?"

"Surface bombardment will commence in two days. Your troops will begin landing two days after that. This time we will not pull them back before the planet is captured; tell them that. They will have full support from orbit.

"The raiders chose this world for their showcase. It was to be the example. They wanted to make it expensive for us.

"It will be."

"Yes, sir," Vai said, ceasing to take notes for a moment. "Will we be landing all four divisions?"

"Yes. I'll have Commander Sh'in give you the landing zones. The campaign should be as swift as possible, consistent with minimal casualties."

There were no further questions.

The small spacecraft carrying John Burt flew out of Jumpspace, spinning rapidly and moving with a great, unbalanced velocity away from its exit point. The microjump had been dangerously short; the four ships that had run from the battle shot, scattered, across the sky above Acheron. With great effort, the pilot of the fifty-meter ship worked the spin downward from an absurd seventeen revolutions per second. Without artificial gravity compensators, the crew would have been thoroughly dead.

Until the spin was countered, there was no way to check the ship's velocity. Distorted radar images showed them heading toward the world at two hundred kilometers per second, on a close skew approach. Through the ship's viewports the madly wheeling starfield reassured Burt immeasurably. He'd had no guarantee of surviving the jump at all.

The other ships, with equally ridiculous velocities, made shift to regain control. They would, at least, be able to land on the contested world, before the Concordat fleet could return to destroy them.

As Burt waited for the ship—his flagship, he sardonically realized—to regain maneuverability, he was joined by Andrew North. They grinned at each other, glad for the moment merely to be alive.

"Hell of a residual momentum we picked up," North said in mock whimsy. More seriously, he asked, "Did the others make it?"

"Who knows. Ninety percent of those of us who started this battle . . ."

North closed his eyes. "Ninety-seven." He shook himself. "You've got one happy gunner below, by the way," he mentioned. "A little wisp of a girl, and a good shot. The port bellygunner, I think, and she put one of the enemy's Heavy Cruisers out of action with the luckiest shot I've seen in years. She hit the hulk in the engine room, just as it swung wide to miss a drift mine. It started a chain reaction and knocked their drives away."

"A good crew. That's all I've ever asked for," Burt sighed. "Give me fifty good men and women, and I'll take this ship anywhere."

"You've got 'em, John."

"We made them pay. That was the whole idea. We made them pay. And when I get down there, we'll keep it up. That planet will cost them dearly."

"But they will take it, won't they?" North gave his leader an almost pleading look. "When things have gone far enough, we will surrender?"

"Yes. I'm no fool. All we can do now is demonstrate our firmness."

North pulled a thermos of cold beer from a wall cabinet and handed Burt a glassful. "To the Outreach."

"To the Outreach," Burt smiled, and drank.

Under Michael's supervision, the drifting bulk of the *Tödlich* was slowed and forced into a high, stable orbit. The operation involved carefully matching courses and stringing massive gravitic towing beams. It took long, weary hours, during which most of the crew and most of the fleet rested. The *Tödlich*, it turned out, would be repairable; within several days it would be as good as new.

The fleet, refreshed, moved closer to Acheron, remaining just out of range of the planetary defense gunnery. Four reinforced divisions, Marines all, rested easily, knowing that soon their turn would come.

The bombardment of the surface was not far off.

"Commodore Steldan?"

Steldan lifted his head from the navigation tank he'd been peering into. The navigator with him frowned at the interruption.

"What've you got, Captain?" he asked Douglas.

"The strength reports you asked for. We've picked up thirty-eight of Admiral Devon's Scouts. Most of them were blockading unimportant planets, but some of them actually had some raiders bottled up."

Steldan considered that. "If we dispatch a few Light Cruisers, with one or two of those Scouts, they could probably clear up any resistance."

"Yes. I'll take care of it." Captain Douglas gave Steldan a weary smile. "We're stronger now than we were when we set out, anyway. If nothing goes wrong, we'll be more than a match for anything we might meet."

"What could go wrong?"

"I'm worried. I don't like the way Admiral Devon has split his fleet. And I most particularly don't like the fact that we don't know where he's gotten to."

Steldan privately agreed, while making a show of disagreeing, for public consumption. Was the command bridge any place to air doubts of this nature?

"I'm confident of Admiral Devon's capability. He can't be encountering any combined resistance, or he *wouldn't* split his fleet. I would like to know, however, why he closed the Courier routes to and from the Outreach."

Captain Douglas said nothing.

"In any case, finding him will be the trick. There are twelve heavily industrialized worlds, clustered within a ten-parsec sphere. He could be at any of them."

"Then how will we choose? Guesswork?"

"I don't engage in guesswork, Captain." Steldan's firm reminder quickly melted into a happy grin. "Because it's *too* productive—who wants to weigh a thousand possibilities when only one is correct?—and because it's too much fun. I've long felt that guesswork should be taxed as entertainment."

"You know where he is?"

"No." He ignored the glare that Douglas threw at him. "Naturally not. Twelve worlds. The centermost of them? Not likely; that's where I'll send some Scouts, to look the place over. The longest-inhabited? To them, with their larger population base, I'll send a cultural-warfare team. We're going to Acheron. Do you know why?"

"No, sir."

"If Admiral Devon is there, we've struck it lucky. If he's not, he'll either have passed through, or will be about to. If he's just been there, we follow him. If he's on his way, we soften up the defenses for him. Clear?"

"Not entirely, sir. The question remains: Why Acheron?"

Steldan shrugged, admitting, after all, the role that guessing had played in the choice. "It's the closest to us right now."

Douglas breathed in deeply and clenched his fists; Steldan affected not to have noticed.

"Blast it, if we've got to fight, why can't we at least help the Concordat?" Denise Voleur fought to keep her voice even, and found herself failing.

"We must not reveal our strength until the right moment," Casadesus responded quietly. Even Denise felt the power in his voice, and hated herself for it.

"Besides, the planetary defense bases are much too big

for us to crack." That was Losse Merent. It seemed to Denise that he had diminished slightly. Probably from following Casadesus. What power did the old bastard have over people?

He did have power. They did what he wanted. Was it his voice? His eyes?

What Denise always overlooked was that she herself had just as much power . . . in reverse. If she wanted people to retreat, it was an easy prediction that they'd attack. Now, when she was committed to an attack against her will, her pleas for a determined effort were met with too damned much caution.

"Gentles, the time has come." Casadesus rose tall, then leaned forward over the chair before him. "In only a few hours, the bombardment will begin. Missiles from above will fall like black rain, and where they strike, nothing can endure."

Nothing can endure, nonsense! Denise jeered silently. She knew that hardened planetary defense sites could survive. True, the cities would burn at the touch of the missiles, seething with nuclear wildfire. They would *if* they were targeted, and it was well-known that the Concordat was not genocidal. The cities would be spared. That was clear.

The cities would be spared, so that Casadesus and his combine could rise from their shelters and take control.

Like black rain, the missiles descended. Falling at high velocities, driving columns of superheated air before them, they howled through the skies, spreading their devastation across the planet below. From sweeping orbits, the thermonuclear explosions were visible as small sparks on the surface.

Aboard the *Philomela*, the tension was muted, and the alignments were confused.

Joan Rogers selected targets, transmitting the coordinates to the missile bays. Relentlessly, almost cruelly, she chose the target points. If she was aware of the questioning looks bestowed upon her by Captain Edwards and Engel, she gave no sign of it.

Coolly, she turned to Sh'in and asked for a report on missile stocks. Sh'in stared at her for a time, and finally complied.

On the command bridge, Michael was very much in charge. He stood tall, his blond hair crowning him. As he snapped orders, the bridge crew sprang to obey them. Commander Beamish was always among the first to respond to Michael's commands, Captain Edwards noted. Worse, he obeyed with a dignity that was far more dangerous than a fawning subservience would have been. Michael was not the sort of man to be impressed by obsequiousness; he virtually worshipped strength. Strength of character, followed closely by strength of physique, were his standards.

Captain Edwards counted on that to regain his place as leader. He'd been watching, waiting . . . and it looked like his opportunity had at last arrived.

"We'll need heavier warheads," Michael suggested.

"I'll prepare them," Beamish answered. Michael half turned.

Beamish recalled, too late, that this would require the Captain's authorization. The ship's computer was still under the impression that Edwards was in charge.

"You'd have a bit of trouble doing that, *Commander.*" Captain Edwards barely recognized the voice as his own. "It might do you a little good to remember who captains this ship."

Beamish turned to face Edwards. He couldn't see Michael behind him, across the bridge, watching alertly. Edwards could see them both. He met Beamish's heated gaze, and tried to ignore Michael. *One thing at a time.* The bridge crew watched with fascination.

"I'm *sorry,* sir," Beamish drawled sarcastically. "I'd *forgotten.*"

"Yes. You had." Edwards saw Michael, standing motionless, merely watching, letting his subordinates work this out for themselves. And yet Beamish, could he have seen the Admiral just then, would have been stopped dead in his course by Michael's expression.

"Commander Beamish," Edwards continued in a businesslike tone, "you're relieved. Go get some sleep. I'll see to things here." It was asking too much; Edwards did this deliberately.

"I'm fine." Beamish half turned away.

"It wasn't a suggestion," Edwards said gently.

Beamish never considered for a moment that Michael wouldn't back him up. This cowardly maggot masquerading as Captain could only nauseate the Admiral as he nauseated him. It was time to humiliate the yellow bastard once and for all. He spun back to Edwards and placed a hand on the Captain's chest. Pushing just hard enough, he snarled, "Get off the bridge, boy!"

It was all Edwards needed. With three short, straight punches, he had Beamish floored. Beckoning a crewman from the radar boards to watch the dazed first officer, Edwards brushed back his hair. "Send for a squad to take this man to the brig."

Gods, that could have gone so badly wrong. What if Beamish had grappled with me, trying to throw me to the deck? We'd have rolled back and forth, destroying forever any dignity we might have had left. What if Beamish had stuck to words? He might well have won.

He still had to beat Michael to the punch. Speaking easily, he addressed the silent bridge crew. "It's been a tough campaign. Nerves are tense. I'll let Beamish cool off in the brig for a couple of days, and then the incident will be forgotten."

Only then did he allow himself to look at Michael. What he saw there froze him momentarily. He saw appraisal, approval, and acceptance in Michael's gaze. It struck Edwards with the force of a hammer blow that he had himself used Michael's methods against Beamish.

He'd set himself on a course from which there could be no returning. It was going to be the hardest work he'd ever needed to do, retaining his upper hand. "I believe you mentioned something about increased megatonnage, Admiral?"

"Yes, Captain. Commander Rogers needs your authorization."

Edwards nodded. "I'll see to it."

That evening, Edwards met with Commanders Sh'in and Rogers, and with Captain Engel, in a now-deserted officers' lounge. Joan watched with reserved amusement as Sh'in and Engel congratulated Edwards on his handling of the unpleasant situation. Both wished they could have been present.

"Beamish is a toadying, beggarish little snot," Sh'in smiled, sitting catlike on the edge of her chair. "I really would have liked to watch you smash him."

Engel, infected perhaps with Joan's more quiet mood, simply squeezed Edwards's forearm in approval. The smile they shared came from deep within them; it was evident that Engel, at least, didn't have to be present at Edwards's triumph to share in his joy.

Joan frowned. Should Michael's favor be fought over? The indignity of that seemed, in her mind, to cheapen the loyalty these officers should feel for their commander. It occurred to her that her silence could be misread, however, and that the others might take her withdrawn mood as a sign of disapproval. Raising her glass, she proposed, in a forced voice, "To the Captain of the *Philomela*."

The others knew she was all right when they turned to her, causing her to blush. The toast was drunk in grinning silence.

Chapter Ten

The reserve fleet fell out of Jumpspace through the rift or singularity that starships' engines can pull open. Some minor discrepancy in the fleet coordinating computers imparted a small residual rotation and large unbalanced velocity to the formation. Captain Douglas cursed silently as the fleet began to drift apart from centrifugal acceleration. Somebody had been neglectful, not paying his status board the attention due it. The ships emerged high above the planet Acheron in a randomly selected orbit.

The drift mines in this area had not been cleared.

"Captain, we're under—" The first officer's statement was interrupted by a concussion and by a flash of blue light from outside the ship. One of the drift mines had decided it was as close to a target as it was likely to get and had detonated itself.

"Drift mines," the first officer stated quietly. "No damage."

Captain Douglas looked about. The flagship of the reserve fleet, the Attack Cruiser *Illuminator,* was safe for the moment, according to the radar board. Some of the outlying ships, including the Scouts gleaned from the blockades Admiral Devon had posted them to, were already taking action. "Have the gunners stand by." He strode through the passageway to the fleet command bridge. Where was Commodore Steldan?

There he was, watching over the backup status board for the battered hulk of a Dreadnought, the *Resolute.* The obsolescent ship was good for little more than launching Fighters, and at this point, it had difficulty doing even that.

As if divining his thought, Steldan smiled at him and interjected, "At least its drives are in tune."

Douglas lowered his brows. He certainly had no wish to wait for the wreck to climb laboriously into Jumpspace each time their course was altered.

"At least. I'd be happier without it along."

Steldan shrugged and indicated the radar board, where coded lights indicated the *Resolute*'s Fighters were at last beginning to launch themselves to clear away the pestering drift mines.

Soon, from the scraps of wreckage swinging in odd orbits, visible by radar from high altitude, it became very clear that a heavy battle had been fought above this world. A growing cloud of stray radiation, strewn from shattered and blasted reactors, helped indicate the magnitude of the defeated side's loss.

Not long after, the radar operator found Michael's fleet, swinging low over the planet and seeding it with missiles.

The Fighters opened a path for the inward-hurtling fleet. A communications officer, on Steldan's order, sent a message in proper naval security code, with recognition signals. After the eleven-second time lag had run out, there was still no response.

Steldan looked at Douglas. Douglas had nothing to say. Steldan returned his attention to the communications board. Admiral Devon should have responded by now.

Five minutes later, he did.

Quietly unfolding itself from the planet-spiraling orbit, the revenge fleet led by Admiral Michael Devon began pushing itself up the long gradient toward the small reserve fleet. In twenty minutes, their formation was unmistakable. Admiral Devon intended meeting the reserve fleet with his full strength. Still no radio messages had been answered.

"Can he mean to attack?" Steldan asked.

"It's an attack pattern. . . ." Douglas said uncertainly.

They both swung their eyes to the fleet status board; the situation was exactly as they both had remembered. The fleet, coming out of Jumpspace, had carried a spurious rotation and velocity. This had carried them far enough into the differential gravity well of the planet so that the climb into Jumpspace was impossible. An hour and a half would be required to come to a stop relative to the world below; another hour and a half to reach the minimum safe jumping distance.

Alternatively, they could drive straight forward for two hours, bypassing the planet and escaping from the far side of its gravity well. This merely involved flying headlong through Michael's fleet.

Steldan and Douglas discussed the options as briefly as they could, and agreed that the latter maneuver was preferable.

"We can't know what he intends. . . ." Steldan pointed out.

"We can't afford to take chances," Douglas returned. "If we scoot away, at least we won't appear aggressive."

"If he intends to attack, he'll catch us whatever we do. This is a nearly unmistakable gesture on his part, but there may be some explanation."

"Sir," Douglas said softly, "he's driving for us at full acceleration, Fighters outspread, under radio silence. He's about to blow us to merry hell!"

"We have no certain indication of that . . ." Steldan began.

Douglas and he spun about at an announcement from a radar officer. "Admiral Devon's fleet fire control radars are sweeping over us, sir: he's feeling for the range."

"Tell me that's not aggressive," Douglas snapped.

"Not necessarily!" Steldan responded, yet he didn't believe it himself, not any longer.

"He's got our range," the radar officer said levelly.

"Damn. We'll have to run the gauntlet," Steldan agreed unhappily. "Full emergency speed forward, and try to duck to one side of him." At this point he entertained the suspicion that Admiral Devon was not in command of that fleet. Who then? "Hold all fire until we know for sure what exactly is going on."

Michael stood stiffly in the fleet command bridge of the *Philomela,* watching carefully the actions of the two women. Joan Rogers worked steadfastly at her board, trying to learn all she could about the strange fleet. Sh'in, however . . . Sh'in worked slowly, clumsily, darting ever more frequent dark glances at him. Let her. He was damned if he'd explain his every order in baby talk for any Commander that failed to appreciate his tactics.

Captains Edwards and Engel also plainly disapproved, but had learned enough in the past weeks to keep it to themselves. They deserved a little more consideration, he decided, and spoke in an even, low voice.

"Their recognition code is proper, of course. Does that prove anything?"

Edwards frowned, and moved closer to Engel. Engel started, as if Michael had just read her mind.

"It does not," he continued, answering himself. "Any saboteur who could plant those bombs aboard the *Vostigée* and the *Tegula* could also lift recognition codes from the computer. I have to be certain."

"Yes, sir." To Michael's surprise, it was Engel who had answered. Was she going to start to shape up and act like a loyal officer? If so, that left Sh'in alone as a recalcitrant, and he knew damned well he could handle her.

"The *Vostigée:* seven thousand dead. The *Tegula:* nineteen hundred. What kind of leader would I be if I took chances now?"

Edwards cleared his throat. "You could answer their calls."

"What could they say?"

While saying nothing himself, Edwards thought of dozens of things that would be in any Concordat ship's computer. Surely no one could have lifted *everything*. With a dull certainty, he knew that Michael would disagree. The calls went unanswered.

Soon it was plain even to Edwards that the strange fleet behaved in an unusual fashion. It drove forward at high acceleration, as if intending to bypass Michael's fleet and make planetfall. If it had been a Concordat fleet, it would have hung motionless, away from the world, to avoid giving false impressions.

"Something is badly wrong," Captain Engel said to Edwards as they stood together on the command bridge. She edged nearer to him, seeking comfort from his presence.

Edwards's sleeve brushed hers as he gestured. "Michael may be right. I wish I knew."

Together they watched the shifting figures on the display. "In less than an hour," Engel muttered, her voice pitched low, for Edwards's ears alone, "they'll need to make fleet turnaround. But we'll be in missile range before that. We can't stop what's about to happen. . . .

"Come along," she said quickly and stalked to the fleet command bridge, not looking behind her, as if afraid to see Edwards standing motionless with indecision. She had nothing to worry about; he followed promptly.

They found Michael watching over Joan and Sh'in. Michael turned, sensing the onrushing confrontation. Sh'in looked up from her board, hoping for fireworks. Joan kept her eyes firmly on her display; in the half-light, her ears could be seen burning fiercely.

"We have spotted several inconsistencies in the messages from the new fleet," Michael said, getting to his point before his subordinates could get to theirs. Sh'in, seated before him, recognized his haste as a sign of weakness. It filled her heart with savage glee to discover that the mighty warrior could be uneasy.

Captain Engel flicked her eyes to Captain Edwards. Neither spoke.

"They claim to be a Concordat fleet out of Tikhvin Sector, under the command of Commodore Athalos Steldan. This is the kind of cover story the saboteur might have gleaned from a half-ruined ship's computer. The *Tegula*'s, perhaps, or the duplicate data we drew from the dying bulk of the *Vostigée*.

"You see, there is no Commodore Steldan, and the Tikhvin Sector—itself a misnomer—was virtually bare when we left."

"Is there an Athalos Steldan listed at all in the files?" asked Engel.

"Yes: a Captain in Intelligence. A physician, which means torturer. . . . But he has no command experience. I doubt that the person out there is truly he."

"I wish you'd talk to him and check out his story more carefully," Engel suggested.

"Pointless." Michael turned away, turned back. "These worlds, now in revolt, were of the Concordat once. They had all the recognition codes, and more than one naval base. We simply can't rely on what they may say."

"What should we do?" Sh'in asked. Was there a snarl in her voice? If so, Michael let it pass.

"We close with them, and demand their surrender. If they refuse, we destroy them."

The two fleets would pass by each other at high velocity in less than half an hour. In fifteen minutes, they would be within missile range.

Two fleets, neither particularly large by the standards of the day, drove toward each other on tails of gravitic glow. Spread out, dispersed for action, each had a small cloud of one-man Fighters keeping an outlying formation.

Large bays, recessed into the sides of the capital ships, lay open to the vacuum, the gigantic machinery within protected by stress fields that kept the atmosphere inside. People moved about, tending to the demands of the machinery.

A standard missile, first of fifty on its launching rack, was armed and levered into position. Its electronics were reprogrammed, and its automatic self-destruct frequency was changed to foil the enemy. The computers had been warned that the opposing fleet might know too much; the precautions seemed natural.

The missile was launched. Magnetic differential slung it outward until chemical drives could be activated. After the small reserve of fuel was exhausted, it switched over to gravitic drive. Pushing forward at six standard gravities, the twelve-meter cylinder decided that it was far enough from its point of origin and quietly armed itself. The few kilograms of plutonium, deuterium, and lithium at its tip were transformed from a slightly radioactive sandwich of light and heavy metals into a thermonuclear device ready to destroy anything it came near.

It selected a target. . . .

Only the fact that the fleet command bridge of the *Illuminator* had no anti-concussion field saved Athalos Steldan from a slow death. The battle had raged for nearly three minutes when a salvo from the *Philomela* contacted the smaller ship. The Attack Cruiser had died, unevenly, noisily, and from the prow backwards. On the command bridge, the anti-concussion fields had dutifully snapped on, freezing the bridge crew in place, keeping the officers from flying headlong forward through the heavy bulkheads. Slowly the fields had built up in intensity, while elsewhere aboard the ship unprotected crewmen fell forward to swift deaths, or were crushed by the incredible accelerations the ship underwent.

Steldan, in the fleet command bridge, lay motionless against a bulkhead, endeavoring to breathe as his weight, now equivalent to hundreds of kilograms, sat on his chest. On the command bridge, the anti-concussion field eventually worked its way up to point nine nine seven: the value at which the partial pressure of oxygen made the very air poisonous. Physical motion was impossible; trapped in limestone, fossilized, the officers died, one at a time, drowning.

The pressure on Steldan eased until finally, with a sudden wrench, he was in free-fall, sprawling weightless across the fleet command bridge. Every telltale before him glowed red. No systems active; no reports from the fleet. The emergency power flickered, steadied, then cut itself off without any fuss. Batteries took over. It seemed he would live.

Gathering his strength, he eased into the command bridge, where the anti-concussion field had at last died. Three persons yet lived, and gasped spasmodically. Steldan dove to the nearest of these and, upon turning him over, discovered him to be Captain Douglas.

Steldan's medical training took over. He tried to aid Douglas to breathe. *Why am I helping him,* he wondered. *I should let him die . . . I can't. I'm trying to save the life of the man who doomed my fleet.*

Why did he fire the first salvo?

Did he panic? Did he realize something that I overlooked?

Douglas's face burned cherry-red; his bloodshot eyes rolled. Steldan felt the Captain's heart flutter under his fingers. Groping for the correct spot, he cupped his hands, pressed. Douglas's heart failed to respond. Try again. Douglas tried to speak.

Steldan, alone on the bridge, worked with the dying man, not certain if anything could be done at all. Douglas managed to force out a few words.

"Sorry . . . Commodore."

"Why?" Steldan felt the arrhythmic pulse, and gritted his teeth. "Why did you fire the first shot?"

Douglas moaned. "For the same reason that I planted the bombs that destroyed two ships already. I'm not on your side."

Not willing to let the man die—not now, when there was so much to be learned from him—Steldan fought to hold back onrushing death. He fought in vain. Douglas fell swiftly into final unconsciousness.

Steldan, numbed, moved to help the other two survivors.

The two fleets passed by each other at incredible speed. Beams blazed threadlike between opposing ships, gouging huge scraps of metal and ceramic out of armor plates and breaching unprotected hulls. Michael's general order went out: aim for engine rooms.

The killing time lasted for fifteen minutes; after that, the two fleets were again out of range of each other. Michael's fleet turned and began decelerating, seeking to match the enemy's course. The enemy was generally without maneuverability. As they swept apart, Michael ordered a full fleet volley of missiles to be fired at the rapidly departing enemy.

Every ship but the *Philomela* obeyed.

"What the hell is going on up here?" Michael demanded as he burst onto the command bridge of the *Philomela.* "Why are we withholding fire?"

The bridge crew looked to Captain Edwards.

Edwards stood his ground. "I've just had a brief conversation with the computer. It now believes, as I do, that those ships are—or were—friendly."

Michael's shoulders slumped. "So you've sabotaged the computer. Can it be repaired?"

"For now, sir, it refuses to recognize your orders."

"Why? Why have you done this?" Pain showed on Michael's face.

"Sir," Edwards pleaded, "that fleet was on our side. If you'd only listened to them—"

"They were attempting to confuse us until they could get close enough. Damn it, Edwards, they fired first!" Michael's burst of rage passed. He turned to one of the bridge crewmen. "Have Captain Edwards taken to the brig. I'll interview him formally later."

Two Marines came forward and respectfully escorted Edwards away. He made no resistance or further comment.

Michael stood straight and addressed Commander Beamish, who watched with stunned incomprehension. "You'll be the Captain until Edwards is cleared. If he is." He waited. Beamish gulped like a fish.

"May I remind you that I outrank Beamish?" The voice was that of Captain Engel. Michael turned to her and glared, as if daring her to speak further.

She did. "Damn it, I'm not sure I don't agree with what Captain Edwards did—" She stopped. Too late.

"Marines, take her to confinement with Edwards." *Gods*, he breathed. He turned about and looked to the doorway where Commander Sh'in watched, fascinated. "Have you anything to add?"

She shook her head contemplatively and returned to her station.

Michael took a turn of the bridge, inspecting each of the several boards scattered there and the officers manning them. Each of the several rows of consoles was carefully watched by the crewman posted there, none of whom dared meet Michael's gaze. When he came to Beamish, now Captain, he beckoned him aside. In the privacy of a corridor, he took the younger man by the jacket front and held him closely with an iron grip.

"I didn't put you in command over Engel because you are in any way better than she is. I put you in command because you will obey my orders without question. I want you to know that whether or not Edwards is a coward or a traitor, he's twice the man you are. Get out there and do your duty, but by the gods, keep your mouth shut. Understand?"

Beamish understood.

Steldan's reserve fleet drifted, the engines of the ships generally blown away. The one ship that had best weathered the passage was the already unreliable *Resolute*. Although battered by time and neglect, its heavy armor had spared it the damage that the rest of the fleet had felt. Its massive beam weapons, never removed from it because of their bulk, had made up for its lack of missiles. As soon as the battle had closed to short range, Captain Walter, commanding, had ordered the untrustworthy weapons primed and targets to be selected.

At that point in the battle, he had assumed fleet command in the absence of communication from Steldan and the *Illuminator*.

The *Illuminator* had loosed the first salvo. Captain Walter had seen that himself, watching from his command bridge. Immediately after, the general orders had come across on the fleet radio band: attack. And after that, the *Illuminator* had been taken out of action, along with nine other ships and two dozen of the Fighters.

Captain Walter wondered what he was supposed to do next. No shuttles could be launched; his shuttle bay had been taken out by a stray beam from one of the enemy's ships. He sighed, and routinely supervised repair efforts and Fighter retrieval.

A damage-control report came to him after a time: while the *Resolute* had held onto its maneuver drive, its jump drives were trash.

"How did that happen? They weren't hit."

"They were taken out by the hit that knocked out the number-five missile bay," answered the damage-control chief. "Some of the secondary explosions reached as far as the drives room. If we'd had missiles in that bay . . ." He shrugged.

"Scratch one Dreadnought." Captain Walter considered. "So we can fight, but not run."

"That's about it. The power plant is in fine shape, so we can power the beams. We'll be in fighting shape in no time."

"What exactly do you mean by 'no time'?"

"Um . . . about ten more minutes."

Captain Walter raised an eyebrow. Not bad. No enemy could possibly come within combat range in ten minutes.

Instead it took them an hour.

Aboard the lifeless, drifting corpse of the *Illuminator*, Commodore Steldan rounded up the few survivors. Five had medical training, with two of them being full surgeons. In an improvised operating theater, their lifesaving efforts proceeded under hastily rigged lights and with what little equipment had survived the explosions.

Elsewhere, engineers under Steldan's supervision probed backward through the dark corridors, looking for the backup life-support systems. Unless these were repaired, the ship would become uninhabitable within the hour. Steldan, in his vacuum suit, drifted along passageways open to the outside void, trying not to look at the gently floating bodies. Very, very few of the ship's complement had survived.

In places, pockets of pressure remained, some with people inside. If they had suits, they were collected and passed forward to the command bridge/operating room to assist. If not, they were freed by means of portable, collapsible air locks. Two more doctors and seven engineers were recruited this way.

Sooner or later, Steldan knew, they would be picked up, either by their side or, more likely, captured by the enemy. Would they be in time? That question could only be answered by the *Illuminator*'s surviving engineers.

Within twenty minutes the auxiliary life-support room had been reached, and a temporary air lock installed. Three life-support engineers entered. After another five minutes they radioed out their findings. As soon as some sections of piping and wiring could be patched, the air plant would be ready. Lights and heat would have to wait, but the latter could be conserved simply by moving the survivors into a small enough room. One average man's body warmth was sufficient to keep a rather sizable room at a constant temperature; lights could be produced by hand flashlights, or they'd do without.

"Ladies and gentlemen," Steldan cheerfully announced on the command frequency, "we are going to live." A relieved babble of voices rose to fill the general communications frequencies. Steldan himself wasted no time returning to the makeshift operating room to lend his own medical skills to the general effort.

Nearby in the ruined remnant of the command bridge, two engineers tried to piece together a workable radio with which they might contact whatever was left of their fleet. Very little of the communications board remained that was recognizable. A new antenna needed to be extended through a newly fabricated shielded air lock—the surface of the hull was dangerously radioactive—and Steldan was needed to give an okay to the project.

He lost track of time in his lifesaving endeavors; he failed to fully appreciate the organizational efforts expended by the engineering crew, until eventually they interrupted him to inform him of the ship's final status.

The woman that caught his attention was of average height, with a full, round face and dark hair. "Commodore Steldan?" she asked hesitantly.

"Yes?" He left off his work, allowing another to complete it.

"Life support can't last more than another ten hours, sir. On the other hand, the ship is stable. Should we bring the bottled air in from the lifeboats, or do we plan to abandon ship?"

"Bring in the air. We'll stay in this one large lifeboat." He paused. "You are . . . ?"

"Lieutenant Commander Emily Young, ranking engineer. We've got seventy-three survivors, including fifteen wounded. In a few minutes we'll have a radio working. Life support is decaying—with the extra air, we'll have thirty hours. I guess you're in charge, sir."

Steldan considered this, fatigue slowing him a bit. "When you get the radio working, try to contact whatever fleet we've got left."

"Yes, sir."

"Is there anything else?"

"Well . . ." Her face betrayed a little distaste. "You'll want to know about our fighting capacity." She rushed on, avoiding looking at him. "The guns are so much pot metal now, but fifteen missiles are ready to fire. The magazine feeds are useless, of course, so fifteen is all we have."

"Unless, under weightless conditions, we wrestle more up from the hold." Young's expression was unmistakable. "Ms. Young," Steldan said firmly, catching her gaze, "I doubt very much that we'll be doing any fighting. Forget about 'fighting capacity' and put your engineers where they'll save the most lives."

Young looked at the deck. "Thank you, sir," she whispered. "I'd thought . . ."

"I know what you thought. And in most cases, you'd be

right. But I'm not that kind of fire-eating fleet captain, to want to fight on when all's lost. The moment we drop a missile, we become a legitimate target again. And we can't take any more damage. Whatever fighting's to be done will be handled by the active elements of the fleet."

"Thank you, sir," Young said again and quickly spun and left, heading for her work. Steldan watched her for a moment, then returned to his duties.

Captain Walter of the *Resolute* responded quickly to the message from the *Illuminator*. Through a telescope, the shattered wreck could be seen drifting in an almost parallel course several hundred kilometers away.

"We can't pick you up," he informed Steldan.

"We'll live. What is the tactical situation?"

"Dead astern is the entire rogue fleet, driving at us at full formation acceleration. Nearly every ship we've got has got its drives blown out. We're not going anywhere."

"How long till they catch us?"

"Over seven hours yet. Some of our ships still have jump capability. What are your orders for them?"

"They'd best stay with us, and leave after it's all over."

"That won't take long, once that Battleship gets within missile range."

Steldan had to agree. Silently he broke contact.

Fifteen minutes later, radar operators aboard the *Resolute* spotted the Heavy Cruiser *Tödlich* bearing down upon their port flank.

Chapter Eleven

Grand Admiral de la Noue reviewed the orbital defenses above the planet Tikhvin. The twelve fortresses circled the dark planet in endless, carefully interlocking paths, each at all times within supporting missile range of three others. With abundant missiles, backup fire-control computers, and small antimissile lasers, the structures were armored and internally segmented.

De la Noue felt no great confidence in them. They were nonmaneuverable, confined to their orbits. She wished strongly that she had a fleet. With even a small one, the fortresses would have the close-range screening they needed.

She wondered whether she was imagining a threat, borrowing trouble. Two fleets had disappeared into the Philomela Outreach, and nothing had been heard of them since. Dutifully, Commodore Steldan had sent Couriers back, detailing what little information he had. Now even those reports had ceased.

What could come from the Outreach? Had the two fleets contacted a previously unknown enemy? Or was she, as she halfway suspected, working herself into an alarmed state for no reason?

Decision crystallized in her. What she planned could prove her downfall; by no means, however, would she wait inert while events moved dangerously fast. She prepared messages to each of the bordering Sectors.

It came to her that her office had never before been as insecure as it was now.

"What's happening?" Michael demanded of Joan Rogers.

Without looking away from her board, she answered him. "The *Tödlich* is back in action. It's closing with the enemy, on a matching course. The enemy is now aware of it. Do you have orders for its Captain?"

Michael permitted himself a tight grin. At last, a bit of unexpected good luck. The *Tödlich*, back in the fray, could prevent the escape of the few enemy ships that had not yet been disabled.

"Yes. Tell him to aim for jump drives. Keep anyone from getting away."

"Yes, sir." Joan applied herself to the instruments before her, her eyes intent. Michael may have acted wrongly—she wouldn't judge him—but he acted decisively. She had to admire his calmness under pressure.

Sh'in worked rather more sullenly, typing in instructions to her machines one character at a time, jabbing with a pencil. She still made too much of a point of her passive resistance, Michael thought with amusement. But, dammit, he liked them both, as officers and as people. Rogers, it seemed, was actually loyal to him when she wasn't being subverted by Edwards and Engel.

Together, the three of them watched the Heavy Cruiser swing into action against the enemy ships that still had jump capacity.

Can one ship assault a fleet? The Captain of the *Tödlich* seemed to think so. In his favor was the state of the enemy, scattered and depleted from the beating that Michael had given them. Their Fighter screen was five times decimated, the flagship wrecked, their reassigned lead vessel a disrupted pile of scrap barely holding itself together. Agreed, the old thing was still a Deadnought, armored protectively and bristling with beam projectors. It had no missiles, however, and lacked jump drives.

All the *Tödlich* had to do was stay back from the decayed hulk and throw missiles into the ships that it vainly tried to protect.

It dove across the trail of the coasting enemy fleet and settled into a pursuit curve. Michael's fleet sped nearer by the second.

Fire-control computers wrestled with probabilities; launching racks in their bays loaded, armed, readied their missiles. From the *Tödlich* three dozen sleek missiles leaped, spitting fire. If it was merely a ranging salvo, it was none the less deadly against ships that lacked maneuverability.

Captain Walter of the *Resolute,* made fleet captain *pro tempore* by Steldan, understood the enemy's strategy and fumed at his own helplessness. One Heavy Cruiser, decently armed and armored, was going to bag his entire fleet.

There was nothing for it, then, but to take out the Cruiser himself. Quickly he coordinated an improvised battle plan.

As the *Tödlich* prepared a second, more massive salvo, the *Resolute* turned over and applied full acceleration back toward the pursuer. Many times as massive, very nearly as agile, the Dreadnought, with its thicker armor and heavier armament, even in its decline was an equal match for the Heavy Cruiser.

The two capital ships neared each other, the crews of each showing open disdain for the danger, hiding private misgivings. Aboard the *Tödlich,* missiles were levered into launching racks by automated magazine feeds; the *Resolute*'s beam projectors were carefully primed, with new firing templates fed them through the fire-control computers.

Entering optimum range, the *Tödlich* dropped its salvo of ninety-six standard missiles. On-board tracking units took over; on tails of flame the weapons raced toward their target.

The *Resolute* refused to swerve. Counter-missiles took out twelve of the oncoming warheads; beams, sand-shot, and electronic countermeasures knocked down fifty-eight more. Of the remaining twenty-six, twenty-four blossomed brilliantly against the Dreadnought's armor plates, incandescing away whole layers of ceramic-plastic sandwich. Radiation and particles were stopped just beneath the surface. One missile collided with an armor plate, failed to detonate, and was shattered wholly by the impact, leaving its section of target totally unaffected.

The last missile slid between two gigantic plates, flew headlong through a radar bay, and opportunely detonated itself only a few dozen meters from the ship's main power plant.

Anti-concussion fields contained most of the direct blast,

while nuclear dampers filtered out the bulk of the radiation. No force known, however, could protect a ship completely from a ten-kiloton explosion in its interior. Decks buckled and conduits separated, while blast doors slammed shut against the loss of air. Much of the fireball was blown by its own pressure back out through the breach; a great deal of it hungrily consumed bulkheads and machinery before cooling.

Inside the shielded pressure vessel of the ship's power plant, the constant fusion fire flickered momentarily, then steadied. When the fire flickered again, automatic countermeasures were initiated, too late. Four-tenths of a second after the enemy's missile had detonated, the multitrillion-megawatt fire burst loose from its confinement, adding for another millionth of a second its energies to those of the warhead.

Despite this, because of the cunning compartmentalization of the massive ship, some areas of the ship remained livable. On the command bridge, Captain Walter and his crew survived; several gunnery bays were not only livable but functional. Cut off from any contact with the bridge, each bay commander had his own choice of whether or not to fire, and at what target.

Only one target presented itself. Seven guns from a forward bay, retaining their firing charge, unleashed their beams upon command. The thick beams flicked across the distance, holding within them just under a billion megawatt-seconds of power.

Four of the beams struck the enemy near the bow; the other three missed cleanly. The first of the four scored a deep groove into one of the armor plates protecting the Heavy Cruiser. The next three each pierced a plate and transferred their residual several trillions of watt-seconds into the interior.

The shock wave of superheated, ionized air inflicted more damage upon the *Tödlich* than had the thermonuclear burst upon the *Resolute.* Two separate chains of blast doors and anti-concussion fields failed to activate, overloaded and ruined before they could react. Sensitive, supercooled machinery died, leaving the Heavy Cruiser without controls. Its engines, sensing the loss, shut themselves down before the explosion could reach them, leaving the ship to drift maneuverless on its previous course.

Although it was severely crippled, it could yet fight. By the time it had expended its last missile, it had disabled all of the remaining jump-capable ships left to Steldan.

An exhausted calm returned to the spreading fleets. The *Tödlich* drifted slowly forward through the scattered formations, while the *Resolute* fell away to the stern. Michael's fleet, under full acceleration, neared steadily. Radio messages flashed back and forth between Steldan's ruined flagship and the other ships that yet had crews. The decision to surrender was uncontested.

The first shuttle flights transported the wounded of Steldan's fleet to medical stations aboard Michael's ships. Subsequent flights carried those remaining to their captivity.

In the gloom of the wrecked bridge of the *Illuminator*, Steldan and his surviving crew members stiffly greeted the section of Concordat Marines that boarded. Their presence destroyed the last remnant of Steldan's theory that the ships had been captured by some unknown enemy. At this point it was obvious that he and they were on the same side. They, however, couldn't know it. To the Marine Captain that commanded the boarding party, Steldan made his surrender a clear statement of whose side he was on.

"Commodore Athalos Steldan of the Concordat of Archive, commanding."

The Marine glanced at him and said nothing. He gestured to his men to remove the wounded, assigning three to stand guard.

Steldan held his peace. Soon he'd have his turn to explain Douglas's treachery.

The shuttle departed; another approached. Steldan and his crew were escorted, none too gently, toward the passenger compartment. At a gentle acceleration, the trim vessel bore them away.

"The prisoners are all aboard, sir," General Matthew Vai informed Michael. His expression was worried; he seemed unsure of where to place his hands. Carefully, he continued. "The ships' Captains were to a man confused.

All claimed to be on our side. They claim no involvement in the decision to fire first."

"When we find the man that gave that order to fire, then we'll have the main tool of the traitors. Most of these Captains are just what they seem." Michael, having secured his victory at scant cost, was relaxed, expansive. He prepared to continue, but was interrupted by the entrance of Joan Rogers and Arbela Sh'in. He and Vai made room for them at the table, welcoming them to the nearly deserted officers' lounge. Joan sat by Vai, glancing nervously about her and sitting gingerly on the chair. Sh'in stalked, catlike, across to the dispenser for coffee.

Michael was as surprised as anyone else at his own good mood. How long had it been, he wondered, since he'd been able to simply sit and talk? Here there was no pressure, and he was at ease with his subordinates . . . his friends. He and Sh'in had been head-on just hours ago, and would be again just hours from now. For the moment, though, he was satisfied to rest with her and speak quietly of the battle just past.

Sh'in, he decided, judging by her expression, hadn't forgotten their differences. How very like her. He knew that her anger was brittle and could be swayed by a little logic and a good dose of persuasion. It would be worth the effort, especially if he could get her to back him up when the crisis came. And the crisis, when he revealed his plans, could not be far off. More was at stake than the fate of the Philomela Outreach; he was amazed that no one saw this but him.

Sh'in came over to the table and sat by him, positioning herself as far away from him as she could. Michael carefully controlled his expression to hide his amusement. To avoid staring at her, he switched his gaze to Joan. Her eyes met his, and dropped in embarrassment. Michael wondered how she saw him. Was he apish in her view? Masculine? Threatening?

He sipped at his coffee. *Where to begin?* he wondered. He took a deep breath.

"Matthew, how much of the strategic situation in this area are you familiar with?"

Vai thought it over. "Not much. I leave the strategy to the Navy. Taking planets is my job."

"You'll be getting a chance soon, never fear. Joan?"

Joan Rogers blushed at the familiar use of her name. As Michael's intelligence chief, she was more used to strategic concepts than was Vai. "There's the developed core of the Concordat, thinning out toward us. Sectors Tikhvin, Triangle, and the District are the latest-organized, incorporated units. They bound the Philomela Outreach . . ." She broke off and blushed further as she realized that this was all too well known.

"Go on," Michael said. From his voice, she drew the strength to continue.

"That's that. Almost all of our naval strength in this entire area is here right now, in our two fleets."

"One fleet," Michael stated firmly. He instantly regretted his sharp tone.

"What does this have to do with a . . . traitor?" Vai asked. Michael was thankful for the cue.

"That fleet was plainly sent here with orders to cripple mine, with no thought to its own losses." Again he hesitated, unsure of how best to proceed.

"That fleet, commanded by Commodore Steldan, was the reserve fleet from Tikhvin Sector. With it destroyed, and with us hamstrung, as was intended, this entire frontier would be defenseless.

"Who benefits most from a demonstration out here with our side having nothing to defend itself with?"

The three considered, approaching the problem silently.

"The Sonallans," Michael answered himself.

"But they're all the way across the Concordat," objected Joan. Michael waited for any other responses.

"Where is the Navy's biggest current concentration? Holding the Sonallan sphere in occupation. Where would a detachment come from, then, if there were a perceived threat out here? The same place. It directly benefits them to have us in trouble here."

Sh'in was unconvinced; that was no surprise. Vai and Rogers remained silent, deep in thought.

"I don't know where the threat was to come from," Michael went on. "Perhaps we've just defeated it. Probably the raiders were stirred up by these traitors; certainly they've been left unchecked too long. That's what I find the most suspicious: the raiders were left alone, free to gather their strength, but when the decision was made to crush them, it took almost no time at all to prepare. Who makes decisions at that level?"

Vai seemed about to speak; instead he drank deeply from his rapidly cooling coffee.

Michael summed up. "I need to be prepared to make war on an unknown enemy, back home. I need to be able to expose the traitors, some of whom perhaps hold high-level offices. I need to be able to uncover the truth behind all these unexplained coincidences." He looked around him. "Is there any question but that we've been lied to? Isn't it evident that we have enemies other than the obvious ones? I need to find out, soon, before things become dangerously overt. The danger, you see, isn't out here. It's back home."

Sh'in cleared her throat. "Could it be that you're wrong?"

Michael rejoiced, showing nothing of his exultation. Sh'in asking a serious question? That was indeed a victory. "It could well be. Do you want me to take the chance?"

Sh'in had no answer for that, but was plainly unconvinced.

"Now that we've got a Scout fleet again," Michael continued, "I'm going to have to let Captain Engel out of the brig. Captain Edwards is a different problem. It didn't prove all that difficult to persuade the computer back to proper loyalty, but Edwards's actions were meant to take the *Philomela* out of action. What should I do with him?"

Joan wouldn't meet his gaze. Vai seemed lost in thought. *Is it up to me?* Sh'in wondered. "Do you intend to press charges when we've returned?"

"No." Michael's response took Sh'in by surprise. "As it is, it's permanently on his record that I removed him from command, and why. I don't need to harm him further. As soon as we've pacified Acheron, I'll let him out of the brig and ask him to confine himself to his quarters."

"He really did mean only the best," Sh'in said cautiously. *Damn him! He's being reasonable! How can I deal with the big bastard when he's being reasonable?*

"He meant the best? Perhaps. The same is true for all

the Captains in the fleet that attacked us. They, like Edwards, won't be punished. They simply had to be stopped."

"What remains to be done?" asked Vai.

"You'll be landing soon. At this point a whirlwind bombardment will be more effective than a prolonged one. We'll try to find you a good jumping-off point."

"Very good, sir."

"Joan, you'll shuttle over to the wreck of the *Illuminator* and draw what you can from its computer. The data we need is probably there. I want proof of who the traitor was."

"Yes, sir." Joan glanced up at him, then dropped her gaze in flustered unease. She wondered if she would always be so awed by this man.

"Any other questions?"

There were none.

"Remember always," Michael summed up, "that I'm in command. I can't function without your help and advice, but my orders are to be obeyed. I'm afraid that we will have disagreements, some serious, in the future. I expect each of you to do your duty."

Sh'in stood aside to let him pass, but would not meet his gaze. Joan Rogers walked to the dispenser to refill her mug, returning in time to nod an uncertain farewell to Michael and to Vai, who likewise nodded as he left. Alone, the women settled.

"How much of what he said did he really mean?" Joan asked in a reserved whisper.

"Either all of it, or none," answered Sh'in. "And I don't know which."

"Who gave the order to fire?" the flat-voiced interrogator asked of Captain Steldan. He watched the meters on the voice-stress analyzer rather than his prisoner.

"Captain Douglas did."

"Why?"

"Because, I believe, he was loyal to the Philomela Outreach, and its ideal of independence."

"What is your role in this?"

Steldan closed his eyes. This was the fifth repetition of the question. "I am loyal to the Concordat of Archive. I will follow any legal order given me by my superiors."

The grueling questions continued, sometimes fast, sometimes slow.

"What is your relationship to Grand Admiral de la Noue?"

"Advisory."

"Did you advise her to initiate this treacherous attack?"

Steldan considered that a leading question, to say the least. Was it worth dignifying with an answer?

"No."

"Who did?"

"As far as I know, Captain Douglas was acting on his own."

"Ridiculous. You know better."

It was a standard interrogation technique: refuse to accept the answers given you. Steldan knew it well, and a hundred others, all equally effective for being so very rude.

"Douglas acted alone."

The weary time passed. Finally, in disgust, the interrogator gave up. "That's all, then," he muttered, gathering up his equipment.

Ten minutes later, Admiral Michael Devon arrived at the confinement level.

Joan Rogers breathlessly caught up to Michael at the cell door. "Sir!"

"It can wait, Commander Rogers," Michael said without turning.

"It's important!"

"I said it can wait." He strode forward to the security doors separating the small antechamber from the cell where Commodore Athalos Steldan waited. Joan barely had time to open her mouth; the doors slid wide. Steldan stood, watching Michael enter.

Joan looked first at him, then at Michael. The two men studied each other appraisingly. Were they allies? Enemies? Both and neither, it seemed.

Michael's blondness radiated, glowing in the air before his captive. Undaunted, Steldan returned his gaze. To Joan it appeared as if the darker-haired, green-eyed prisoner kept fires brighter than his captor's shielded behind curtains, which themselves were hidden by his very openness.

Suddenly embarrassed, Joan closed her mouth and stepped back. The doors slid shut. In the antechamber she paused, then turned and sat on a low seat against the wall. Near her shoulder was a recessed keylock.

Michael dismissed me; he didn't want me to witness the interview with Captain Steldan. Why?

Breathlessly, hesitantly, she reached out and switched over the keylock. *He never ordered me not to listen . . .* From a speaker grille above her head she heard the two men within speaking.

"Greetings," said one of them. Joan was unsure which. Had Michael intended her to overhear? She felt totally out of her depth.

"Why did you attack us?"

"I could ask you the same thing."

Joan shivered. Their voices were so much alike—in very different ways. One was more friendly; it also had a sharper edge. The other was forbidding; it was that one she trusted. But which was Michael's and which was Steldan's, she had no way to guess.

"What are your plans?"

"I haven't made any; it would depend on you."

"In what way?"

"Which of us is the more helpless?"

No hint of humor. "Whose side are you on?"

"There are four sides. De la Noue's. Yours. Mine. And the Outreach raiders. We're both against the last one, I trust."

"Captain Douglas—"

"Is very dead, and thus of no use to this discussion."

"He probably wasn't on de la Noue's side."

"Sabotaging two of her ships? One would think not."

"And only four sides? You overlook the Sonallans."

"I assure you, I would never do that. Strange that you should mention them—"

"Being all the way across the sphere from us. You can see why it would be to their advantage to have us divided."

"Not only to *their* advantage."

"Who else would benefit?"

"There are powerful interests within the Concordat, any of which might gain from dissent in the Navy."

The sound came across of one of them pacing, relentlessly, the length of the room.

"Are the people on the planet below to suffer needlessly to advance your plans?"

"The Outreach's revolt was not at my instigation. I don't see what you imagine it gains me." He sounded honestly surprised. Joan listened carefully, trying to distinguish between the voices. "Doesn't my very presence here prove that?" He was not answered. "I see that it doesn't."

"I don't know who you serve," said the first, the one who paced. "Damn it, we're supposed to be on the same side!"

"Shooting at each other is a novel way of demonstrating this."

"Neither of us is responsible for that. That is totally beside the point. We've got . . . well, you might call it an intelligence problem."

"For the record—"

"This is not on the record."

"Hmm. Agreed."

"Why waste the time? Neither of us will believe the other."

"True. The facts will be revealed, however, in the end."

"In the end. How many must die first?"

"Too damned many have died already! Forgive me—"

"What do you have to gain?"

"Until a very few hours ago, I didn't know—I didn't have proof—that I had anything to lose."

"Now?"

"All or nothing, I guess."

"Correct."

A long silence followed.

The doors slid open; Michael stalked out. Ignoring Joan, he left the area, face averted. Behind him, Steldan motionlessly gazed at the floor, lost in thought. He looked up as the doors shut themselves. For a moment, he met Joan's gaze. Then he was locked in, and she was locked out.

I never told Michael my news, she agonized. *I found it in the computer aboard the* Illuminator; *I found everything! The location of every bomb aboard every ship in both our fleets. I found locations, detonation sequences . . .*

And I can't tell Michael.

The thought froze her. One of the two men might—

might!—be a servant of the enemy. Which enemy? Joan stood very still, trying to sort out what she'd heard.

Decision came to her.

With a secret this dangerous, the only person I can trust to keep it is myself.

Is this disloyalty?

She didn't know.

Commander of Gunnery Ruth Noel took several turns about the busy command bridge of the *Resolute*. Most of the circuitry had survived, including the main and backup computer accesses. Since she had been given command of the wrecked Dreadnought, the fact cheered her, if only slightly.

Formerly in charge of a laser bay on the *Philomela*, she had been chosen by Admiral Devon to oversee the repair of the drifting, gutted hulk. It seemed like an impossible job. That portions of the ship yet held air amazed her; to expect it to someday return to active duty was insane.

The drives were wrecked. The power plant couldn't light a flashlight; the maneuver drive couldn't propel a rowboat. Nothing remained of them but pools of once-molten metal, splashed and plated across buckled and twisted structural members. She mentally cataloged the remaining ship's systems, using the exercise as an excuse to avoid real work.

Artificial gravity: working, somewhat, and in selected places, thanks to a portable small-gauge power plant on loan from the *Philomela*.

Life support: the same.

Passive defenses, anti-concussion fields, antimissile batteries, nuclear dampers . . . all dead. Ruined beyond her ability even to imagine repaired. Only the ship's thick armor still survived, and that had a gaping hole in it amidships. How could a ship be expected to fight with a chink in its armor the size of a large building?

On the bridge, technicians worked with little enthusiasm, splicing control linkages that led nowhere. Commander Noel had ordered that the ship be made ready for the installation of new engines and systems. They considered her to be unrealistic. They obeyed their orders, however, all the time convinced that the twisted wreck would never again jump.

Touring the gunnery bays, she felt a little more optimism. The heavy lasers were in quite good shape. Without a power plant, however, they would be useless. And without maneuver capacity, there would be no way of bringing them to bear upon an enemy.

Did Admiral Devon know something she didn't? Was there a scrapped Dreadnought on the planet below with a power plant and maneuver drive ready to be cannibalized?

As a matter of fact, there was. At the weed-grown construction yards of the decaying Acheron Spaceport, the unfinished bulk of a *Cathedral*-class Improved Dreadnought rested, laid down several years ago during the height of the Sonallan crisis. Michael, with access to computer records aboard the *Philomela,* had discovered the project, and planned to boost the stern half of the uncompleted ship into orbit, to be rudely attached to the bow half of the *Resolute.* The resulting hybrid, overengined, unstable, and dangerously weak along its join, would nevertheless be a welcome addition to his fleet.

When General Vai captured the planet, the Spaceport with this wreck in it would be among his highest priorities.

Michael knew full well that his voyage was far from over; he already knew his next target. It was the desert world of Tikhvin.

Chapter Twelve

Interrupted for several days, the savage bombardment of the planet Acheron resumed. The first few days' rain of missiles went toward recovering lost ground, knocking out planetary defense lasers that had been repaired during the lull. Using almost surgically precise missile fire to deliver fractional kiloton fission warheads, Michael made certain that the collateral damage was kept to a minimum. He did not unleash the multi-megaton city-shattering weapons; those were for enemies, not for one's own rebellious citizens.

"The duration of the surface struggle is to be minimized," he said, addressing the assembled troops of the 44th Marine Division. "We'll land you right on top of the enemy troops, in a good position to swoop down into their primary city. This is an almost undeveloped, back-cluster world that the raiders have decided to make a stand on."

His voice rose. "You've fought the Sonallans on their home world. Compared to Tenh Sonallae, this is a village-world, a weed patch, scarcely an outpost. You're the best; they're nothing. Nothing whatever.

"So to hell with subtlety. We'll drop you in their laps, and let them try to figure out what to do with you. If they're lucky, they'll be allowed to surrender. If not, if they try to resist . . . then it'll be their own fault, won't it?

"The First Regiment will land on the hilly uplands above the city, with most of the heavy weapons. The Second and Third Regiments will land beside the city, up- and down-river. The 1071st Marines will land, dispersed, to keep the countryside secure. And, never fear, you'll have air and close orbit support from above."

At an officer's surreptitious signal, the Marines, veter-

ans all, stood and barked a brief cheer for their leaders.
General Matthew Vai stood to dismiss them. Together he
and Michael departed.

A subtle change took place in the tempo of bombardment. The impotent planetary defense lasers, now silenced
if not destroyed, were passed over as targets in favor of
troop and equipment concentrations. *Soon,* the missiles
wailed as they fell from the heavens; *soon.* The defenders,
dug-in infantry, armor dispersed for survival, and artillery
emplacements, sensed impending glory or defeat. First
they must survive the bombardment.

Missiles swerved in mid-flight, homing in on radar stations and radio relays. The electromagnetic noise gen-
erated by almost continuous thermonuclear explosions
disrupted all but the most powerful communications, save
in the few prepared positions where lines had been laid for
field telephones.

Commando units waited, entrenched, ready for infiltra-
tion sorties behind the enemy's expected front lines. Their
job would be to prevent the Marines from linking together
their many isolated landing zones.

Men took to scanning the skies, vainly and helplessly.

A point of light was seen. Was it a transport?

Instead of the slow-moving, easy target the tense defenders expected, the spot dissolved into a squadron of Fighters, diving down from low orbit to hit targets the missiles
had missed.

Lieutenant Jaquish hated working within atmospheres.
The sticky, soupy, viscous turbulence interfered too much
with the free maneuvering of his Fighter.

The squadron soon reached its assigned post over the
green surface of the planet. Breaking up into several two-
man flights, the larger formation ceased to exist. When it
eventually reformed, several pilots would be gone. Lieutenant Jaquish had no intention of being one of them.

Doctrine said to fly low, but not too low. Lieutenant Jaquish didn't feel there was such a thing as "too low." If
every meter he rose above the surface increased his theoretical horizon by roughly two kilometers, he intended to
stay mighty damned low. And of course the geometry of

the horizon only applied to a perfectly smooth world; here he was able to take full advantage of ground cover.

The result was his flying at nearly a thousand kilometers an hour, dodging smoothly between trees, buildings, and low hills. If his mission was to knock out a laser anti-aircraft battery, then that was all the more reason to play it safe.

His wingman didn't see it that way and coursed above, varying altitude and path to avoid danger, but still visible for a greater distance than Jaquish was. *Fine,* Jaquish thought. *Let him be a target if he wants.* He sang through a stand of tall trees, leaving them whipping in the gale behind him.

Only a few minutes from their destination, they flew over an entrenched company of armor. Before Jaquish was even consciously aware of the gray tanks below he had released three of his seven missiles. The camp was gone again, and behind him the small valley erupted in flames. The automatic cameras placed about the small craft would have recorded the action for review by a computer when he arrived back at the *Later.* He hoped his quickness would earn him a commendation.

Over two more ridges he flew, with his wingman above, now to the left, now the right. The fool was going to give the target an extra few seconds of warning, Jaquish knew. Just short of the laser battery's kill-zone, he swerved to the right, letting his wingman take the direct run if he so wished. There it was, to his left.

The battery was a cluster of tracked vehicles facing outward in a small circle scattered through a stony outcrop amidst the green fields. Already they fired, their steady orange beams swiftly flicking back and forth like long fencing foils. The threadlike beams sought the wingman, matching their radars and computers against the Fighter's electronic countermeasures and its pilot's skill. Each time the beams deftly snicked back and forth, their target was miraculously somewhere else. Lieutenant Jaquish, from his unexpected approach angle, knocked out two of the firing vehicles with perfectly placed laser shots of his own. He buzzed over the encampment and through the danger before any of them had a chance to aim at him.

Zigzagging crazily, he returned over the rock-strewn

field, flying right into the muzzle of one of the laser vehicles. At that range, neither could miss. Jaquish fired first. The vehicle quietly died, its front armor glowing blue-white where the beam had punctured it.

Once more he was past the battery. Where was his wingman? There was no trace of the lad. It didn't matter. Jaquish knew himself easily capable of taking out the few remaining lasers. At this point only one could fire in any given direction. For them to regroup to double-up their fire would be insane, inviting an attack upon their rear. If even one more of them was destroyed, the remainder would be left completely defenseless.

For the third time he flew low, this time in a straight line, heading dead-on for his chosen laser vehicle. He fired his own pulse laser, and threw the small craft into a jacknifing climb, to level off at an altitude of forty meters and just as precipitously dive again.

And there was his wingman, methodically beaming away the four surviving targets while taking no risks himself. Jaquish couldn't blame the young man. He flew between the low-flying wingman and the ground in a gesture of bravado, and, angling his craft's nose into the sky, blasted away straight up, eventually escaping the atmosphere altogether. In the stark blackness of vacuum, he radioed a brief congratulation to his wingman, who paralleled his course a few kilometers behind. They headed for the Mothership.

Half the squadron failed to return. Jaquish and his wingman made up the only two-man team to return intact.

Some would call it luck.

The transports landed in the valleys that had been prepared for them. Accompanied by swarms of Fighters, the large landing craft settled roughly to the scorched earth, raising swirling clouds of ash. Armored soldiers flung themselves out of the several doorways that opened in each ship. Scurrying, they rushed forward to the tops of the low ridges that formed the landing valleys.

The 44th Marine Division landed in twelve separate spots, unloaded, and prepared to effect linkages between their neighboring enclaves. These were spread, as Michael and General Vai had planned, in three dispersed groups of four units, surrounding the city.

There was fighting immediately. Two of the landing craft had come down virtually on top of defending units. Laser hand weapons and ordinary slug-throwers sent their charges back and forth, soon defining a front line between the mingled troops.

Support from the swooping Fighters helped decide the issue in the Marines' favor. Soon their perimeters were secure, allowing them to begin consolidation and expansion. General Vai and his staff landed not long afterward, then set up a working command post and radio relay station.

Colonel Sheffield had his hands full. His duties included setting up the command center, overseeing the three landing regiments' radio reports, and relaying General Vai's orders. This was the work he was best trained for; he almost enjoyed it. First Regiment, under Colonel Joshua Crater, expanded almost unchecked. They had managed to link together three of their four landing enclaves and raced ahead of their heavy weapons support.

General Vai came up behind Sheffield, peering over his shoulder at the tactical abstract on the computer. The Second and Third Regiments had more trouble, spread out on lower, more level ground.

"Tell 'em they've got support when they need it," Vai said unhurriedly. In the nearby valleys the heavy artillery casters were setting up. Occasional muffled explosions could be heard as the large transmitters slung test masses toward the enemy target zones.

Soon orbiting observers signaled that proper range had been found; not long after that, packages of high explosives were placed on target by the primitive teleportation devices. Forward observers confirmed the orbiting sighters' reports: the bombs materialized, distorted but still explosive, directly on target, detonating perfectly.

Overhead shimmer told of incoming bombs: counter-battery fire. The weapons burst as they materialized, showering the gunners below with bits of burning casing but nothing worse. Smiling grimly, the gunners kept transmitting. The enemy's aim would improve, given time. That time must be denied them. Tons of explosives were fed into the transmitters, arriving at their destinations without traversing the intervening space.

"Beats the hell out of line-of-sight shooting," said a young artillerist. Due to the volume of the departing bombs' transmission bursts, he was unheard. He'd never known about arched, indirect fire; he'd never known about twisted rope ballistae, either. More packages went into the teleporters; more were carted from the landing boat to be transmitted.

The enemy's aim was improving.

The Marines infiltrated expertly, working about strong-points in small detachments, putting their firepower to maximum effect upon the rearward areas. Caster fire intensified as targets became available, clearly defined by orbital observation.

As Harold Court, ground troops commander for John Burt, watched from his hilltop command post, he could see a segment of the battle develop. A flight of enemy Fighters descended from the sky, swooping almost to the ground before scattering. The thin-faced Captain beside him called in the sighting. Within minutes the sky was a spiderweb of dancing red threads. Several Fighters were intercepted by the deceptively weak-looking laser beams, which sliced through metal and plastic to cut at the delicate systems within. More Fighters completed their missions, however, inflicting severe damage upon sensitive targets.

The pace of combat quickened, and Court, helpless, was made aware of the fact that a full, reinforced Marine division was concentrated within less than two hundred square kilometers. His plans had been made long ago; he was not now able to change them. His several planned counterattacks were either repulsed or called off at the discretion of company leaders.

To his surprise it was already noon. The fields and hills below showed green and beautiful from the rocky hilltop where he sat. *Ground troops commander,* he thought wryly. At the scale of this battle, he couldn't even exercise command over his headquarters company. Each unit now fought on its own, surrounded by probing Marines. The heavy rumble of the artillery casters died away as friend and foe closed to near mingling.

"What about us, sir?" asked the Captain.

"Eh? Oh, we'll wait here. Nothing more we can do anyway, wouldn't you say?" Actually, the fight was far from over. What remained to be done, however, would be done under Burt's personal direction. That the terrorist tactics he intended to use were illegal mattered not a bit to him; the Concordat already wanted his head. Letting Court surrender was a kindness to him.

John Burt and Andrew North are down in that damned city, putting together a small collection of hells to greet the Marines. That'll only earn them a quick death . . . and maybe will enable their successors to win the peace, after we've lost the war.

From the left, a detachment of Marines spread out and sprinted up the hill toward the rude shelter where Court awaited them. The surrender was brief and to the point.

"We strike!" shouted Losse Merent. "We strike!" echoed his fifty volunteers in a ragged battle cry. Rising from cover, they swarmed across the quiet service road and through the trees, knocking down the previously weakened sections of the security fence at the rear of the city's main power plant. They had no chance of fighting their way through to the huge underground fusion generator itself; that wasn't their plan.

Sprawling over several small hills and cool valleys in the parklands below the city, the power plant complex was like a town with no inhabitants, or a fortress with no defenders. This was an illusion, Merent knew, born of the installation's vast area and its stark, geometric concrete layout. Inside this large fenced-off plant were numerous security personnel, well-trained and ready. The illusion of desertion persisted; where in this jungle of piping and of block structures could a person find shelter?

He led his team scrambling to the previously chosen building; while all other doors slammed themselves shut to the accompaniment of intruder alarms, this door was jammed in its slot. Merent's inside man had done his job. The crew, alert, followed him inside and took up positions beside the door, ready to repel any relief efforts.

The small building, containing automated switching apparatus, was unmanned during this shift. Soon the main power supply to the city dwindled, died. Merent watched the meters, and sighed his relief. The damage they'd done was fairly easily repaired; the city was not powerless for any real length of time.

Neither was the building they occupied defensible for long. If most of the planetary militia was out in the hills vainly contesting the Marines' landing, there were still enough troops within the city to evict the counter-rebels handily.

But, Merent hoped, by now Casadesus and his strike team of four hundred had fought their way into the government office building, taking at least symbolic control of the planet. With the main power to the building's defenses cut off, and with the backup power disabled by another inside man, all that stood between Casadesus and H. Anselm, the planetary president, was a very small bodyguard formation.

Was John Burt there also, to be captured? If so, the rebellion in the Outreach was dead and buried. If not, if he escaped, Merent predicted trouble ahead for the counter-revolt.

He had no more time for reflection. Outside, dodging from cover to cover toward the small outbuilding, armed troops closed in. Enough, Merent judged, to defeat him and his fifty after no more than half an hour of firefight. Or —he smiled—after five minutes of support weapon fire. And that would ruin the equipment inside for good. Days would be required to replace it.

He took position behind a heavy conduit and began to fire upon the advancing enemy.

Perfectly in accordance with Casadesus' plans, eight men entered the lightly guarded main portals of the government office building, successfully giving the impression of men with legitimate business inside. Together with the five men and women who worked there, recently subverted by Casadesus' machinations, the building had a substantial unknown strike force stalking its halls.

Denise Voleur had been given control of the force whose duty would be to storm the rear of the building. She and her fifty waited inside several buildings across the wide street from the heavy stone facade of their target. Plans prepared many months in advance were proceeding rapidly.

The lights shining within the building faded; although it was day, the large rooms and chambers inside became quite dark. Officials looked about in distress. The skeleton staff, covering mechanically the duties that twenty times their number normally oversaw, were assailed with doubt. Were they in danger? How could the invaders be as close as the power plant?

In his private office, H. Anselm, white face suddenly matching his hair, gave himself over for a wild moment to his fears. *We are invaded. I will be shot as a collaborator. . . .*

John Burt, beside him, suffered no such paralysis. Grabbing his pistol, he leaped toward the window and carefully peered out. What he saw filled him with a rage he'd never imagined himself capable of. His folly returned to him in a rush.

Nearly fifty men and women dashed across the street, people armed for an assault upon this building. Burt took it in in an instant; they weren't his troops. It was painfully obvious how deeply his policies had failed.

All I've done for this damned world, he snarled to himself, *and there are still Concordat traitors among us.* North had always told him to work harder on internal security. *I never took him seriously. What did he know of the political situation?*

Anselm approached, trying to look out the window.

"Get back, idiot," Burt snapped. Stunned, Anselm jumped back. He'd always known he was nothing but a figurehead for Burt; of late he'd grown to imagine that he had some power of his own. Burt's words shattered that illusion, quickly.

There was gunfire in the building. Small-arms firefights rang the length of the hallways. There was nothing whatever keeping the counter-rebels from coming directly here.

Was I a fool for underestimating the loyalist sentiment? Burt wondered. Scant time was left. Against the horde he'd seen charging across the open street, the small bodyguard platoon would be helpless.

Someone was at the door. Burt looked at Anselm, who

shakily gestured an okay. "Come in," called the figure-head president.

The leader of the bodyguard platoon entered, pale and broken in spirit. "We'll have to run," he said, unsure of whom to address.

"Let's go, then," Burt said, and motioned the two men toward the roof, where an aircar waited.

It proved to be a mistake. As the elevator opened, letting them out on the rooftop, they were met with a heated crossfire from neighboring rooftops. Already the aircar had been disabled, its hull riddled and its cockpit wrecked by small-arms fire. Burt hastily led the two back into the elevator. A whoop of triumph followed them, cut off by the closing doors.

Below, the security platoon still held back the determined assault, primarily through the intrinsic advantage always held by the defense, and aided by better equipment and training. Time was on their side. If the engagement lasted much longer, reserves could be brought up from nearby city defensive positions.

John Burt rounded up five soldiers and tried to make his way to the escape route he should have thought of first: the basement. Tunnels there gave onto a number of bolt-holes, many of which were defensible by one man against an army. If they could win through to the basement, they were free.

The darkness of the corridors was relieved only by the dim light that seeped in through high windows intended for ornamentation rather than for illumination. The painted portraits of previous, Concordat-loyal planetary presidents gazed down placidly from their heavy frames, unimpressed by this ill-timed revolution. A figure ducked out of sight behind a doorway, and from cover opened fire. Three shots from John Burt silenced the would-be assassin. Their progress through the labyrinthine building slowed now that they were aware of the need for caution.

Would I have been better off with a secret police? Burt wondered painfully. *Was I too respectful of people's rights?* He had never intended to be a dictator, only a deliverer. It occurred to him that a covert agency, spying relentlessly on the loyalists throughout the Outreach, would probably have uncovered this damnable plot in time to have coun-

tered it. All it would have required was a massive disre-
spect for personal privacy, property, and liberty. *And that
would have made me as bad as the damned Concordat,* he
thought savagely.

A part of his mind mocked him, charging him harshly
with believing his own propaganda. Did he really have any
evidence that the Concordat employed illegal methods?
Could it be true, as they claimed, that the massive conscriptions and trebled taxation in this area were necessary
to fight an alien threat on another front? His spirit re-
coiled from these doubts. *I'd rather believe my own propaganda than the lies told by my enemies.*

The elevator that would take them to the basement was
guarded by a team of counter-rebels. Scarcely pausing,
Burt and his hastily formed guard team opened fire,
downing two and scattering the rest. From the crossing
corridor echoed a fusillade of ill-aimed shots. Burt, the
guard officer, and two soldiers made the crossing unharmed. Anselm and three others failed to make it to the
elevator by the time the doors closed.

I hope the poor fool lives, Burt growled to himself, unaware of the prayer behind the statement. He had been
more than just a tool used by Burt to advance the revolution. His leadership had kept not only Acheron but half the
industrial planets of the Outreach organized, cooperative,
and faithful. The man was perhaps doomed to be remembered as a footnote, as one of history's many men of average talents. They, however, kept civilization running.
Brilliant men, Burt knew, including himself, caused almost as much trouble as they ever remedied.

The resistance in the heights evaporated. The Marines,
moving ahead of their artillery support, approached the
city's outskirts, moving cautiously yet swiftly along broad
avenues and past homes, some abandoned, some not. Civilians had been warned by both sides to stay out of sight;
most of the men and women of combat age had been taken
into one or the other of the armies, either to fight the Sonallans far away or to man the revolution.

The hardened Marines, most from interior Sectors,
didn't really care who they shot at, especially if the target
was shooting back. Snipers made the streets hellish; when

located, they were given no opportunity to surrender. Colonel McBain hoped that this harsh treatment of last-ditch defenders would discourage other would-be heroes. Instead, however, it brought out a fatalism in those people misguided enough to become snipers in the first place.

Under the sporadic fire from unseen, solitary enemies, armed with silent weapons and telescopic sights, the Marines grew surly. They advanced by turns, keeping to maximum cover, and fired indiscriminately at anything suspicious. They were slowed, but they were not stopped. As always, extraordinary tactics could not prevail once orthodox combat had failed.

The Spaceport, fallen into disrepair from lack of use, was swiftly bypassed, according to General Vai's orders. No one wanted to cross the huge landing field, an open area with no cover. Vai's orders were welcomed. What use could the Spaceport be anyway? The boost-grid was intact, perhaps, but weeds pushed their way up through the concrete. The Marines moved on, glancing only casually at the decaying complex.

Working up the steep gulleys and canyons below the sprawling Spaceport, the Second Regiment of the 1071st moved toward the city's heart. On the other side of the port, the lead elements of the 44th maneuvered down built-up hillsides, crossing streets only with care, heading for a linkup with the other division.

The leaders of the revolution claimed that they worked to free the Outreach from the Concordat's repressive economic policies; that they would increase trade by throwing off the larger system's regulation. In the meantime, a Spaceport that formerly handled millions of tons of cargo, raw and finished materials, the wealth of the Outreach, now sat idle, growing weeds, contributing nothing.

Behind the high wire fence protecting the Spaceport, in the rusting construction yards, sat the rear half of an uncompleted Improved Dreadnought, the *Basilica*. At present only a few people on the planet knew of the plans to boost the hulk into orbit. The fighting moved past, slowly, in fear and in hatred, until the Spaceport once again lay silent.

* * *

The city was all but taken. Nowhere was any resistance more organized than wandering fire teams to be found; even those tended to avoid Marine detachments. Dusk fell swiftly over a planet largely untouched by the fighting. Like many colony worlds, Acheron was completely dependent upon its capital city for communications, transport, and administration. While the lesser cities might complain, they could do nothing now that the central heart of their economy was taken.

General Matthew Vai strode through the gathering gloom toward the massive government office building, where his troops had found an unusual situation. Sheffield, beside him, was no more certain than he as to the exact meaning of the events here.

A Marine noncom saluted, indicating that the building was clear. Vai nodded. Sheffield motioned the bodyguard squad to wait and followed Vai inside.

In the large central hall they found a section of Marines guarding a tall old man, white-haired and somber. Beside him was a young woman, fiery-eyed and defiant. Several of the other prisoners were plainly their subordinates.

In another part of the room, medics put the finishing touches to their minor surgery on a wounded man. Vai recognized him as H. Anselm, the planetary president.

A guard sergeant approached and saluted. Quietly he informed Vai of what had happened.

"When we got here, this man"—he indicated the elderly Casadesus—"was here first, and let us in. They'd been holding out against a half-assed relief effort by some planetary troops who were trying to take the building back. We scattered 'em, and he let us in. He says his name's—"

"Casadesus," the man intoned. Vai glanced at the sergeant, who shrugged. Approaching the counter-rebel, Vai took stock of him. Even surrounded by Concordat Marines, the man gave the impression of being in command. Sheffield hung back to converse with the guard sergeant.

"I represent the legitimate Concordat-loyal government of Acheron," Casadesus stated clearly. "Unaided, my volunteers have recaptured this building, with its equipment and files intact, in the name of the Concordat of Archive.

We have also captured the traitor Anselm, leader of the collaborationists in this world."

Vai stood silently for a moment, considering. Sheffield approached him from behind and respectfully caught his attention.

"From what Sergeant McAnnister says, this Casadesus"—he swallowed his mispronunciation unhappily—"could be just a local petty tyrant with some devoted troops." With difficulty he kept his voice to a low whisper.

"Come along," Vai said and pulled Sheffield away from Casadesus' hearing. "He may or may not be legitimate, but have you taken a look at this place?" Sheffield shook his head.

Vai took a deep breath and spoke quietly. "This place was fairly secure, and yet they took it away from its defenders with ease. This is no pack of backyard terrorists. They know what they're doing." Worry crossed his face. "That's why I don't know how to decide. If I choose wrongly, I could foul things up pretty good locally. Admiral Devon wouldn't like that at all."

Sheffield raised an eyebrow.

"If they were a simple gang of homegrown hoodlums," Vai went on, "I'd put them in charge straight off, knowing that they could be thrown out at leisure. But these people are organized enough to entrench themselves in office. On the other hand, Michael told me that he didn't want us to run the planet like a captured enemy world."

"You can ask him, can't you, sir?"

Vai looked carefully at Sheffield. Shrugging, he agreed. "I can ask him. Why not?" He signaled the man carrying the orbital uplink radio.

A few minutes passed while the connection was steadied. Michael Devon's voice came clearly over the link. "General?"

"We've got the city secured. I'm in the government office building with the planetary president. We've also got an old man with an armed following claiming to be the legitimate planetary government, loyal to us. They rose up in counter-rebellion, capturing the building and holding it for us. I thought you'd best speak to their leader before I made any decisions."

"A good idea, General. Congratulations on a well-executed campaign, by the way."

"Thank you. I'll put the fellow on the link. He says his name's Casadesus."

"I'll wait."

Casadesus approached with grave dignity and asked General Vai for privacy. Put off by the man's effrontery, Vai nevertheless stepped away, out of hearing.

"What do you think will happen?" Sheffield asked.

"I'm unable to guess," Vai confessed.

Several minutes later Casadesus drew back from the radio and gestured to Vai. Shrugging, Vai took the microphone from the aged counter-rebel. "Sir?"

"I've given him official recognition as head of state, Matthew. You'll have to help him, of course."

"You've made him my superior?" Vai asked incredulously, glancing sidelong at Casadesus.

Michael's voice was relaxed, confident, over the radio link. "I think we can trust him. He's not the type to begin massive purges or roundups."

"Sir, somewhere on this planet John Burt is hiding. If we can capture him . . ."

"If you can, fine. But don't assign too many of your troops to the hunt. He's not our prime enemy right now. The people of this planet are. Until we can establish a cultural-warfare team here to stabilize loyalties, it'll take force. The only problem is, I can't spare the troops to hold this planet forever."

Vai was honestly surprised. "We have other targets? I'd thought that our campaign was over. Certainly the raiders are broken."

"We have other targets. I can't speak further over the radio—I'm sure you understand—but perhaps you'll remember our conversation in the officers' lounge.

"For now, help Casadesus put together a durable government, preferably with a broad base. He's no fool, but he may be overzealous. Try to keep your soldiers in line; the rebels will be looking for provocation."

"I'll do my best," Vai promised, and signed off.

Within minutes, Casadesus was installed as planetary president, with Denise Voleur as his first assistant. Soon calls for support flew across the planet, seeking to build up a basis for legitimacy. Former rebels were promised a secure place in the coalition if they would forswear the revolt; John Burt was promised a complete pardon if he would surrender.

Few of the appeals were answered. To General Vai, it seemed that Michael's plans for an end to the military occupation were overoptimistic.

On the outskirts of the town, the 1071st Marines found that their cordon was permeable and reported this fact to General Vai. Sheffield, as always, was quietly concerned.

Shortly after midnight a series of explosions ripped through the center of the city, tearing great holes in the roadways and shattering windows for several blocks. The power net serving half the planet faltered, then cut itself off. In the darkness, Marine platoons scrambled, dutifully combing the streets, knowing full well that they'd find no one.

By dawn, Casadesus' provisional government found itself under a different kind of attack; noncompliance. The outlying regions quietly resisted the new leader's directives, passively fighting him in lieu of carrying on a hopeless uprising. Although the action in no way directly threatened the new order, it seriously undermined its legitimacy. In the city, under Casadesus' and General Vai's direct control, things were more subtly wrong. The ministers of the enacting house, although accounted for, refused to allow themselves to be associated with the upstarts, while the many enforcement and civil service officials scattered throughout their precincts found excuses not to report for work.

Vai struggled valiantly to avoid imposing martial law. He and Casadesus knew that to govern by force would forever destroy any hope of a popular recognition of the new regime. The ideal solution would be for him to leave a sole battalion behind to quietly maintain the status quo while the bulk of the divisions pulled off the planet. Objections intruded, first among which was that without massive invasions of the privacy guaranteed by the planet's Enabling Charter, one battalion could never hope to stop the terrorizing raids that John Burt had begun.

General Vai, Casadesus, and Admiral Michael Devon

secretly discussed the situation at length one evening in
the government office building. In contrast to Vai in his
tunic and tight, flat tabard and Casadesus in a shapeless
coat of a dark color, Michael wore sharp dress blues with a
crisp high collar, white pants, and gleaming black boots.
Even in repose, he was very much the center of the room. It
seemed to Vai that Michael was the center of any room he
entered, no matter what the situation. Was Michael himself aware of this? No one could ever be sure.

"This planet is the home of the rebellion, gentlemen."
Michael's bright blue eyes pierced through whomever he
spoke to; not even the enigmatic Casadesus could long
meet that gaze. "If it surrenders peacefully, the rebellion
collapses. If we are forced to crush it, however, the resent-
ment will haunt us forever.

"We must pacify this world in both senses of the word.
How will we proceed?"

Vai couldn't force his eyes above Michael's Admiral's
chip, shining white upon his breast. The chip seemed to
swell, to dominate Vai's universe. Although Michael often
asked much of him, he'd never asked more than Vai could
deliver. His demands took on more of the character of a
test than an ultimatum. And yet . . . for the first time in
years working with Michael, he was unable to find any answer. Was this what failure felt like?

"You ask too much," Casadesus said softly. "We cannot
gain their respect without force, force which you refuse to
allow me to use."

"What happens when one demands respect?" Michael
asked, just as softly. "Is he likely to get it?" He didn't look
at Vai, but the state of his leading General was on his
mind. Vai, tough and trim, slumped in his overstuffed
chair like a rag doll. Was it merely the post-battle depres-
sion that some officers felt? Michael determined to spare
Vai whatever pain he could.

"You can't buy respect, either," Casadesus responded,
flushing. Admiral Devon was the first man he'd ever met
who was totally impervious to the image projected by the
elderly man. Wasn't the wise elder, white-haired yet
strong, supposed to be an archetype? Weren't archetypes
universal? How could the younger man, strong in exactly

the characteristics that the archetype spoke most strongly to, be immune to the appeal?

"Their grievances are imaginary," Michael said placidly, inwardly pleased at having nettled the strangely compelling Casadesus. Contrary to what the latter thought, Michael was not unaffected; he merely concealed his own thoughts from those around him. "The conscriptions and taxes are borne without complaint by other Sectors. The Outreach, being slightly more self-sufficient than internal Sectors, wants self-determination. We can't afford to give it to them."

"Unless you allow me force, I can't stamp out the last traces of the rebellion."

Michael looked at him, amused. The wise old man, the paradigm of wisdom and gentleness, recommending force? "Do you think reprisals, searches, and raids are going to bring the populace around to our side?"

"Can we afford Burt running around free, bombing as he pleases?" Casadesus was unpleasantly aware that he was losing control of this conversation.

"General Vai," Michael said, ignoring Casadesus, "can you mount a low-key effort against Burt? Low-visibility, low-impact, and yet effective?"

Vai thought. "We can make it harder for them to operate, but we can't stop them. Not that way."

"Starting tomorrow, begin working on it. No point in letting them run around unopposed." He turned back to the president. "If the bombings don't sting us into taking rash actions, the people will start seeing us as the reasonable ones."

Casadesus spread his hands. "So you say. *I* think it makes us look weak. If we seem unable to counter threats against us, it only inspires more subversive activity."

Michael spoke to Vai. "Did you catch his operative word?"

" 'Seem'?"

"Exactly."

"It's true. Without taking actions of the type you're forbidding, we *are* vulnerable."

Michael frowned at the unexpected seconding of Casadesus' opinions. "Reprisals would drive the people of this planet, and of the entire Outreach, into further pointless rebellion. This is the place to end it, once and for all. We'll either leave behind us a seething vat of unrest, or one of the Concordat's more loyal Sectors. It all depends on how we handle things *here,* on this world."

Casadesus remained silent. Michael's tone left him uneasy.

"We've avoided purges so far," Michael continued. "If the government here isn't working, at least it isn't our fault. We're going to have to lay it on the line: we're here to stay, and the only way to adapt is to work with us. We'll need to recruit able personnel who'll work with us—"

"Traitors, in other words," Casadesus interrupted.

Michael looked at him carefully. "Traitors, then."

Vai, watching his commander carefully and with experienced eyes, saw a resolve that Casadesus missed. *So,* he mused. *The old man won't last. Who will Michael replace him with? And how will the transition go?* He did not for a moment suspect that it would be smooth.

Chapter Thirteen

"Commander Noel," Michael greeted her, his expression an honestly happy one for once. "And Lieutenant Commander White. Have you put together a construction crew?"

Noel answered first. "Yes, sir. We've pulled out all the stops. The very notion—"

White interrupted. "The *challenge*, sir!" His eyes danced. "We're not just welding two half-ships together; we're breeding an entirely new *class* of ship."

"Have you recruited a crew yet?"

"We're turning people away," White exulted. Michael gave Noel a supporting glance. She had done well in instilling enthusiasm among her officers.

"We've prepared the front half of the *Resolute*, putting computers and controls into first-rate condition, and we've retuned the engines of the grounded rear half of the *Basilica* to perfect pitch . . . although we haven't fired them up yet."

"Mass-balancing? Jump-field-tune?" Michael asked quietly. "You may be, indeed, designing an entirely new type of ship; are you keeping the dangers in mind?"

White was not to be deterred from his exuberance. "Have you *seen* that rear half? Armor plates twenty meters thick! You could swim halfway into a sun with that thing and never feel it. I've never seen the like."

Michael, smiling, gave it up, and determined to leave the reconstruction of the two ships in the capable hands of Noel and White. He smiled again as he walked away; the happy sounds of the two discussing engineering details followed him down the hallway of the *Philomela.*

* * *

Noel's part of the task was aboard the forward fragment of the *Resolute;* during her four-day stint tending the repairs of the systems circuitry, she forgot more about synthetic-aperture waveguides than most engineers ever learn. Small, uncontrolled charges of static electricity made touching anything a sticky, sparky adventure, and provided opportunities for practical jokes. People jested that Noel had an unbalanced magnetic charge, explaining her undeniable and attractive popularity. When field stress gauges began to register her presence, however, she agreed to the expense in time to install antistatic area decontaminators. These didn't always work, and touching metal remained an occupational hazard.

Within four days, the computer and its associated control systems were operating at over ninety percent accuracy.

Among the gleaming consoles of the torn-up command bridge, Noel conversed with Commander Bolsa.

"Lovely," Noel said caustically, gesturing about her. Cables snaked across the floor; equipment cabinets swung open and empty, and the sound and sparking light of microwelders were everywhere. Datascreens that ordinarily would have shown tabulated displays of system statistics now wriggled with test patterns. On the station displays that were active, more red lights shone by far than amber and green; four-fifths of the orbiting fragment of a ship was yet open to vacuum.

Bolsa replied carefully, "We're ahead of the schedule that Admiral Devon set for us. The equipment seems to work."

"But here," Noel sighed. She slapped her hand on a gunnery console, then snatched her hand back from the discharge of static electricity that delivered her a minuscule shock. "This station registers a laser battery on line. It's shown as charged and ready. Here, this indicator tells of a full missile bay ready to fire. But there aren't any lasers or missiles."

"We've got simulators hooked up to the controls," Bolsa said, holding his hands open before him. "That's to test the systems. When the rear half of the ship is shoved up here into our orbit, we'll unhook the simulators and put the real things on line."

"Great. Fine. And your simulators are being calibrated to the voltages that White is measuring, downside." She laughed, a happy, meaningless, joyful laugh. "What we have here, then, is the most expensive flight-training-simulator in history." The notion cheered her.

She ambled toward the flight control station. "Commander Bolsa, fire up the engines."

Bolsa, eager to demonstrate the efficiency of the new controls, entered commands from a separate keyboard. The screen lit up with an animated visual of the orbit.

Noel smiled thinly. "I want one G of thrust, in that direction"—she indicated where on the screen—"for twenty seconds."

Bolsa complied. On the screen, the ship was portrayed as shifting its orbit; in reality, the ship fell unheeding through the same stable orbit it had been towed into.

"What do the radars read?"

Calling that information to the screen, Bolsa's face fell. Radars were control systems, and no simulator had been linked in.

"And what happens when the computer tries to reconcile the two inputs?" Noel asked, driving the point home sharply, although not maliciously.

Bolsa finished the calculation. The datascreen turned red, and error messages swept upward faster than the eye could read.

"It looks like I neglected to inform the computer exactly which systems were simulated," he concluded lamely.

Noel clapped a hand on his back. "Initialization will be easy, once we're operational. The radars work. We've got decks to stand on. I'm favorably impressed."

"You are?" Bolsa asked awkwardly.

"This is a lot of controls to have built in four days." She wandered off, her hair lifting slightly from the monomagnetic charge the console had given her.

Returning to the console, Bolsa frowned and began running through diagnostic checks.

On the ground, White oversaw a task force composed of half the engineers of the fleet and as many technicians as he had been able to recruit from the planet's citizenry. The towering mass of the *Basilica*'s unfinished stern lay nestled on its side in its construction cradle.

"You want to tell me how I'm going to get this thing onto the boost-grid?" he asked aloud.

Two engineers began to answer him, both talking at once, each waving rolled-up prints and charts.

". . . We drag it out there . . ."

". . . And boost it whole . . ."

". . . Negligible surface damage . . ."

". . . Sliding over the hardened armor . . ."

"Whoa!" White called. "We do what?"

"Drag it."

White turned to the technician on the left. "Can we do that?"

"Yes. The armor plates will hold."

"I don't believe it. Technology has come full circle. From travois, to wheel, to glideplate, to gravplate, to—"

"What's a 'travois'?"

"That, my dear friend, is what you have just reinvented. We'll hitch ropes to it and get ten thousand people out in front, and all will pull to the timing of a drum. Have you got someone who can handle a whip?" He didn't give them time to become confused. "Do you both agree to this?"

Both nodded. White looked from one to the other.

"Fine. The odds that both of you, two highly trained and competent engineers, are both crazy in exactly the same way must be no more than one in two or three. I'll play those odds."

Any response the technicians might have made was forestalled by the passage of a carrier, loaded high with missiles. White's cheerful mood was gone in an instant.

"See to it," he muttered; the technicians scuttled.

The missiles, twelve-meter shafts, gleaming, polished, dark gray, sat stacked, six high by six across. The carrier slid to a halt. White ignored the driver and came up to stand by the missiles. He moved around to the end of the load and peered into the television eye in the front of one weapon: its optical guidance system. In his imagination, he felt it looking back at him.

Around the eye lens were three ports for gravitic radar, and surrounding them, three neutrino detectors. Just behind the nose of this stellar bloodhound was the encased warhead, the thermonuclear death punch that the missile existed to deliver.

And this ship of marvels, this whole new breed of ship, is still no more than a warship. The thought unsettled White, who had, until now, been happily engrossed in the engineering details of the job, for the intellectual joy of it.

Sighing, he returned, soberly, to his work. This ship, which he had come to think of as his, existed to kill other ships, and thus to kill people. But, by heaven, it would be built well. It would be a damned fine ship; so insisted Lieutenant Commander White's engineering pride.

Commander Noel visited him, and they took their lunch together in an unlikely location: the interior of the ship's main power plant. White had laid out a small table in the center of the fusion engine's containment vessel; open sandwiches and coffee, sweet rolls and spice cakes, a salad and a bowl of fried crisps, sat in a mouth-watering array, with dishes and flatware for four. Above, lights blazed, shining from the burnished magnetic heads; injection needles jutted from the coppery metal of the walls; exhaust ports yawned.

Noel and White sat down to dine with the two technicians whose job it would be to start up the fusion fires at the right time.

"Think of it," White said happily, looking about him. "Here, in only a few days, hydrogen will die in agony to power our starship. Hydrogen will transcend itself, will aspire to something greater—"

"Depleted helium," muttered one of the technicians, folding a sandwich into his mouth. "That's all. No need for poetry."

Abashed, White lifted his glass and touched it to Noel's in salute. The two technicians were already well into the spice cakes.

"To this ship . . . whatever its name shall come to be."

"To the ship," Noel responded. They looked at one another, glanced at the technicians, and dove into the sweet rolls in order to get a few before the technicians nabbed them all.

"I assume we don't have to worry about crumbs?" Noel asked somewhat later.

"We'll flush the chamber," one of the two engineers answered, his mouth full, "with fluoride-tet. Then evacuate it to complete vacuum."

White amplified. "It will produce about as much terawattage as the plant on the *Philomela*, but more of that will be consumed by the plant itself. This version runs hotter than the latest models, and less efficiently. The three streams of plasma will be circularly polarized . . ." He saw that Noel didn't understand.

"Well"—he blushed—"we could have done a lot worse. This will be more than enough power to run the final ship's configuration. We'll have beam power to waste."

"And defenses?"

"I've been over the armor. Not a crack; not a mousehole. I was speaking literally, not figuratively; we could take this ship more than halfway into a sun." He grinned a foolish grin. "Getting it *out* again . . . that's *your* problem. We could stand the temperature, just not the friction."

"And I learned about that kind of orbit," Noel retorted. "Thank you, but I'd rather have my dinner cooked before I eat it."

The rest of the luncheon was eaten in silence.

The main Spaceport, on the outskirts of the city, had been carefully cleared of resistance, and certain buildings and systems put into repair. The gigantic landing field, some fifty square kilometers in area, had been re-smoothed, the tenacious weeds burned from its now-polished surface. In the main control building, the computers had been set right, as had the boost-grid controls.

Set into the field's surface, the thick boost-grid railings gleamed. From the city's power plant the energy channels were clear, and billions of kilowatts waited patiently on call.

From behind a seven-story hangar, the stern tubes of the wrecked mass of what one day might have been an Improved Dreadnought protruded, edging forward, urged on by swarming teams of tractors. Three large trucks sprayed streams of antifriction foam beneath it, lessening the damage done to the ship and to the field by the scraping of the multi-million-ton bulk.

More and more of the unborn ship came into view, rear first. It was incredible that such an ugly load, dragged bodily across the ground, could some day leap between the stars. It continued to swell. Gun emplacements and bays crept out from behind the hangar. The size of the thing was astonishing.

Finally it was completely revealed, the jagged, unfinished front edge visible, a painful, crippled amputation of the front half that would have completed the whole. Closer it was dragged, crews working on the engines even as it traveled.

Growing always, it was positioned at last in the center of the boost-grid. The tractors withdrew.

For several hours the bright sparks of welding lasers were visible, dancing, crawling, moving in their patterns over the surface of the giant, beached corpse. Deep in its interior, similar rituals proceeded, preparing the hulk to rise again.

The sun, so much like the sun of home, crawled with unnerving rapidity across the sky; thick shadows crept.

Energies beyond conception channeled themselves through the heavy rails of the boost-grid; the very stuff of gravity, of weight, of mass itself, was focused upon the quiescent bulk. With a stately slowness, a half-bow of almost pedantic formality, the rear half of the ship rose. Computers shifted the focus; the ship rose more swiftly. The strange levitation of half of a ship seemed unlikely, calling to mind eldritch visions of the dead that walk again.

From deep in the memory of a computer that was programmed long years ago, a brief ceremony was dredged. With mechanical precision, the forms were filled out, filed, and a mention noted on a terminal. A technician spotted it, smiled, and acknowledged it. The rear half of the ship had been cataloged, enlisted into the First Fleet of the Concordat of Archive.

It was now listed under the name with which it had just been christened: the *Basilica*. Aboard it, another technician received the notice, frowned, and carved the name permanently into a bulkhead with a welding laser.

It approached the orbit occupied by the ruin of the *Resolute*. It approached reanimation.

The two halves eased together, slow centimeters per second of relative velocity given them by impellers. Spacesuited figures swarmed about and within, watching to see that every tube, conduit, wire, and cable spliced neatly. Against the sun, which cast each detail into sharp relief, the rear half slowly eclipsed the front half. Floodlamps slammed on.

White gnawed his lip as the first rumbles and clangs vibrated forward through the metal and plastic of the hull. He felt the shivers—birth pangs—through his gloved hand where it rested on a stress-beam. The noises swelled into a firecracker series of poppings, then an all-consuming shudder, finally to diminish into a separate series of cracks.

The *Basilica* was one.

In the pressurized command bridge, Noel listened with gritted teeth to the wholly audible roar of metal grinding against metal. *I must believe that no one is stupid enough to risk his life for no more than a better fit of some water pipe.*

Despite the temptation to make last-second adjustments of matching parts, no one was injured. Noel remembered historical tales of the launching of seagoing ships from their slips, and how the one to knock loose the last prop had been, all too horribly often, an unintentional human sacrifice to the juggernaut as it slid into the bay.

The roar muted, and slowly ceased.

Another five days yet remained—of welding the computer links into the engines and guns that had been prepared. Although the job would be much simplified by the installation of modular connectors, there would still be the great, time-consuming, finicky labor of checking every data-bus, every control linkage.

Nevertheless.

"We've got ourselves a ship," she said quietly, her words carrying over the command frequency to every radio headset aboard.

Three cheers resounded: for the ship; for White and the engineers; and for her.

The *Basilica,* commanded by Captain Ruth Noel, was in action.

Chapter Fourteen

In a safe hideout in the home of a trusted friend, John Burt angrily paced the floor before a group of allies and advisers. The latter, all loyal men, wore worried expressions and frequently glanced at each other. Andrew North, just returned from a recruiting mission in the countryside, sat nearest Burt's unoccupied chair, anxiously watching his boss.

"We're not winning," Burt said sharply.

"We're not losing, either," North responded.

"If we can't find some very damned effective way of hitting them, we'll lose all respect."

"Agreed."

Burt spun. "Well, damn it, do something! Blow up another of their ships!"

North looked away. The others in the room looked sharply toward him. This was the first that any of them had heard of a saboteur; all wanted to hear more.

"He's dead. That's all." *What in hell do you want, John? That man, that loyal man, all alone, destroyed as many as twenty-three ships by setting the enemy to fighting themselves. I give thanks for having been privileged to know Irwin Douglas—"Captain Douglas," loyal to our cause.*

From the center of the crescent of allies, Robert Bishop threw a sharp question at North. "Why weren't we informed of this?"

North turned his head partway toward Bishop and answered gently. "You didn't need to know." He returned his attention to Burt.

The leader's rage passed, fading swiftly as he saw what it could lead to. If he couldn't inspire solidarity among his immediate followers, if his anger could wear off onto

Bishop and the others, how could he hope to hold an entire planet together?

"We need to hit them, and *hard!*" He surveyed his crew. Survivors all, they were still a scant cadre for the kind of plan he needed. "No more of this small-time bombing and sniping. We have to show them that we mean it. Either this world is freed, or we'll burn it once and for all."

Abruptly, he turned and felt for his chair with his eyes closed. What had he just said? Had he meant it?

The memory came to him of an endless day, several years ago, when, having nothing better to do, he had spent long hours looking over the surface of the planet Acheron through the telescope of his ship. Even now he felt echoes of the intense emotional revelation he'd felt that day.

From low orbit, the image intensifier revealed clearly every detail of city and town, of empty kilometers of wasteland and forest, bush and bracken. As he swung around to the night face, he could see the quiet glow of civilization's many lights as a cool glitter in the hills that marked the capital city.

With a little effort, he'd worked the telescope around to where it revealed a tiny, isolated spark of light high in the mountains on the western continent. He'd stepped up the photomultiplier and the gain until he saw, as if from the treetops, a small campfire surrounded by several amateur explorers, most likely students on a field expedition.

Looking away, oddly ashamed, he vowed then to protect the planet always, in order to be at all times worthy of the soul-shaking sense of responsibility he felt at that moment. No man, he knew, could look down from such a godlike height onto the peaceful and trusting innocents below and then order a missile fired at an inhabited planet.

Over the years the memory faded, and the determination. Several times it was very necessary to bombard a planet. But always he felt protective of the planets that were hit.

We'll burn it once and for all?
Never!
He raised his suddenly flushed face to the assembled

men who were his allies, subordinates, friends. Each of them watched him closely.

"Any ideas, gentlemen?" he asked in a subdued voice.

Day by day the new government gained in popular legitimacy, both through Casadesus' clever manipulations and by the unpleasant reminder provided by Burt's aimless bombings. When the latter ceased, the former continued, making the most of the return to normalcy. Given enough time—Casadesus estimated that several months would suffice—Burt's last-ditch campaign would be virtually forgotten, or remembered in the company of other, doomed fights that had continued overlong. Casadesus judged that within two years, John Burt himself would be, in the popular mind, a tragicomic figure, an archetypal fool, never accepting his defeat even when it was obvious to everyone else.

For Admiral Devon, the process moved along too slowly.

"Commander Sh'in," he snapped icily.

From her chair in the fleet command bridge, Arbela Sh'in waved a languid hand toward Commander Joan Rogers, indicating insolently the true source of any irritation. She had become expert, in the several weeks of waiting, at metering Michael's anger, and at knowing just how much affront she dared offer him.

Contrary to her intention, Michael retained his composure and offered her a sardonic "Thank you very much." Sh'in's eyebrows rose; only with effort did she avoid spinning in her chair to look at him.

She couldn't help overhearing his conversation with Joan.

"As soon as we get that battalion aboard," he began, standing behind her, "we can move the fleet on to our next target."

"I've said it before, sir, and I'll stand by it." Joan forced herself to meet Michael's cool gaze. "It's too soon to leave this planet ungarrisoned. The rebellion is too fresh in everyone's mind. The government needs the support."

"The battalion has had nothing to do for days."

"I disagree, sir." Seeing the tableau from the side, Sh'in could see Joan's lower lip tremble. Michael, standing tall above her, seemed unaware of her distress. Unlike Sh'in,

Joan at least had a good reason to turn away from her superior; her attention was pulled away from him by a signal from her display screen, which proceeded to show a column of figures that crawled slowly upward. Sh'in, from her vantage, could see Michael's deadly calm, far more threatening than his open anger ever seemed to be.

"That battalion," Joan continued, "serves as a police force that Casadesus doesn't have to be responsible for. More importantly, it serves as a symbol. The populace won't soon forget the 'ten hours' battle' that took away their freedom. It's vital that they remember it in the correct light. When we pull that battalion away, it can't look even slightly like a retreat, or we'll lose them again."

"We have other enemies," Michael suggested gently.

"You're in charge, sir. It's completely up to you whether or not you listen to me." She spun back to face him. "But I was appointed your intelligence chief, and that means political adviser too."

"We can't delay much longer," Michael said distractedly.

"Can we afford to have enemies behind us as well as in front?"

Michael looked at her quizzically. "Our enemies *are* behind us; soon we'll return to meet them."

"The rest of the Outreach—"

"Can be discounted. Now that we've put an end to the rebellion here in the central worlds, the fringe will swing into line on their own."

Joan looked at him wide-eyed. He had to be imagining things. The notion of an enemy back home could not be a true one. Where could she turn for advice?

John Burt's final plan was so simple, so logical, that it amazed even himself. When a tactic works once, the odds are good that it will work again. When an enemy succeeds with a trick, the same trick will often work when used against him.

Fifty men were in position behind the line of trees along the access road to the power plant. When the correct moment came, they would leap forward, plant explosives to breach the security fence, and rapidly penetrate one of the outer circuit-control buildings of the sprawling complex.

Their job, just as Losse Merent's had been, was to put out the power to the city.

Across from the government office building, Burt himself waited with two hundred handpicked volunteers. Inside the building were ten plants, people chosen for their loyalty and for their hatred of the damnable, usurping Concordat. Earlier experimentation had shown that the basement escape tunnel had been found and blocked. Burt and his engineers felt that it could be blasted open. The odds were more in his favor, he felt, than they had been for the counter-rebels. If the traitors had succeeded, why shouldn't he?

The sun sank swiftly, descending behind the government office building as seen by Burt, behind the distant reactor buildings as seen by the team leader lying beneath the trees. Soon they would both be in action; soon they would have their planet back.

The moment came. Silently, in the deepening dusk, the power-plant team scuttled across the access road. The explosives were in place; the troops spread out along the wall. In the distance, an alarm bell rang insistently; plainly they had triggered some hidden sensor.

The explosives burst, neatly prying the heavy wire net from its posts. Immediately, three men leaped forward and wrestled it out of the way. Far across the compound, the attackers heard the shouts of well-drilled Marines scrambling to the defense.

"Come along, men," called the attacking team leader. "Let's show them how free men die!"

Free men, it turned out, die just like conscripts, only to less purpose. Despite this, the power to the city was severed for two long hours.

The careless sentry patrolling the corridors in the government office building could not be blamed for his lapse. The person he passed was familiar to him: a minor functionary in the Courts division. In the bundle of papers she carried, however, was also a long, thin knife.

Into the small room serving as the building's security center burst four men, shouting angrily. "What did you mean by this outrage?" called one, raising an envelope.

The security officer and his men wasted the last seconds of their lives trying to read the meaningless scrawl that had been dashed upon the clean surface. Silenced weapons aimed with skilled accuracy took the defenders out.

In the basement, an explosive fluid, poured into the cracks in a steel doorway, cleanly bent the door back from the frame. Within minutes, seventeen men and women, all slightly built and agile, clambered through, tossing each other weapons and equipment. As they moved rapidly down the tunnel, now inside the building, the overhead lights dimmed, flared up again, and dimmed, finally dying altogether. Hand flashes came on, guiding the way for the intruders.

John Burt, having nothing to lose, charged across the street with the foremost of his volunteers, kicking down the front gate and leading his troops into the traitor-held government office building.

He had no way of knowing how futile the attack was. He himself, when occupying this very building, hadn't had a direct line to the power plant. If he had, he too would have received the eleven-second warning that the current occupants had. When he held the building, he hadn't arranged for the security antechamber to contain a backup deadman alarm switch. If he had, his troops could have been ready, or at least more ready, instead of being caught weaponless, unprepared. He could have had the grand hallway completely covered, just as the current occupants did.

Eleven seconds' warning to the command room, and seven to the troops. Concordat Marines had faced tougher ambushes, with far less notice, and won.

John Burt surrendered, his only intelligent option, before the firefight had a fair chance to develop. The lives he saved included his own.

General Matthew Vai, when informed of the conference of senior officers aboard the *Philomela,* had been unpleasantly aware that things would be brought up of a more than slightly controversial nature. During a small conference of his own, with his staff and with the commanders of the other divisions, he'd done what he could to prepare for the blow.

Now, sitting toward the side of the large conference room of the Battleship, he tried to believe that Admiral Devon would not declare the things Vai expected him to. It was a losing battle of self-deception.

Across the table, Commanders Arbela Sh'in—languidly relaxed, smiling too widely—and Joan Rogers—red hair flaming above her red-trimmed uniform, her small body tense and desperately taut—sat together. With them were Captains Edwards and Engel, Edwards slouching unhappily in his uniform, Engel, ready for a fight, as always, and knowing that she could never win this one. It was plain that they were out of favor and were present only by Michael's magnanimous permission. Their opinions would bear little weight, and their advice would not be sought.

Despite Vai's unwelcoming expression, Captain Beamish, the de jure commander of the *Philomela,* had approached him and seated himself nearby. Vai wondered if the two empty seats between them insulated him from the taint. Four others were present: unimportant people, minor figures. Probably Michael had invited them as witnesses who'd spread the word quickly to the rest of the crew. A rumor net is only useful if you make the most use of it, exploiting its involutions. Michael would enter soon, say something noncommittal about keeping this meeting confidential, and before twenty minutes had passed after its adjournment, everyone aboard would know every detail.

Exactly on time, Michael entered. Beamish, from his seat, all too plainly wished he could have entered at the Admiral's heels, favoring the conference with a superior, restrained grin, rather than be seated far enough away from Michael to give a general impression of independence. But, to his chagrin, Michael had arranged to enter alone.

Alone. Joan Rogers, off with her faction on Michael's left, seemed to be the only person in the room who knew just how alone the Admiral was. Standing comfortably in his duty uniform, he seemed, as always, the living personification of strength. His decisions, however, were his, and only his; should everyone else in the room disagree, the decision would be carried out, forced through by Michael's sheer force of will.

Just before he was ready to speak, the doors slid open again, and the slight figure of Captain Ruth Noel ducked inside, walking with a trace of embarrassment to an empty seat at the far end of the table. A great deal of tension was dispelled, an effect that even the tardy Captain Noel sensed. She smiled, and nodded her apology.

Michael raised his arm to call for attention, looked in pretended expectation over his shoulder as if waiting for another interruption, and began.

"Does anyone know what day this is?"

Although three other people present did indeed know, not even Beamish was churlish enough to answer.

Michael smiled. "By the ship's clock—which is reasonably accurate, I think—today marks the end of exactly three months of operations on our part." He indicated the fleet's orders lying on the table before him. "When we set out, we were given three years in which to pacify the Outreach. I claimed that it could be done in three months.

"As usual, I was both right and wrong."

Joan, without moving, came to full alertness. This was where the first crucial point lay. Would Michael come directly to it, or would he approach it cautiously? Everyone else in the room shifted, or changed expression. None but Joan and Vai were aware of what was to come.

"Our operations here are over. We've finished with this part of it. But we're not done. The planet Acheron was the center of the rebellion out here. I'm going to leave a small team of political experts behind to try to hammer things into shape.

"I'm also going to change the terms of the planetary presidency. The old man that led the local counter-revolt isn't capable of running things here all by himself, nor is his staff enough. Acheron needs a government with a broader base of support, or else it may fall again into rebellion.

"I've named John Burt planetary co-president."

Vai nodded wearily. He'd prepared for that. He'd arranged things so that the announcement would trigger neither revolt nor collapse, neither loyalist nor raider dissatisfaction. The new coalition of bitter enemies would be at worst impotent, but it would be stable. By the time it fell, the planet and the Outreach would both be fully integrated into the Concordat.

He did wish that Michael had seen fit to warn him, however.

Joan Rogers took the revelation in the same way that Vai did. She too, in her capacity as Michael's intelligence chief, had carefully prepared. Working through the higher echelons while Vai had worked through the lower, she'd managed to warn everyone except the strangely naive Casadesus that such an upset was in the offing. The only person who'd actively aided her in her preparations was the slightly aloof, slightly abrasive Denise Voleur. A survivor, she, Joan suspected. With care she would succeed Casadesus as co-president when the latter angrily resigned. How would he take the seeming defection?

Around the table, the remaining officers were shocked, stunned, or bemused, according to their natures. To Joan's relief, no clamor ensued, but rather a cautious silence. The officers had finally learned that their approval or disapproval meant nothing to Admiral Devon. Later, though, when he opened the floor to questions, comments, advice . . . Joan almost felt that she could enjoy the upcoming scene. On the other hand, Michael still had his other bomb to drop.

Golden-haired, shining-eyed, challenging, Michael waited.

"I've spoken with Burt," he said after a moment, "and with the men of his staff. They have no love for us, but they have for their homeland. They'll give us no further trouble, because they know what we'll do to these worlds if they try again.

"Further, they have much to offer the Outreach. Their experience, their expertise, and their loyalty will be needed. Having failed in their bid for independence, they'll do all they can for these worlds by acting within the laws." He grinned. "And perhaps a bit beyond them.

"On the other hand, we have not won the final peace. Another enemy awaits us.

"Several years ago, at the First Battle of Binary, a powerful Concordat fleet was betrayed by an unscrupulous and highly placed man. Some of you have heard the story; others have not. It doesn't matter. The point remains: we can't afford to trust our superiors just because they are our superiors.

"The Concordat of Archive is ruled by the six-man council, the Praesidium. How does the Praesidium select its members? The members themselves chose their replacements. We who serve them have no say in this selection. And poor choices have been made in the past.

"Recently our fleet was attacked by the Tikhvin Sector reserve fleet. It was commanded by a man who was directly sent to disable this fleet, acting under higher orders. By his testimony, those orders were from the person who was the chosen replacement of the man who destroyed the fleet at Binary."

Of all the officers present in the conference room, only Commander Joan Rogers and General Matthew Vai were unsurprised. For a moment, Joan felt that she understood Michael; for a moment, she too was totally alone.

Vai looked down at the tabletop. Some frightening responsibilities had just descended upon him; he had decisions to make that most generals never think about.

Michael's voice overrode the growing murmur of shocked voices. "Grand Admiral de la Noue attempted to wreck our fleet, even though we travel under her orders. Why? I believe I have part of the answer; the remainer will be gotten from her when this fleet lands, whether opposed or not, on the planet Tikhvin!"

The meeting dissolved into knots of officers intent upon hearing the details from the few present who knew the true history of the Sonallan wars. Michael made no effort to restore order.

". . . Security classification. I don't remember the code . . ."

". . . Grand Admiral Telford? But . . ."

" . . . The fleet? Betrayed? Surely . . ."

Joan carefully held herself away from the discussions, many of which were not much better than rumor-bruiting. She, with a rather higher security clearance than most, knew the truth. The fleet had been betrayed at First Binary, and the traitor's last action had been to appoint Jennifer de la Noue to succeed him to head the Navy.

The conference room slowly quieted. Soon Michael had

recaptured the officers' attention. He stood motionless before them and waited for total silence.

"This isn't going to be easy." His voice was composed; his hands were on the table in front of him. "Already I have enough problems with you, my officers. The operation smells too much like mutiny. Because I'm determined to see this through, and because I'll need your help, I'm willing to make the effort needed to convince you of the need for action.

"One at a time, please, give me your opinions. We've got all day." He pointed to Sh'in. "Commander?"

Sh'in smiled up at him, eyes wide. "I think you're nuts. I think you've flipped your wig. I think your uniform's too tight, and vital circulation is impeded." She slouched back in her chair and grapsed her knee. "I'd like to request an immediate transfer to the medical section, preferably to work with a psychiatrist. That way," she purred, "we'll meet again."

Michael heard her out, his own slight smile undiminished. "Commander Sh'in, as always, speaks her mind. Transfer denied. Has anyone anything useful to say?"

Captain Edwards looked gloomily to Captain Engel. Understanding passed between them: no point whatever in taking a stand. Michael would cut them to shreds. Disloyal officers are not privileged to hold opinions.

Ruth Noel, now the Captain of the new *Basilica*, felt herself to be outside the circle of people here. In her, however, a sense of being excluded by her newness often brought out her participation. In places where she was unknown, a careful aggressiveness was her usual tactic.

"We'll need hard evidence," she tossed in.

"To a large degree, of course, that will be lacking. Admiral de la Noue has covered her tracks quite well. On the other hand, I will be able to offer you some documentation.

"To begin with, I have the transcript of the interview with Commodore Athalos Steldan, who commanded the fleet that tried to ambush us. There are some questions he was unable to answer, and, although I can't prove this, I believe him to be concealing facts deliberately. More interviews will be necessary."

"Anything else?" asked Noel.

Michael regarded her. Without realizing it, Captain

Noel was asking exactly the right kind of questions. Rather than attacking the very concept of further operations, as Sh'in, Engel, or Edwards would, Noel was opening the way for him to introduce his evidence.

"Yes, there is. Much of it is subjective, I'll warn you. Taken together, it adds up to a total that cannot be ignored."

"Couldn't you use a truth drug on Steldan?" Beamish interrupted.

"Commodore Steldan is from the Intelligence branch," Michael answered without looking, "and has been immunized to anything we have."

Beamish cast about him and discovered by the knowing expressions of the officers that he was the only one present who didn't understand. To ask for a clarification would only embarrass him further; he remained silent.

Captain Edwards again considered throwing in his opinion, futile though it would be. He subsided, distracted by a tug on his sleeve. He turned and looked at Captain Engel.

"What?" he whispered.

She leaned close and spoke softly. "Don't intervene. We're less than nothing here."

"Can we stand by and watch? Can you?"

"We'd better. He's not going to listen to us, and it's idiocy for us to try anything."

"I *must.*"

"In that case," she said resignedly, "let me, instead."

Edwards nodded.

To Michael's surprise the questioning still followed Captain Noel's line. He was being asked for reasons to go ahead rather than being offered reasons not to. As he had hoped, Sh'in's unsubtle remarks had tainted that particular line; when it eventually came up, it would be more reserved, more tactful.

I must leave them the illusion that it's their decision, he astutely judged, *while guiding them to the point I desire.*

"We were sent out on a mission helpful to the Concordat," he said calmly, picking up the initiative. "The developing rebellion in the Outreach was of the sort to eventually be a threat to the stability of the entire region. Left alone, it might have drawn entire Sectors along with it.

"But the Navy's reaction—and that means de la Noue's—was uncharacteristically rapid. Instead of the time-honored tactic of waiting too long and then overreacting, we were sent out quickly. Very quickly indeed.

"I believe that Grand Admiral de la Noue not only knew in advance of the rebellion, but that she had a hand in its instigation." He looked about at his officers. All of them, save Sh'in, listened carefully. Sh'in, of course, made a great show of not listening, which was infuriating to Captain Beamish, but which the others ignored. Michael knew the importance of keeping the attention of those others; his revelations were of such a sensitive nature, and so contrary to what they wanted to believe, that it would take all his care to keep them listening with open minds.

"Consider: sending our fleet out on a three-year campaign effectively weakened the Tikhvin Sector, a Sector that is not yet fully established in its new capital, Tikhvin itself. While the decision seems strategically unsound, at least there are no known enemies in the area.

"There we would be, out of the picture for three years. Except that we were soon far ahead of schedule. It suddenly seemed to our Grand Admiral that we would be back soon to interrupt her plans." He stopped, noting Captain Engel's upraised hand.

"Yes?"

"How could Grand Admiral de la Noue know we were ahead of schedule when you'd cut off the Courier link?"

Michael smiled. "Good question. I have evidence that she had a link to the Outreach's rebellion and that information came to her from them." He held up a hand to forestall Engel's objections.

"You are about to ask why I believe she knew at all; why I'm convinced that Commodore Steldan's story is false.

"If he came into the Outreach in order to find out why we had failed to report, as he claims, then how did he know exactly where to find us?"

He looked about, letting that sink in.

"Was Acheron the only logical choice for our destination? Plainly it was not. None of us knew where our campaign would take us. How did Steldan know we'd be there?"

He waited a moment.

"Did he just guess? Was he just lucky?" He smiled a lop-sided smile of self-mockery. "He might have been."

His expression regained fierceness. "And he might not have been. How did he know?"

No one had an answer for the question. Looks of uncertainty passed back and forth between the officers present. Sh'in looked disgusted.

"I have been criticized for my warlike disposition when we first detected Steldan's fleet. The question I've just asked you was the uppermost thought in my mind. How did he know where we were? His very presence verified several of my suspicions."

"Why did you sever the Courier link in the first place?" asked Captain Noel.

"I suspected de la Noue from the moment I met her," Michael answered simply. "Her explanation was too pat, while admitting of several conceptual flaws. Why send a fleet this size after a pack of underequipped rebels and freight raiders? Why include a first line Battleship that should more sensibly have been kept back at Tikhvin as a reserve? What kind of coincidence was it that a brand new Battleship of this quality was available, not even named yet, ready for this very low-level mission?

"When we were sent out, I cut the relay link, knowing that with this kind of firepower the campaign would be over in months rather than years. I hoped to return ahead of schedule to avert whatever strange plan de la Noue had for the Tikhvin Sector. I admit I erred in boasting of our ability to beat the deadline; I thought it might serve as a warning to her that I knew of her plans."

He paused again and surveyed the wide-eyed faces before him. Even Sh'in was paying attention, he noted with amusement.

"I knew from the moment we set out that our return would be as her enemies, not her returning allies."

Joan Rogers watched him carefully. Did he believe what he said? Did it matter?

"When we've returned, what do we do?" Captain Engel asked, almost awed.

"That depends on what de la Noue has done in our absence. If she's taken the kind of steps I suspect her to be capable of, we'll have to fight. On the other hand, we may be in time to abort her schemes, in which case we land and report as if all were normal. In private, I'll confront her with my evidence and give her the option of resigning her office rather than have all the dirt brought out in the open."

"And you feel that she's nearly ready to move?"

"That is the one thing I'm most certain of."

Soon he had them convinced. Although they were uncertain, they fell into an uneasy agreement. The facts that he represented—or misrepresented—to them were clearly indicative of the wrongness of the situation. That Michael never claimed to know exactly what was wrong only aided them to agree to his plan.

His personal force of leadership carried them. To salve their aching consciences, he allowed them to withdraw from duty if they could not agree to serve him. Captain Edwards had already been relieved of his post. Captain Engel accepted Michael's offer.

And through all the pressure he put upon them, no one, not even he, knew exactly what this campaign was in anticipation of.

Later, carefully examining his motives in the privacy of the deserted conference room, he could find no real guilt in himself. The dread word "mutiny" simply could not be applied. Certainly he'd oversimplified the case to persuade his officers. They, however, were protected. The responsibility, and blame, if it came to that, were his alone. Alone.

In the electronics-deck officers' lounge, Joan Rogers, Arbela Sh'in, and former Captain Engel sat silently, each painfully poring over her own thoughts. Edwards joined them sometime later, and could bring no cheer with him.

I couldn't stop him, Joan thought to herself. *I should have fought him . . . but I would never have been heeded. How many ships will I need to destroy to stop him?*

Chapter Fifteen

Uncoiling itself from about the blue and green world of Acheron, the fleet moved spaceward. Soon the vanguard caught up with the Battleship *Philomela*, itself moving outward from its higher, protective orbit. Combining the best of two fleets, the rededicated armada sailed to the will of its Admiral, arranging itself in an orderly way for the trip outward to safe jump distance.

Behind it, the drifting remains of several ruined ships orbited inertly, wrecked, stripped, and abandoned. These were the grim legacy of the two fleets' joining, a combination that left the new sum greater than either of its parts, even after the substantial losses.

Passing further out, the fleet cut safely through the several belts of mines and high-velocity sand-shot. During the three weeks of inactivity, the fleets' computers and radar operators had carefully tracked every mine and every sand-burst, allowing safe passage through the inevitable gaps in the purely defensive rings.

One ship in the fleet was more carefully watched than the others: the *Basilica*. The odd-shaped hybrid, its join still not fully completed, seemed as maneuverable as any other ship in the formation. It put the long kilometers behind it with capable ease. Would it be able to jump? The construction engineers said yes, although they admitted that the jump's precision would be lacking. For this reason the lumpish Dreadnought was to be the linchpin of the formation jump.

Captain Ruth Noel personally oversaw each detail of the upcoming jump, hovering over the readouts in the fleet command bridge for long hours and checking on all facets of the engineering section. It occurred to her that Admiral

Devon might have wanted this ship put together more as a target than as a fighting vessel. Certainly, gunners and missilemen aboard enemy ships would see it and the *Philomela* as the two main threats. If the limping *Basilica* was put in the vanguard, it would clinch Noel's suspicion. She resolved to review the tactical setup that Michael ordered as soon as the lines were drawn.

Although the entire fleet's jump was to be based upon the *Basilica,* the ship was not indispensable. As soon as the fleet was free of Jumpspace, control would revert to the fleet command bridge of the *Philomela.*

The piecework Dreadnought moved with reasonable smoothness. Although the bridge and the engine room were completely unrelated, and although virtually no two sections of controls matched, the ad hoc mating held together. In just twenty minutes, the laboriously contrived contraption would enter Jumpspace. Captain Noel wondered if her first command would be her last.

"Safe distance achieved," announced a worried-looking Lieutenant Commander White.

"Everything set?" Noel asked of the fleet coordination officer; the young man looked up and nodded.

"Let's go, then."

White, looking thoroughly nervous, prepared to put his engineering skill to the final test. He tapped into his display the final string of commands. On his data display screen, a reassuring line of green squares flashed, to be replaced by a confused graphic schema of the non-Euclidean, nonrational Jumpspace matrix local to this area of normal space.

The gyrating lines on the screen seemed somehow to comfort White. Turning around, he gave Captain Noel a wide grin and a thumbs-up gesture.

The *Basilica* skittered twice, executing neurotic microjumps in response to the titanic energies marshaled by the ship's greatly oversize power plant. Compensators cut in, wrenching the interface between normal space and Jumpspace into a more mathematically flat surface. Instead of the usual large gap through which the ship would normally be drawn, dozens of smaller rips appeared, neatly aligned, but each only marginally wider than the bottom-heavy ship itself.

In the fleet command bridge, the fleet coordination officer gasped at the view of the several gaping rents visible on his screen. Glowing with the oven-red of Jumpspace, they appeared far too much like wounds, cut into the very stuff of normal space. Automatically, he checked the fleet status; the other ships each slipped neatly into their own Jumpspace gaps. Although tied to the *Basilica* in their destination and their course, they were in no way impeded by the difficulties now facing the larger Dreadnought. Even the *Philomela* moved gently into Jump, its computers hastily recalculating fleet status in case it needed to pull coordination duty from the ailing current flagship.

At the next station, Lieutenant Commander White, once recovered from a split second of indecisive panic, applied himself frantically to his keyboard. He almost wished for the good old days, when a helmsman had something physical to wrestle with. When "starboard" meant "steerboard" and when a desperate man could throw his weight onto a pilot's wheel to save his ship.

Instead, manual dexterity and hand-eye coordination were the requisites; how fast a person could type on a vibrating keyboard, making the fewest possible errors, thinking just ahead of his fingers. The frustration welled inside him. Why couldn't the damned computers take this run? Computers that make all the decisions a man might make in a long life in five crawling minutes. Why couldn't the damned things *think?*

Under the guidance provided by the young man's damp hands, the slightly rolling ship edged through one of the many smallish rips and into the rich red of Jumpspace. The insane conditions that composed the edge of the rip foamed by within meters to each side; the ship barely missed intersecting with what mathematics alone could deal with. One touch of those visibly curdling boundary-value problems would have churned away any portion of the ship, volatizing it into component quanti and beyond.

From the other side, the holes looked, acted, and interacted in totally different fashions. Under the decreasing, although still carefully balanced, stresses issuing from the titanic, throbbing engines, the holes gently sealed themselves, leaving the ship precisely positioned in Jumpspace, exactly where it was supposed to be. Around it, the rest of the fleet was visible, if only as point-singularities in the non-Einsteinian starfield outside.

Captain Noel, having witnessed the hellride from the viewpoint of the fleet coordination officer, was understandably relieved that no communication was possible between ships while in Jumpspace. She had a fair idea of what Admiral Devon would have to say.

Commander Bolsa, Noel's recently appointed first officer, approached, a tiny, metallic, glinting object in his proffered right hand. With an ashen face he presented it to his Captain.

Noel looked at it. It seemed to be a small Concordat symbol pin, cut neatly in half. She looked up from the small semicircle to the Commander.

"Um . . . tradition, ma'am. For a Captain's first jump. Half now, and the other half when we break out."

Noel nodded, then turned and pinned the silver and green half-pin to Lieutenant Commander White's jacket.

Commander Bolsa thought of the other half of the pin that waited in his quarters, and managed to avoid shuddering.

"Why is it," Sh'in asked, "that the first thing a new, vital colony Sector does when it gets a shipyard is to try to build a big warship?"

Beside her at their usual table in the officers' lounge, Joan Rogers laughed gently. Sh'in didn't let it show, but she was relieved that the overserious kid could still laugh. She slitted her eyes. Was Joan going to be all right?

"By building a capital warship," Joan explained, "they can get Concordat naval construction contracts to make up for the money they're losing by not building a merchant fleet. Also, this way, they can feel all the more cheated when they're taxed to pay for it, and when their young are conscripted to crew the damned thing!"

Sh'in blinked; Joan's voice had cracked; she'd almost shouted the last two words. No, Sh'in judged, Joan was not going to be all right. *I wish I could help her. But she's got her problems all bottled up, and I haven't got the bottle opener.*

She spoke on, continuing as if all were normal. "Really, though, why do they always make such a production of asking for the permission to build capital ships?" She hurried on. "I can see all the immediate advantages: a Dreadnought with the colony's name on it; the glory; just a little bit of real power. What I want to know is: can't they ever see the long-run problems?"

Joan stared at the table top. "Of course they can. But they also see the longer view yet: examples such as the Line Worlds. Jewell has forty shipyards, each as big as the city we've just left behind. They throw tonnage around at an unbelievable rate. This ship, for instance. How many Sectors could donate a brand-new Battleship, combat-ready, just out of trials, with no strings attached?"

Sh'in laughed. "No strings?" She watched Joan like a hawk.

Joan smiled, still looking down. "None. They're so damned powerful that they can write their own rules. A little largess, however, is good for their public image. Not even the Praesidium can push them where they don't want to go. And the newer Sectors see that, and hope someday to wield similar power."

"And instead, they get absorbed by other institutions."

"Like the Opifex Group," Joan agreed. "Owned by a consortium of Line Worlds concerns, and heavily subsidized by the Jewell government." She seemed back to normal, but Sh'in realized that this was a brittle normality.

"What's a small Sector to do?" she wondered idly.

"Persevere." Joan's answer was deadly serious. "The Philomela Outreach will be powerful of itself someday. If Burt and his rebellion have set the area back a bit, it will pick itself up again. The Concordat will give them the aid they require . . . *with* strings attached. As much as Burt did to damage the Sector, he's in the best place to help restore it. Knowing that rebellion is useless, he'll push all the harder for legitimate competition."

"It was still a poor choice, leaving him in charge. He should have been executed." Sh'in said this almost randomly, still keeping an eye on Joan.

"Bloodthirsty, aren't you?"

Stung, Sh'in muttered, "And you, of course, agree in full with Admiral Devon's every decision."

Joan blushed, and lowered her head. "Of course not." This was scarcely audible. "For as long as we've worked for him, he's made the right decision in every case, but always for the wrong reasons. He could have done a lot worse than choose Burt.''

Sh'in returned her attention to her coffee.

In the waiting room outside the office where John Burt met with Denise Voleur, Andrew North waited patiently, trying to pretend that he couldn't hear every word spoken within. Burt and Voleur had been going at each other hammer-and-tongs for over an hour now, sometimes shouting, sometimes whispering in deadly seriousness. North was amazed at how remarkably similar their viewpoints were.

This time it was over a new enabling document for the world of Acheron. Burt wanted to scrap the old one and start afresh, while Voleur insisted that the older document could be modified to the necessary degree. It took a detached observer, such as North now was, to realize that the final result would be the same in both cases. Each of them believed in statutory safeguards and in balanced government; their argument over form seemed ludicrous.

North sighed. Last time it had been over Burt's raiders. Should he be allowed to keep the group, hamstrung though it was, as a cadre, or must it be disbanded? Burt only intended it to be a party-style organization, it turned out, which would be specifically legal under the laws that Voleur argued for. That fight, which wasted the better part of three workdays, had been for nothing, just as had been the one before that, and the one before that.

Behind the closed doors, Burt ranted, while Voleur icily ignored him. *Damned childlike,* North mused. *But what can you expect from two paramilitary adventurers put against their wills in charge of a planetary government?* He was glad that he'd convinced Burt to put away the two pistols that the leader ordinarily carried. Probably he'd have stopped short of shooting the younger Voleur. Probably. But right now, for emphasis, he'd be waving the heavy slug-throwers around, gesturing with them, pointing them rudely at her. Would that intimidate her? North felt that it wouldn't. Rather, it would move her to a stiffer, if inwardly fearful, defiance.

A loud slamming noise echoed from inside. Burt banging his hand onto a desk top, North judged. The poor man never had known how to deal with people diplomatically. That had always been North's job, when the raiders were still in business.

He checked a wall clock. Fifteen minutes early . . . Oh, well.

Rising, he strode to the door and tapped deferentially.

"What the hell do you want?" Burt snarled.

"We've got a meeting with the roads department, sir," North called calmly.

Burt stomped out, leaving the door open behind him. North saw Denise Voleur inside, face flushed, eyes bitter.

"Come along, then," snapped Burt, heading for the waiting room door.

"Yes, sir." *Am I an intelligence chief or a baby-sitter?*

"Where are you parked?"

"Basement Two."

"Damn it, she makes me so angry. . . ."

"Better her than Casadesus."

Burt smiled then. It was one of his fondest moments, the day that the elderly Casadesus was informed that Burt was to be co-president. The white-haired man had stood, mouth working like a fish's, and only after a long minute of unhappy expressions had he been able to speak. Just as Burt hoped, he announced his inability to work with Burt, whom he categorized as a "terrorist," a "barbarian," and a "criminal with no true soul." With his passage, loud and self-righteous, Burt had thought himself alone, as full president.

Then that Voleur wench had stated her intention to stay on as Casadesus' replacement. *I fought it,* Burt recalled. *I fought it as I'd never fought anything before.*

Admiral Michael Devon was also like nothing he'd ever fought before. The man had a surpassing gall completely outside Burt's experience. *I'd like to meet him alone, some dawn. Man to man, with no fleet for him to hide behind. No pistols; no knives. He, and I, and our fists.*

It was as well for Burt that he never got his wish.

Breaking into his leader's moody silence, North brought up a delicate subject.

"Sir?"

"What?"

"Did you tell Admiral Devon anything about the saboteur?"

"Of course not. Why? Are you wondering why you're still unhanged?"

"There is a death penalty for what I've done, sir. I was wondering what you'd told them."

"The subject never came up during the reconstruction talks. Since they didn't ask, I didn't talk."

"I'm safe?"

"You better believe it. It never happened, and to hell with it. We've got better things to waste our time worrying about."

"Yes, sir."

Burt turned and faced his most loyal follower. North had risked more than his life in Burt's service; he had never disappointed his leader in any way.

"We dared to face the Concordat, Andrew. We met them, and the meeting was on our terms, not theirs. They won. Or so they think. But we proved strong enough that they realized they needed our help.

"Now I'm stuck running this one damned planet. Soon we'll start to put the whole Outreach together under a more central control . . . for the Outreach's own good. This world will be a power within the Concordat someday. That's not what we wanted, but it's not so bad.

"And I'll need your help. Do you think I'm going to let them take you away from here on so little a pretext as 'war crimes'?"

"Well—"

"Hell, no! Now come along. I've got the roads department to scream and shout at; when it gets too heated, drag me away, okay?"

"Yes, sir."

Chapter Sixteen

Once again Joan Rogers was asked to accompany Michael as he interviewed his ranking captive. Once again she was bluntly asked to wait in the antechamber while he conversed with Commodore Steldan. And once again she eavesdropped upon the entire conversation, listening to it through the speaker grille overhead.

This time, however, through increased familiarity with the two men, she was able to distinguish Steldan's voice from Michael's.

Inside, the two opponents gazed at each other, calmly, neither giving nor asking for recognition. If Michael was physically more powerful, Steldan had the greater willpower, having been tested against challenges Michael had never needed to face.

The captor saw that his prisoner was somewhat drawn, though otherwise healthy and well-groomed. He'd adjusted well to the confinement of the security cell; it was the inactivity that tore at him.

The captive saw his warder, tall, golden-haired, intense, and determined. Nothing could ever stand up to him for long, Steldan knew. Few enemies had ever tried.

"I need further information," Michael spoke at last. "What exactly is de la Noue up to?"

"Running the Navy," Steldan answered shortly.

"Where was the demonstration to come from?"

"Would it upset your view of things if I were to say—"

"Come off it, mister!"

"—that I don't know what you're talking about?"

"You play a very dangerous game."

"And you."

Michael slumped. "Agreed." Silence hung heavy.

"When do we arrive back at Tikhvin?" Steldan asked.

Michael glared at him. "How do you know my destination?"

"It was a guess. Your response verifies it." Steldan's smoothness took the sting out of the trick.

Or was it a trick? Michael wondered. *He must have known already.*

"The last time I saw a clock," Steldan continued, "two months and five days had elapsed since your departure. My fleet had an estimated relativity differential of less than a day. Does yours?"

Michael didn't answer.

"Since then I've been here for twenty-seven more days. I assume that you've met your boastful three-month deadline, and that we're on our way home. Your tenseness when I asked about Tikhvin betrays your guilt.

"Guilt, Admiral. What are you up to? What crime are you contemplating?"

Michael heard him out without comment. *He knows far too much, I fear; more than he's letting on.* He silently scourged himself for revealing himself the way he had. And yet it went deeper than that; it cut straight to the heart. *If I'm wrong, if I've jumped to the wrong conclusion, then I am contemplating a crime.*

Steldan abandoned his accusatory tone and became completely serious. Rising, he faced Michael sternly. "Don't do it. Neither I nor Admiral de la Noue are planning anything."

"What makes you think *I* am, then?" It was Michael's turn to mock.

"Your fleet can easily match what she's got on hand at Tikhvin—which is exactly nothing. My fleet was the full Sector reserve fleet. The Sector's helpless." He kept his voice even, although it was difficult.

" 'The Sector's helpless.' I know." Michael looked at Steldan quizzically. "That's part of the plan, isn't it? What do you think I intend? To break out with missiles flying and beams tracking anything in sight? If it's necessary, I will, because *I don't know what I'll be facing.* I know just two things: the Sector was weakened, and something is planned to happen *soon.* I suspect a great deal more than that, and I must be ready to act swiftly."

"You're wrong."

Michael ignored that. "Tell me what I need to know, and lives on both sides will be saved. I'll suspect you of lying, of course, but I'll take what you say into account."

"You've told me a lot."

"Yes, I have."

"Enough to put your neck in a noose when I report it."

Michael took a deep breath. "Yes, I know. I may well be wrong. I don't know whether to hope I am or not.

"Consider: if I'm wrong, then I'll charge in, looking like a fool, and spread accusations indelicately, which will be refuted. I'll be stripped of rank and either imprisoned, or, depending upon how much damage I do, executed.

"But if I'm right! A well-timed attack through the stripped Tikhvin Sector could peel two or three layers away from the Concordat frontier. We'd lose not only the Philomela Outreach, but Sectors Tikhvin, Campanile, Triangle, and the District. Maybe more!

"Can you blame me for taking this chance? Would you respect an Admiral that held back? I'm risking my life for the good of the Concordat!"

Steldan couldn't meet Michael's intense gaze. For the moment, the blond Admiral's fires blazed higher than his own, and all he could do was look away.

"I swear to you that nothing of the sort is being planned," he murmured.

"But there are things you won't tell me?"

Steldan blanched. Yes, there were. There could be no hiding that. For a moment he was tempted to tell everything.

But how could he? The odds were too high that Michael would misinterpret it. Misinterpret? Steldan felt like laughing. There could be only one interpretation of his illicit conversations with Joan Rogers. The two of them had planned mutiny. It was undeniable. What would Michael make of that? He'd see it as the confirmation of the whole structure of conspiracy, only the scaffolding of which he now glimpsed. The only possible interpretation of the truth would be totally damning.

"Aye. I can't even tell you why." He turned a grim face to Michael. "Can't you trust me when I swear it has nothing to do with Tikhvin Sector?"

Michael was not unmoved. He wanted to trust this man. But over his impulse to believe, the greater weight of duty descended. He could not afford to take the chance.

"No. I cannot trust you."

"I have to try to stop you."

"You're in the brig," Michael noted, "which effectively limits your resources."

Steldan dropped to his chair, exhausted. "Yes, I know. But you must be stopped."

Michael stood for a moment, then spun and left. Outside, in the antechamber, Joan Rogers stood when the security doors opened and fell in behind him. The second set of doors slid shut behind them.

"Will I end up like him?" Michael wondered aloud. "Locked up in a security cell?"

Joan had no answer.

The sun shone brilliantly over the drab, lifeless bleakness of the planet Tikhvin. Black gravel stretched from the jagged horizon to the unfenced edge of the naval base; from the windows of the office building, the empty desert and the empty landing field seemed horribly alike.

Grand Admiral de la Noue looked out over the burning rocks and shivered in the chill draft from the overworked air-conditioning system. Outside, the temperature was over eighty-two degrees centigrade, hellishly hot, while indoors the air chiller kept it at a thoroughly uncomfortable eighteen. Her several requests to the physical plant managers were apologetically turned down; they didn't dare turn the heat any farther up for fear of damaging the base's computer systems.

No one expects these distant planets to be comfortable, de la Noue thought, *but if we must travel out here and plant ourselves, why can't we build for us instead of for our machines?*

A chime sounded from the intercom on her desk. Pulling her uniform tighter about her, she wandered away from the illusory warmth of the distant desert.

"Yes?"

"Message, ma'am, from the commander of the Triangle Sector reserve fleet."

Relief washed over de la Noue. She'd been afraid that

the Triangle Sector authorities wouldn't act swiftly enough. Although she controlled the Navy, outlying Sectors were often fussy about releasing their reserves. Triangle's Sector government could well have delayed.

"Put him on."

"Yes, ma'am."

After a long moment while contact was transferred, the voice of the fleet's commander, Captain Norman, boomed jovially over the intercom.

"Captain Richard Norman reporting, ma'am, with fourteen of the nicest Light Cruisers Triangle Sector ever laid hands to, plus two Heavy Cruisers in really good shape. Shall I bring 'em in, or do I stand off and hold high guard?"

De la Noue smiled. She would remember Triangle Sector, and sometime, in some way, repay them.

"Since we don't know what the problem is, I think you'd best stay out there and be ready."

The two-second transmission delay elapsed while de la Noue waited.

"Sounds good to me, ma'am. What exactly should we be ready for?"

"We don't know. Maybe something big enough to have eaten two fleets, or maybe nothing. I don't want to take chances."

Two long seconds, so disruptive of normal communication.

"Just stopped sounding good." His voice was still cheerful, belying his grim words. "O' course, I couldn't hold something like that back for long, but I might be able to give you enough time to evacuate the planet. Not that that world's much to look at. Do you know how long we might be waiting here?"

Remembering Michael's boast, de la Noue checked the calendar. Three months and nineteen days had passed. Even allowing for a fleet's relativistic differential, it seemed certain that Michael was overdue. He'd seemed so confident, though. Three months, he'd claimed, was more than enough time to clear out the Outreach.

Could he have run into delays?

What about Steldan?

"I think that if anything is going to happen, it will happen soon."

"Sounds fine. 'Least, we won't have long to wait. Myself, I'd like a good fight." Hastily, he added, "Not without your orders, o' course. Uh, Norman out."

In the office, the chill of which somehow seemed less, de la Noue made arrangements for the fleet's coordination with the orbiting Monitor system and with ground-based weaponry.

Her problems were far from over. Since the removal of her predecessor from office, the Praesidium had been exercising a stricter control over the Navy. Being new, de la Noue hadn't yet built up a power base broad enough to support her against opposition.

Only by lying to the Praesidium had she been allowed to call upon the Triangle Sector reserve fleet, and if she were discovered, she could very likely be out.

It wasn't really a lie, she thought insistently. *I told them that there was a danger somewhere out there, either in or beyond the Outreach.* Something *is preventing Steldan from reporting.*

Now she had two Heavy and fourteen Light Cruisers: enough to defeat just about anything that was likely to appear. Or was it? Even if they were used in a purely defensive array, in full coordination with the Monitor system, any fleet capable of taking out Michael's force could easily batter through.

That was it, then. If nothing appeared, or if Michael and Steldan returned peacefully, she would lose her office and be disgraced. If an enemy appeared, the consequent fight could end with both Tikhvin and Triangle Sectors lost.

She had no idea which to hope for.

Michael's piecework fleet fell from Jumpspace on the very outskirts of the Telosophae system, still well within the Philomela Outreach. Two more jumps would be required to reach the border, and two beyond that to arrive at Tikhvin.

To everyone's great relief, the unpleasantly vibrating hull of the *Basilica* dropped out with almost no ill effects.

Captain Noel stood on the slightly bucking deck of the *Basilica*'s command bridge during the breakout, gripping the edge of her chair so tightly that her knuckles looked like solid knots of bone. Although she knew that the gravity fluctuations were unimportant, that they would be repaired during the four-hour stopover, the changing pressure did horrible things to her madly insisting hindbrain. Half-dreams of falling came to her, and sensations gripped her in her gut, sensations that signaled loss of balance, or a fearful plunge.

From the faces of those about her, she was able to guess how her entire bridge crew suffered. She tried to project the image of control. Her shifting stomach commandeered her attention.

Suddenly it was over, and normal gravity settled throughout the ship, the variations fading like a freshly escaped dream. From the tactical readouts in the fleet command bridge, it was plain that the *Basilica*'s jump-coordination equipment was in reasonable shape; only a slight spurious spin had been applied to the fleet. Within seconds command reverted to the *Philomela;* within minutes the spin had been countered.

"Commander Young?" Noel asked, speaking into her intercom.

"Yes, ma'am?" answered Emily Young from the engine room.

"Don't do that again."

"This?" A split second's gravity pulse flickered through the command bridge, scarcely noticeable.

"Yes, that. Don't do that again."

"All right. I won't."

"And while you're there, how long to fix it?"

"If I can have zero-gravity for a couple of hours, I can patch it together."

Captain Noel looked about automatically for someone to okay the order, taking a moment to recall that she was in command.

"Go ahead."

The warning buzzer sounded throughout the gigantic ship, giving the crew what Young and Noel mischievously thought of as a sporting chance. Then the gravity cut out, leaving anyone who was in mid-motion groping awkwardly through weightless contortions. The entrail-wrenching feeling of falling headlong eased into the normal spacehand's free-fall caution.

When gravity was to be restored, the crew knew, the

warning would be more substantial, more on the order of minutes than of seconds.

Good training, though, thought the commander of the shipboard regiment of Marines. *Captain Noel seems capable.* "Clean up that mess, soldier!" he snapped, and hid his grin when three men leaped to obey.

In the engine room, Commander Young applied herself to the gravitics control board, while several crewmen threaded the access tunnels to the connector points. Just as she'd thought, the problem was where the two half-ships joined. Forward of the engine room and astern of the bridge, linkages had either settled or been severed, pinched between two ill-welded bracing members.

They'd had a bare two weeks to assemble the bottom-heavy wreck. Even with every engineer in two fleets, and with a hundred trained workers from the planet, one could hardly expect the nonstandard bulk to work perfectly. At least the jump drives had been fine-tuned. Commander Young had no desire to enter Jumpspace the way they had the last time, scuttling for it rather than pulling it over them.

Back on the command bridge, Commander Bolsa returned from his brief trip to his cabin, clutching the other half of the ceremonial "first jump" pin. Elaborately, he presented it to Captain Noel, who smiled theatrically and affixed it to her jacket front.

If the crew of the *Basilica* was a piecework group, picked up from Steldan's fleet, from the planet's unemployed, and from Michael's reserves, Captain Noel had nonetheless worked them into a cohesive and disciplined force. Partly through luck and partly by a good working knowledge of command gained during her months as the overseer of a gunnery bay, she had managed to avoid most of the pitfalls that await a Captain on his or her first jump.

Although the credit for the ship's crew's readiness and good morale were hers, the credit for the ship being here at all was due to the quick reflexes of the jump control officer. Noel, looking at the half chip, knew that he deserved the first half far more than she.

This half she'd keep.

* * *

Several kilometers away, on the *Philomela,* Commanders Sh'in and Rogers worked quietly from the fleet command bridge, putting the fleet into formation for its next jump. Refueling proceeded systematically, with the two large tankers that had made this system their prearranged rendezvous moving among the ships, tending them. Michael planned no stopovers along the path home, instead relying on each ship to execute maximum jump in order to arrive back at Tikhvin before the disaster he anticipated.

"You're so certain," Joan pressed him as he passed by her station. "Why can't you—"

"This isn't the time to discuss it, Commander Rogers. We'll have ample opportunity to debate during the next jump."

"Yes, sir." She returned to her board, blushing hotly.

"Why do you bother?" asked Sh'in after Michael had gone. "He doesn't give a good goddamn for what you or anyone else thinks."

Joan didn't answer.

"Don't bother trying," Sh'in continued. "There's no way you'll ever change his mind—if he has one, which I doubt."

Joan retreated for a moment into the privacy of her thoughts. *Michael . . . has a mind. Why must it be that the most brilliant man I'll ever meet is the most wrong . . . for all the best reasons. I can't save him; I'm going to be forced to destroy him.*

Destroy him? I think I love him.

Sh'in's incessant mockery, her flippant jocularity, seemed so totally wrong to Joan that it was the greatest effort for her to keep her voice strictly neutral.

"We have a fleet to see refueled."

Sh'in looked at her carefully. "Yeah, I guess we do."

Chapter Seventeen

The fleet dropped into jump on schedule. The *Basilica* again was the keystone; this time it pulled the jump distortion around itself with classical precision, coordinating perfectly the fleet-formation jump. It looked as if the spurious energy that sometimes manifested itself as fleet rotation might this time be converted into extra speed. The rich, red false-glow of Jumpspace pervaded the universe.

In the carefully neutral ground of the electronics-deck officers' lounge, Joan Rogers met with Michael. She was uncertain as to how he saw her, whether as opponent or ally. While she had indeed classified herself as his enemy, she hadn't declared this. Her conscience charged her with treachery, and she couldn't deny the charge. *Is it treason when one betrays someone who would himself assault the legitimacy of the whole Concordat?* She didn't believe so, but still it haunted her.

"You asked to meet me?" Michael asked quietly.

"Yes. If I was appointed to be your political adviser—"

"Then why won't I listen to you? Is that what bothers you?"

Joan met his gaze, although it cost her. "Partly."

"There's more, then?"

"You know how dangerous this course might be. I think that you haven't taken enough measures to protect yourself if you turn out to be wrong."

"If I'm wrong, they'll string me up. That should please a good portion of my staff."

She did not—she *would* not—let him see how his words hurt her. "You've admitted that you're just guessing—"

"It's not that simple. I haven't any solid proof, but that's not as indicative as it might seem. The preparatory cover-up has swept most of the damning facts out of sight."

"If they're out of sight—"

"You're being oversimple!" he snapped. Sagging back in his seat, he brought his hands to the back of his neck. Joan looked at him with eyes as cold as ice. More bothered her, he saw, than just the plight of the fleet, or even of the Concordat. He felt a tenderness; he wanted to spare her. But there was no sparing anyone who could give him so intense a gaze. "I apologize," he said roughly. "That's no way to persuade anyone.

"I've tried to work this through both ways. I've tried to be fair. I've bent over backward trying to see it from de la Noue's point of view. And it doesn't work. The evidence is too much."

Joan's heart cracked, while she spoke on relentlessly. "You've presented your case sufficiently well that we'll follow you. We, as well, are suspicious, on the grounds of the arguments you've given us. We wouldn't obey your orders otherwise. I need to ask for insurance so that if you're wrong, no damage is done to the fleet, or to de la Noue."

"Only to my career, right?" He thought for a while. "What could I offer? If I'm correct, any delay will be fatal. Already the enemy—and I agree, he's hypothetical—could be in occupation of Tikhvin and beyond."

"Hypothetical?"

"I use the word for your benefit. I'm fully convinced that an enemy is involved. Whether he's from the cold beyond, or is an already known factor, I believe in the threat. I'm also quite certain that the Sonallans are involved. They have the most to gain and the least to lose."

Joan hid the pity she felt. He was wrong. She now knew more than he about the Sonallans; while they were indeed a dangerous enemy, their influence was simply not at work here.

"If we must proceed, then let's get it the hell over with." Nothing could be gained here. Nothing.

"That's what I intend."

Neither moved to leave. Over their coffee, each was alone with his or her bitter thoughts, separated by the wide gulf of duty.

* * *

During the remainder of the voyage, Captains Edwards and Engel found comfort in each other's company, while Commander Sh'in renewed old acquaintances with the junior officers in the radar control bay. General Vai and Colonel Sheffield kept the Marines from losing effectiveness due to boredom. Captain Noel, working with Commander Young, learned more about the finicky *Basilica*, getting to know its quirky moods, its warnings, its needs.

Michael kept to himself, removed from the rumors and the uncertainty. Generally, he left the running of the fleet to Captain Beamish, who, with his handpicked group of cronies, managed to keep order. No one knew what the suddenly reclusive Admiral was up to; no one particularly cared. The general view was that the operation was a false alarm and would abort immediately upon breakout back at Tikhvin. Michael's absence belied this impression, however, and everyone, from the reserve gunners to the command staff, had a deep-seated fear that combat was a real possibility.

Joan Rogers, as well, kept to herself, withdrawn into a shell of defiance, hiding her fears from the others. The few times that Engel or Sh'in tried to coax her into better cheer, she responded, only to fall eventually into her sullen silence. She alone knew the fullness of the mission's folly; she hoarded the knowledge and the responsibility for it, knowing the uselessness of speaking out.

And in the triply locked security of the *Philomela*'s brig, Athalos Steldan sat, or stood, or paced, sometimes restless, sometimes despondent. Always he felt the pain and frustration of his hopeless position, knowing himself helpless and, at the same time, too powerful. Was there any way of stopping Admiral Devon without destroying him? Steldan knew there was not. He ran through the scenarios in his mind, groping for any alternative. There was none.

Time and choices were running out.

In precise formation, Michael's fleet fell though the imaginary boundary and into normal space some million and a half kilometers from the smooth, gray, half-lit globe that was the desert world of Tikhvin. Fleet integrity was excellent, with no spurious velocity or acceleration. Every ship, from the outlying Scouts to the core, formed of the *Philo-*

mela, the *Basilica,* and the three Heavy Cruisers *Clianin, Invariable,* and the repaired *Tödlich,* was in position. The launching tubes of the *Philomela* and of the *Later* were operating at full capacity within seconds after normal space was secured; radar beams scanned the nearby emptiness, frantically searching for signs of possible hostiles.

For once applying herself energetically, Commander Sh'in oversaw the fleet's disposition, redirecting the launched Fighters into the most favorable search patterns and feeding their reports and those of the Scouts through into Commander Joan Rogers's station.

Joan sat carefully forward on her chair, supervising the critical nearsweep of the radars. Four seconds later the report came back: clear. No enemies were within the range of the fast-resolution nearsweep scanners. While she signaled the result back to Sh'in's station, the computers automatically began the mid-range sweep, coupled with a low-probability farsweep.

After twenty-eight seconds, the mid-range radars gave their full report: no enemies nearby.

And within two minutes the long-range radars sent in their word: two Heavy Cruisers and fourteen Light Cruisers, each of which gave an acceptable identification code automatically upon contact, as well as the expected twelve stations of the Monitor belt around the world.

Sh'in, hearing the news, heaved a great sigh of relief. *They're ours. The mission's over. I'll get to get off this goddamned tub and rest for a while.*

"Stay on your station, Commander," snapped Joan. Sh'in turned to her in disbelief.

"Are you corroding upstairs? Those ships are friendly!"

"Recognition codes failed us once before, remember?"

Sh'in stared, suppressing anger. "Whose damned side are you on? *His?*"

Oh, by the gods, if only I were. But I am not. What could she say?

"How are we doing?" Michael asked, striding into the cramped fleet command bridge. His light tone failed to cover for his all-too-evident worry.

What the hell is happening?, Sh'in wondered, her stomach knotting in sudden fear. *Has everyone lost their traction? Can't they see that our campaign is over?*

"The Cruisers all register positive identification," Joan said, carefully controlling her voice. She didn't dare let Michael know how she felt.

"Good," Michael said cautiously. "See if you can raise them, and find out who's in command. I'll be forward, signaling the planet."

"Yes, sir."

As she tapped out the proper radio frequency, she felt the pressure of Sh'in's unhappy gaze. She turned.

"Tell me," Sh'in muttered, "tell me that this is just a nightmare."

"Relax, Commander. If you can't sit your board, you'll be replaced." In a gentler tone, she continued, "It *is* a nightmare. More than you may ever know. Stay in control of yourself, and do your duty."

Sh'in sat back. Joan Rogers, whom she'd once thought of as a kid who needed her protection, had changed. The change struck Sh'in as ominous; the storm clouds gathered.

Joan finished the connection.

"Captain Norman here."

"Commander Joan Rogers, on board the *Philomela*. What is your fleet status?"

"We're holding high guard, under Grand Admiral de la Noue's orders."

Joan tapped the instructions that would record the message; Michael's face on a secondary screen turned to face her. "I heard. Ask him what his disposition is."

Flustered, Joan obeyed.

"Um, standard tactical spread, two in reserve. What . . . ?"

On another subsidiary screen below Joan's main data display, the image of Admiral de la Noue appeared. "Michael? Admiral Devon?"

Plainly, both Michael and Captain Norman saw and heard the transmission, although Captain Norman's reactions were delayed slightly by transmission lag.

"Answer for me," Michael said to Joan. Apparently, he wanted to study de la Noue's expression without being seen himself.

"Commander Joan Rogers, *Philomela*," she repeated. She added, "What are our orders?"

"What happened to the missing ships of your fleet? Where is Admiral Devon? And what happened to Commodore Steldan?"

"Commodore Steldan failed in his mission," Michael snapped, revealing himself to both de la Noue and Norman. Joan watched him watch his screen, waiting for their reactions.

First de la Noue, then Norman, received the word. De la Noue's face fell; Norman's expressed ignorance. Michael, noting this, concentrated on de la Noue. As he watched her on the screen, and while Joan watched as well, seeing exactly what he saw, de la Noue's head turned to the side, listening. Apparently she was receiving an update from someone at the naval base.

Returning her attention to Michael, she regarded his image uncertainly. "My radar officer tells me that you've got several of Commodore Steldan's ships with you. What happened?"

"He found me. I was forced to destroy him." Despite the gravity of the comment, he delivered it offhandedly. Through the pose, he studied de la Noue's every gesture. On one of the subsidiary screens below the main display of the communications station where he sat, the green readout line of a voice stress analyzer quietly quivered.

I must hurry, he thought. *The longer I wait, the more time she has to compose herself, and to prepare a story that will hang together.* As it was, he knew, the voice stress analyzer was countered. De la Noue obviously had cause for anguish whether or not she was lying.

"What do you mean?" Her voice shook with suppressed worry. Michael double-damned her in his mind. Either she was playing for time, or she actually didn't know.

"He came out of Jumpspace and immediately opened fire." Pleasantly, he added, "Now why do you think he would have done that?"

De la Noue frowned. "He wouldn't." She closed her eyes. "Bring your fleet in and make a full report."

The cagey . . . Michael fumed, suppressing the obscenities that leaped, unbidden, into his mind. *She wants my fleet helpless, trapped in a low orbit. At least, although my plan is ruined, hers is wrecked also. I'll stay at a medium orbital distance, with a substantial fighting crew aboard, so that if anything appears we'll have a fair chance of taking it on.*

He was, however, certain that he'd lost. All de la Noue needed to do was wait until he was gone, standing trial for the crimes he appeared guilty of, and signal her invasion while he was discredited. His warnings would be discounted as the ravings of a traitor, until it was too late. The only defense against the kind of operation de la Noue planned was preparedness.

"Coming in," he said, with the full weight of his despair showing in his voice.

Was he actually guilty? Could he have been wrong all along? He grimly admitted to himself that he would not have been the first person to have been blind and stupid.

On his console, the image of Admiral de la Noue blinked off. Out of sheer stubbornness he set the communications console to searching the frequencies for any other radio messages being sent. Soon he found a conversation between de la Noue and Captain Norman. It was encoded.

Michael shrugged, then frowned and put the station's computer to search for a key to the encrypted message. It answered immediately, noting that the code was a standard Concordat command code. Michael looked up, thought for a moment, and asked the machine for a translation.

On his screen, the image of de la Noue reappeared, speaking now to Captain Norman privately, or so she thought.

". . . Destroy him."

Michael came to full alertness. Quickly and precisely he keyed in the instructions to the station ordering it to record the transmission, and to feed a duplicate through to Commander Rogers at her station.

Captain Norman's image appeared on the answering channel. "Yes, ma'am," he said, his expression unreadable.

"No evidence must remain."

"None will."

"What about automatic recordings in the ship's logs?"

"Erasable. With the amount of radiation sleeting through those ships . . ." He looked thoroughly miserable.

"That would work," de la Noue admitted, smiling a

mirthless smile as she envisioned the mounting thousands of casualties. A thought came to her. "Witnesses?"

Norman answered slowly. "In something as confused as a battle, especially between fleets of these sizes, eyewitnesses are very few. It's never hard to persuade people that they've only seen what they want to have seen. I don't think it will be any good to anyone to look for witnesses."

"This is going to be very hard to explain."

"Just say what Admiral Devon said himself a space back. 'He fired first.' "

"I'd like to have proof."

"Hard to come by. Whatever, though. I'm just a reserve fleet Captain. I'm more than a little proud of my Cruisers, but as for myself, I'll do just as you say."

"Why did Steldan fail? What could have gone so horribly wrong?" De la Noue looked down. "I thought I could depend upon him. . . ."

Norman had nothing to say.

"I'll see you, then," de la Noue muttered.

"Right."

The communication ended.

"Did you get all that?" Michael asked Joan over the intercom.

"Yes, sir. Did you get the first part?"

"No." He felt almost elated. It was definitely the proof he needed.

Joan felt otherwise. "It could have been something other than it seemed."

"Not likely!" Michael scoffed. "Check your radar. What is he doing with his fleet?"

"He's heading planetward . . ."

"Yes?"

"On a near-intercept course," Joan whispered.

"Coincidence?"

"It could be," she said defiantly. "It's one of the best ways to obtain close orbit. We're heading inward, and so are they. Why shouldn't we come near each other?"

"Why indeed?" He called an orbital graphic display to his screen, glanced at it, and guffawed. "How very convenient. His trajectory is a classically perfect defense-offense trade-off with respect to ours. Exactly what he needs, if his smaller fleet is to destroy our larger one."

"It's a neutral formation!"

"No, Commander; it's an *alert* formation. If we let them have the first volley, they could destroy us, even though we outnumber them. But if we fire first, it gives de la Noue the excuse she needs."

"So? What do you do?" Joan badly dreaded the answer.

"They're going to use the excuse anyway; why not give them something to complain about?"

"Michael! You can't mean—" He could. Her words were cut off by the strident buzzing of the combat alarm. Admiral Michael Devon was through with waiting. The time had come to act.

Chapter Eighteen

With the *Philomela* in the lead, the fleet spread and charged, its formation and velocity plainly setting it into position for a devastating missile attack. Within fifteen minutes the disposition was unmistakable. The communication board signaled for attention; Michael ordered that no answer be given.

At full combat acceleration, the fleet would take just under an hour and a half to close to missile range. Michael was careful not to waste a minute of it.

The taped evidence was played for the officer staff of the *Philomela*, and copies were sent by shuttle to the other capital ships in the fleet. Michael intended no interception of his communications such as he had used against de la Noue. The uneasy concensus returned; led by Beamish, the Captains agreed to follow Michael. Dissent was suppressed, and several Captains found themselves spectators, relieved of command. Michael was prepared to brook no opposition.

General Matthew Vai, although not a part of the relevant command hierarchy, tried to talk to Michael. He was turned away by a squad of his own Marines. An Admiral, it seemed, outranked a General, regardless of chain of command. Vai, incredulous, marched off without another word.

Full battle drill followed, with the gunnery divisions running through the fire-reload-fire sequence several times. Radar equipment ran through several mock combats, preparing for possible anti-radar measures, and for the type of unorthodox electronic warfare that the Concordat delighted in. Deep in the missile magazines, the destruct frequencies of the missiles were randomly altered, a deviation from standard procedure, although justified. Certainly the "enemy" knew the standard frequencies; the new ones were unpredictable by man or machine.

Command staffs were put through equipment shake-down. Backup systems were tested. No officer was allowed enough time to realize that he or she was deliberately being kept from thinking about the enormity of the coming battle. Were they attacking their own side? Was it truly mutiny? Drill, drill, and more drill drove the straying thought away.

"Admiral Devon?"

"Here."

From her station in the fleet command bridge, Joan read the message she'd found. "It was pinned to my chair when I returned from lifeboat drill. It says: 'Check the power plant on the CR *Clianin*. Unless the current campaign is aborted, similar bombs will burst, ruining your fleet.' "

"The raider saboteur!" Michael hissed. "This is the last proof I needed. Take a team through the *Clianin* at once."

"I've already ordered that. They'll report soon."

"Now can you deny the link between Admiral de la Noue and the raiders?"

Joan lowered her head. "No, I guess I can't."

In seventy-eight minutes, they would be within range.

Soon the message came back from the *Clianin*. A small, conventional-explosives device was insinuated deep within the power plant complex. Although it was easily removed, the Heavy Cruiser would be required to drop back, out of the attack formation.

"Do so, then," Michael snarled. *Similar bombs.* Cold fury ate at his reason, driving away the sudden fear that had sprung up.

Throughout the heavily accelerating fleet, search teams ran through their ships, probing minutely, testing the air for the vapors that explosives give off. Time was not on their side. Soon Michael would be forced to decide whether or not to break off his attack.

"Sir?"

Michael took the call. "What?"

"Three bombs have been found, all on the Light Cruiser *Swift.*" Joan's voice was concerned. "If there are three on a CL, then how many are there on the *Philomela?*"

"Where were the bombs placed?"

"One was set into the main drives so that if it blew, the ship would be lost with all hands. The second was placed against the main power bus; it would have damaged the ship and pulled all power for hours. The third was in a bundle of computer linkages. If it went off, the ship would have been useless, but very easily and cheaply repairable."

"We've got a damned subtle saboteur. Have all ships searched in the same places."

"It won't work."

Even though he'd half expected that, it still hurt. "Why not?"

"As soon as I got the word, I ordered just what you said; nothing resulted. Our chief engineer says that every ship we've got is packed with sensitive areas where a bomb, placed by someone who knew the ship's layout, could destroy, damage, or disable."

"He doesn't think we can predict where the bombs will be?"

"He has some suggestions, and they're being followed. It doesn't look good."

"You found the three on the *Swift* fairly handily." Michael almost whined; with a jolt he reminded himself that he was in command, both of the fleet and of himself.

"That was just as much luck as anything else. Two teams happened to be looking in the right places."

"The operation will proceed." Michael's voice was crisp, vibrant, and in control.

Lieutenant Jaquish, in the cramped cockpit of his Fighter, smiled wickedly and pulled the jar of "brine" from beneath the control board. Spun-column distilled from a select mash of tubers, smuggled here by a good friend, the potent brew was one to tackle one's taste buds, not to tickle them. It was a good deal more than ninety percent alcohol, laced with the very choicest esters, ethers, and aromatics, many with out-of-the-ordinary effects upon central nervous systems.

It had the side effect of increasing hand-eye coordination and decreasing response time by forty percent or more.

"Gee, I really shouldn't quaff this stuff," Jaquish said to

himself, speaking aloud as if arguing. "After all, it's illegal."

"Why not drink it up?" he answered himself, taking the other side of his solo debate. "Even without it, I'm still the best pilot in the fleet. Why not make a good man better?"

"Doctrine, that's why. Our chief ideologist says that anything that alters the basis of human nature is—what was his charming phrase?—'antiprogressive, dehumanizing, and counter-revolutionarily debasing.' Besides, it's inebriating, and that means fun, and that means forbidden."

His second voice spoke again. "It better enables me to serve my fellows. That's what the Concordat is all about."

"But it's against *regulations,*" he entreated, in a mocking voice that left no doubt as to which "side" of his one-sided debate would eventually win.

"To heck with regulations. This is too important." With his free hand, he pulled open the jar and drank deeply.

"Good stuff, Lieutenant."

"Thank you, sir."

There was no one else worth talking to out here anyway.

Another deep draft passed down his suddenly inflamed gullet.

"Just like back home."

"Yep. Jus' like back home."

And another.

"It's empty! How could that have come to pass? If I weren't alone out here, I'd suspect another of having filched some." He looked about him, as if suspicious of the presence of a hitchhiker, a stowaway that had been surreptitiously pulling at the jar while he wasn't watching. No one was with him.

"Anyone back there?" he called over his shoulder to the autopilot computer. No reply came.

"Not talking to me, eh?" He wrenched himself around and faced the impassive computer. "Well, buster, let me tell you a thing or two . . . What's this?"

"This" was a small gray package wedged into the space between the computer and the autopilot linkage cable. It was also a bomb.

Glaring at it for some time, as if unsure of its reality, he decided at last that it existed. Did he? All he knew for certain was that if the bomb went off, he wouldn't.

"Right?"

"Right, sir." Reassured by this seconding of his opinion from a source he knew he could trust, he reached back and pried the out-of-place device from its nook.

"Wow. A bomb. I'll bet most of the other pilots of the squadron wouldn't think to check there the way I did." Delicately he snapped on the radio linking him to the squadron leader.

"I hear you, Jaquish. What report?"

"Uh, sir," he answered, not a trace of intoxication appearing in his voice, "I've discovered a small bomb just under the computer."

"Repeat!" the leader snapped. Jaquish knew he was being recorded.

"During routine check, I found a small bomb, of unknown origin, placed just under my on-board autopilot computer." He was proud that his voice was perfectly unblurred.

"All pilots," the leader announced. "Carefully examine your autopilot computers. Search for an extraneous object just beneath it. Do not touch it, but report, by sequence, if you find anything."

After a long moment of silence, a strange voice came over the common band. "Pilot number one: Castle. I've got one."

"Pilot number two: Brundt. I have one."

"Pilot number three: Davis. I've got one."

"Pilot number four . . ." The full report took some time, but the important idea was grasped soon. Everyone had one.

"All right." The leader's voice sounded worried, and for good reason. He too carried a bomb. "Don't touch them. By sequence, turn around and land back on the *Later.*"

Don't touch them indeed, Jaquish snorted. He'd pulled his loose, and nothing had happened. Should he report this? Well . . .

But it was too late. Already the ships had begun to turn, matching courses carefully with the distant Mothership.

Gosh. If my reflexes weren't hair-trigger sharp from the "brine," I might have spoken up . . . and been discovered in

*my use of the forbidden stuff. But . . . if I had, the fleet
would've had Fighter support. . . .* Should he say something now? Once the Fighters were taken aboard, it would
take too long to launch them again, considering that the
overcautious inspection officials would insist on combing
through each craft for more bombs.

Jaquish managed to hold his speed down to a reasonable
degree, only slightly outstripping his companions. They,
fearful that their bombs might explode, plodded along
with no acceleration, merely coasting toward the nearing
Mothership. As much as it annoyed him, he too had to act
frightened, paralleling his friends' cautious course.

With the slightest of jars, the recovery field gripped the
small craft, pulling it with a gentle gravitic tug toward the
landing bay. Above and below him, Jaquish could see the
titanic curve of the Mothership edging toward him, the recovery bay doors yawning wide to receive him. Warm light
spilled out from the landing deck's floods; already his
craft's gravity field readjusted itself to match the force and
direction of the larger ship's pervading field.

Past the bay's recessed doorway he and his ship floated,
his hands behind his head as the computers handled his
landing. The Fighter sank to the deck without a quiver,
settling into its assigned slot on the gleaming wire-net surface.

Neglecting, as always, the standard atmosphere check,
he blew open the canopy and vaulted, recklessly, from the
cockpit. He beckoned to a flight attendant, tossed the man
his identification chip, and sprinted for the open doorway
to the command center for this deck. He dashed inside,
ducked to the right, swatted the gravitics officer on the
rump, and announced to the deck officer in a voice just
short of a shout, "Lieutenant Jaquish, Seventeenth Squadron, Vaney's Valiants, reporting. First, as always." He
lowered his voice. "I don't know what's keeping the rest of
the guys. Maybe they ran into a bit of trouble."

He shrugged. "Oh well." Reaching into his jacket, he
pulled forth the small gray box that had been placed into
his autopilot. "I found this. Belong to anyone?"

The deck officer, long used to Jaquish's irrepressible
flamboyance, took the whole routine without expression.

Even the bomb, nestled in Jaquish's right hand, failed to move the man from his impassivity.

"Put that thing down, Lieutenant. Outside. And report to Captain Thornton."

"Why?" Jaquish's attitude suddenly radiated defiance. His stance, the positions of his hands and feet, were more impertinent than anything he could have said aloud.

"He needs to know more about how you found the bomb."

"Not much I could tell him." Jaquish yet made no move to leave.

"Every Fighter in our complement was rigged with one of those. You just saved over three hundred lives."

"Oh."

"And when you talk to the Captain, try not to breathe at him, okay?"

Letting a precise sneer be his reply, Jaquish strode off toward the elevators that would take him to the command bridge. The deck officer deftly snagged the bomb, which Jaquish had been about to take with him.

"That's one officer who will never rise to his level of incompetence," he remarked to the gravitics officer as the slightly inebriated Lieutenant left.

"How so?"

"He'll never, never, never get a promotion. The only reason we keep him at all—"

"Is that he's the best pilot in the Navy."

"Right." He glared at her. "Just don't tell him, okay?"

"Oh, he already knows."

"Report from the *Later*," Joan spoke into her intercom. "Every Fighter aboard was rigged with a small bomb."

"Our saboteur is industrious" was all Michael had to say.

"They were small, virtually harmless things. If detonated, they would have rendered the target helpless, without killing or even injuring the pilot."

"That's not what the first reports indicated."

Joan stammered for a moment, until she regained control. Why should it have surprised her that Michael was watching, looking as if over her shoulder, calling a duplicate of her display screen onto his own on the command bridge? He doubtless circulated, backing up first one, then another officer, overseeing the whole of the operation.

"The bombs aboard the Fighters were small, precision shaped-charge packages, designed to penetrate the on-board computer links but not to do any damage."

"You're painting the saboteur as someone interested in our well-being. I urge you to remember the *Vostigée.*"

"Yes, sir." Joan was glad that Michael couldn't see her blush.

On the command bridge, Michael was far more concerned than he let on. If the bombs aboard the majority of his ships were to be detonated, there was no way he could face the nearing Cruisers. Already he was without Fighter cover; fortunately, his enemy had none either.

Captain Norman was no fool. The man had put his small fleet to full acceleration, inward toward the protective ring of orbiting Monitors. If he planned to avoid overshooting them, however, he would need to make a turnover at the halfway point, applying all his acceleration outward. Michael, pressing forward, would be able to close to missile range, staying close to the fleeing fleet for most of the distance to the planet. Nothing of the sixteen Cruisers would be left. Nothing.

But the bombs, the damned bombs. Search teams had combed the colossal mass of the *Philomela* ever since the warning had been received, and nothing had been found. There were hundreds, even thousands of places that a bomb could be secreted, crippling the ship. If the conscientious saboteur really was as kindly as he appeared, the explosions could be arranged so as not to harm anyone while still taking the ship out. Some of the locations of the bombs aboard the *Swift* wouldn't have kept the ship out of operation for more than a day, and would have been easy and cheap to repair.

For a moment his mind toyed with the idea of bombs placed aboard all Concordat ships by the deliberate order of some previous Grand Admiral, to be used against muti-neers . . . just as he himself must appear to be. But this was nonsense. Warships were already dangerous enough, with fuel tankage, arms magazines, and power plants all ready to explode if roughly handled. Placing "loyalty enforcement" devices was an insanity that not even a total paranoid could have used.

Why then the care taken, not only for the crews, but for the ships themselves? Probably the enemy intended to capture the ships, repair them, and put them to his own use.

Who was the enemy? Whom did Admiral de la Noue serve? Again the certainty seized him that the Sonallans were involved. The treacherous inhumans were the only known threat of any real magnitude. Michael discounted the possibility of a truly unknown enemy being involved in a plot of this complexity.

What was he to do?

"Sir?" It was Joan again, on the intercom. Damn her and her intrusions. He shook his head. No, that wasn't fair. She only did her duty, using her full intelligence and imagination.

"Yes?" He hoped his voice showed none of the unease he felt.

"A message from our saboteur. It gives us ten minutes to make fleet turnover or bombs will be detonated, starting with the smaller ships and working upward."

"Gods! Why didn't they do this earlier, when we faced Burt or Steldan?"

"What are your orders?"

"What else? Press onward, at emergency thrust, and destroy the enemy before we ourselves are destroyed."

"That's insane!" Joan's voice betrayed real surprise at this decision.

"We have no choice. We are the last defense for this entire group of Sectors."

"But sir! We can't just—"

"Silence, Commander. We can and we will."

Joan found herself speaking into a cut-off microphone. In misery she stared at the schematic of the fleet's disposition on her datascreen. In less than ten minutes the outer ships would begin to fall behind, their engines blown out by the well-placed bombs aboard. Working inward from that perimeter, more and more ships would be eliminated from the force, although not from existence. Finally, the

Philomela itself would be bombed, its engines severed from its computers at some vital linkage.

The ten minutes expired. "I warned him," Joan subvocalized, and keyed the instruction that detonated the final bomb hidden aboard the CL *Swift.*

Chapter Nineteen

Captain Traforth of the *Swift* retained his balance when the artificial gravity cut off. Some others on the command bridge failed to do so. For half a second everyone on the ship was dragged backward under the ship's driving acceleration of three standard gravities. After that initial lunge, the entire interior of the ship was in free-fall, uninfluenced by the shut-down drives.

Glancing over the duty stations before him, each of which displayed an almost solid bank of flashing red lights, Captain Traforth was at a complete loss as to what course of action to follow. He twisted awkwardly about to check the life-support station. To his relief, only amber lights, with a few welcome greens, glared unblinking across the console.

On the main navigational radar display, the bulk of Admiral Devon's fleet was visible, moving steadily away from the drifting *Swift*. Swallowing his shock, Traforth finally stirred himself. "What happened?" Even as he spoke, he realized how inane the question sounded.

"I don't know, sir," answered the radar officer. While he hadn't been the one Traforth had asked, no one else seemed disposed to speak up at all.

"Well, find out."

"Yes, sir."

"Wait . . . check your screen."

The radar officer spun, and stared unhappily at the display. On it, the Light Cruiser *Start* could be seen slowly falling out of formation, soon followed by the CL's *Dash, Celeritas,* and *Bolt.*

"I . . . don't . . . understand," mechanically stated the

suddenly dizzy Captain. He shook his head. "You'd better report this to the Admiral."

"Yes, sir."

Throughout the fleet, small bombs exploded, shearing with surgical precision through vital cables, conduits, or linkages. No pattern could be found; as often as not the target's power plant was involved, but other sensitive areas were also targets. Soon the entire complement of Light Cruisers was gone, falling slowly behind.

What next? The answer wasn't long in making itself known. Simultaneously, aboard every Scout in the fleet, a tiny device, secured against the main fuel pump, detonated itself, wrecking the pump and cutting all fuel flow off from the power plant. The damage, in real terms, was minimal, almost negligible; the result was the loss of the entire Scout fleet.

"Nice. Neat. No casualties." Captain Engel stood over the display screen that ordinarily she would have commanded. The officer there gave no indication of having heard.

"I'm glad you approve," Michael responded absently, even in this extreme managing a dry tone. To the other officer, he snapped, "Feed the computer reports through immediately to Commander Rogers. If she can't find an answer . . ." His tone of voice made it clear that he felt she couldn't, that no one could, and that he clutched at her like a straw.

Captain Edwards ducked past just then, pausing to give Engel a weary, reassuring smile. Once the master of the *Philomela*, now he ran errands for the radar section, which was commanded by a friend of his. Engel smiled back. She wished for the time to go to him, to talk with him. Time . . . She returned her attention to the fleet status display.

"How long until extreme missile range?" Michael asked tensely.

"Thirty-two minutes, sir." The officer didn't look up.

"Blast."

There could be no answer to that. Even under emergency acceleration, the fleet would be gone before it could release even a ranging salvo.

Michael sat down at the auxiliary station next to the fleet status/radar console and keyed in the instruction calling for a copy of Joan's work in progress. Instantly the screen lit up with a rapidly moving column of figures.

CS Blade: Bomb Sequence	42886-64713
CS Scimitar:	18887-97914
CS Saber:	22377-79962
CS Rapier:	31250-16278
CS Bayonet:	40835-88933
CS Scythe:	77777-77072
CS Broadsword:	09308-59578
CS Edge:	etc.

The list ran on for several more lines. Michael was able to recognize each of the ships, knowing them as his own. Were any left out? No. For a moment it seemed as if Joan was being thorough, perhaps running through the ships for possible inconsistencies in their maintenance records, or some such.

Until the single word:

DETONATE

moved up the screen. Almost instantly the radar operator beside him announced: "We've just lost all our Shock Cruisers, sir."

"Cut off Commander Rogers's board!"

"I can't sir! Hers controls all communications!"

For a long, sickening moment, Michael sat and remembered each instance of Joan Rogers's treachery. She'd fought him at every turn; now those events took on a new and far more sinister meaning. She'd never been the loyal fool she'd seemed. Rather, she'd been like a tumor, growing inside his command staff, infecting them all with the malaise, with doubts, with disloyalty.

On the screen, further characters moved upward.

CR Clianin: Bomb Sequence	21010-62684
CR Tödlich	66213-08595
CR Invariable	79157-56771

For a long moment he sat, motionless, with a sick helplessness paralyzing him. What use to leap, dashing awkwardly through the too-small doorway? With eight swift,

precise finger strokes Joan could type the word "detonate," leaving him standing stupidly, too late. The sense of
distance held him trapped; five and a half meters away
from him, she was as far beyond his influence as if she
were on the planet below.

With a feeling of fatefulness he watched the word forming:

DETONATE

Below it came the inscription:

Philomela: Bomb Sequence   86727-44919

The blood rushed to Michael's face. Desperately, awkwardly, his lethargy gone in an instant, he leeped to his
feet and threw himself past the doorway into the fleet
command bridge. Joan, in the dimly lit passageway,
looked up, eyes wide, at the charging Admiral. If her
mind froze, seeing her doom approach headlong, her fingers did not.

DETONATE

Michael's rough grasp on her wrists, wrenching her
hands from the keyboard, came too late. The lights throughout the bridge complex blinked twice, and stabilized. Tell-
tales on display boards all across the command bridge indicated the loss of drive and power.

"Release me, Admiral."

Michael looked at her, no expression visible on his
unnaturally calm face. He looked down at his hands, still
gripping her wrists. Mechanically he let go. The white im-
print of his rude grasp slowly faded from her skin.

Over her shoulder he saw the datascreen clear itself and
display in red flashing blocks of print the *Philomela*'s
status—drives: down; gravitics: holding; weaponry: down;
defenses: down; life support: holding.

"It was you, all along."

"No, it wasn't." Her voice was calm, contrasting with
his, which was listless, drained.

"Listen to her, Admiral."

Michael spun, stopping short as he saw the man who'd
been behind him. Athalos Steldan.

"You've lost, Admiral. You've lost, when there was never an enemy."

The doorways to the fleet command bridge were filling now with worried-looking officers. At her console, Commander Sh'in stared wide-eyed, having no idea of what to do. In the forward doorway Captain Beamish stood, his face pale, his throat working unhappily.

Michael's head snapped up. His eyes gleamed.

"Not yet." He brought his fist down upon Joan's console, jamming several of the keys. Leaping up, he pushed Steldan out of the way with a vicious straight-arm block and dashed away, past the startled bridge crew.

Recovering swiftly, Steldan threw himself at Michael's back, shifting his weight expertly so as to floor the fleeing Admiral. At the last moment, however, he himself was dropped by Beamish, who, roused from his stupor, saw Michael as the one who needed his help. Steldan flailed with his elbows at Beamish, failing to dislodge the wiry little man from his back. Michael used the distraction to make good his getaway.

His quarry gone, Steldan ceased to struggle; Beamish took advantage of this to catch his helpless victim in an extremely secure headlock.

"Release him," snapped Joan. Beamish made no move to do so.

Rising lithely, Arbela Sh'in strolled over, bent, and thumped Beamish solidly behind the ear with her knotted fist. It didn't bother her that the man was still, legally, her superior; she smiled and struck him again. After the third time, he released Steldan.

Sh'in looked up at the gaping officers of the bridge crew. "May I remind you that we each have assigned stations?" she said sweetly, and seated herself at her board.

Joan knelt by Steldan, ignoring the somewhat wobbly form of Beamish. Steldan waved her back. "I'm okay. Stop him."

She wasted several moments trying to clear her board, to no avail. Reaching below the panel, she tripped the release and levered the keyboard loose. With a well-trained economy of motion she handed the dead unit to Sh'in, who accepted it automatically. From the cabinet below their side-by-side stations, Joan pulled a replacement and settled it into place.

44TH MARINES SHIPBOARD TROOPS/SECURITY DETACHMENT

she typed.

FULL ALERT
DETAIN ADMIRAL MICHAEL DEVON: EMERGENCY.

Following that message, she tripped her intercom and signaled General Vai. His unit answered with the message that he was not to be disturbed.

"Damn it to . . ." Joan muttered, and gave an override command. *I would have been faster running after him.* Impatiently, she pounded the keys, instructing the unit to sound an all-ship red alert due to loss of hull integrity. It wasn't true, but it was a sure way to keep the airlocks shut.

"What?" snapped Vai over his intercom. He'd been in conference with Sheffield and his field commanders, trying to decide what to do about Michael.

"The Admiral's lost control. Commodore Steldan is taking command. Find Michael and stop him."

"About time, legal or not. We were just coming to the same conclusion. What'd he do, run away?"

"Yes!"

"He can't get far, can he?" Vai paused. "Okay, I'll have my men in the corridors fast. And erase this conversation!"

Steldan returned at that point; Joan hadn't even noticed him leave. "I couldn't find him," he said, and stretched. "He and Beamish caught me pretty good in the ribs. I probably couldn't have outfought him anyway." Gesturing absently with one hand while holding his side with the other, he made his report. "I put the bridge crew to either tracking him down or closing him off by remote control."

"We've got to stop him, Athalos. We've got to. Do you realize where he's going?"

"I'm afraid I do." He sighed. "The *Basilica,* with its new stern portion, doesn't have any bombs aboard."

* * *

With the detonation of the bomb in the main power-plant control mechanism of the *Philomela*, the security overrides throughout the huge ship automatically triggered. As with most emergency devices, however, manual releases were to be found at every location.

The delays were sufficient. Michael found a vacant shuttle bay, threw the release, and stole a high-velocity courier boat. With a gust of condensing air, the small craft blew itself through the half-open bay doors and careened off at five gravities of acceleration.

He'd come to the same conclusion that Joan Rogers and Athalos Steldan had: no bombs could possibly be aboard the new portions of the *Basilica*.

Captain Beamish was still nominally in charge of the *Philomela*. Michael wondered if he would prevent a message from being sent to Captain Noel. It didn't seem likely. To everyone aboard, Michael's flight would be taken as an admission of guilt. *It was no such thing,* he angrily thought. *We simply didn't have time to stand around arguing while the* Basilica *moved away from us faster every second.*

He knew well that most of the officers aboard the *Philomela* were actually loyal, and that only Joan, Steldan, and perhaps a handful of others were in the pay of the enemy. By delaying, however, even those few could cause the operation to collapse.

We haven't lost yet! he exulted. If one crippled Dreadnought couldn't face down two Heavy Cruisers, fourteen Light Cruisers, and a Monitor system, then his personal guidance and command skill weren't worth what they once had been.

Within ten minutes his fast courier had caught up with Noel's *Basilica*, made its turnover, and slid into a docking bay that gaped to receive him.

He was met just inside the ship by Noel, who was accompanied by several shipboard Marines.

"What the hell is happening?" Noel asked, her eyes clouded with suspicion. "Why have I received orders to arrest you?"

"Disregard them. The *Philomela* is in the hands of the mutineers who've been setting off the bombs."

"The orders claimed that Commodore Steldan was in

command, and that your orders were the ones to be disregarded."

"We haven't time for a tribunal! If you haven't decreased your ship's acceleration, we can still catch those enemy Cruisers."

Noel blinked several times in surprise. "This ship can't outfight—"

"Why not?" Michael's attitude was challenging. Inwardly, he already celebrated his victory over the pliant Captain Noel. Once she had begun responding to his sharp questions instead of asking her own, she was lost.

"This wallowing beast is a patchwork, jerry-built lump of lard. You can't ask me take it against first-line ships!"

"This ship is the last remnant of the fleet. It alone has survived to face the enemy. I see no reason for it not to triumph."

"But we're untried, uncalibrated . . . I won't have it."

"You have no choice, Captain. Unless you wish to be relieved of your command."

Captain Noel turned away and paced anxiously for a moment. Returning, she waved the Marine guards back, tacitly accepting Michael's dominance. The issue of his arrest was forgotten; the issue of the upcoming battle took precedence.

"This ship has maintained full emergency speed without difficulty—"

Noel looked up. "Without—Ha! Our compensators are melting as fast as they can be replaced, fuel consumption is phenomenal, and the damned power plant is set to explode, bomb or no bomb."

"Can we catch the enemy?"

"If nothing's changed since I left the bridge . . . yes."

"When we catch them, can we fight?"

Grudgingly, she admitted that they could.

"Let's get up to our stations, then. We've got a job to do."

On the way, Noel belatedly remembered her orders from Steldan. "What exactly is your status? And what is Steldan's?"

Michael stared straight ahead. "He is at the very least a traitor. Probably he's a mutineer as well. I am the commander of the fleet."

"Some fleet. A decrepit hybrid Dreadnought."

"Officially, the *Basilica* is classed as an Improved Dreadnought of the *Cathedral* class. It should be fairly capable of handling the enemy."

Noel said nothing, preferring to keep her thoughts to herself. Privately, she admitted that with its missile-fire capacity, which had been lacking in the old *Resolute,* the *Basilica* had a chance. Improved Dreadnoughts were among the best missile-flinging vessels in the Navy; the *Basilica* would perform, unless some small yet vital linkage decided it was overworked and burned itself out.

On the command bridge, they were met by Commander Bolsa and Lieutenant Commander Young. Young spoke first. "The compensators are lasting longer now that we've got the secondary power plant on line. Four engineering crewmen are dead and seven injured, from working too near the powerscreen. Everybody in the section will need radiation treatment."

"Is he . . . ?" Bolsa began, indicating Michael.

"Is our thrust undiminished?" Michael asked, interrupting Noel's attempted answer.

Lieutenant Commander Young gave him a glare of contempt. "Yes. We're still headed nowhere, at full emergency acceleration. Are you in command?"

Surrounded by disrespectful women, Michael thought. *What is the Navy coming to?* "Yes, Commander, I am. Get back to your post, and give me all the acceleration you can." His expression quelled any further comment. Young departed, and Bolsa, his questions answered, turned back to his station.

In fifteen minutes the hurtling ship would be within missile range of the fleeing enemy. Would they turn and give fight or flee, hoping vainly to ride out the attack until they came within the monitor system's covering range? For the moment, Michael didn't give the slightest damn. He had a fast, powerful ship, a tangible enemy, and the courage of his convictions. More than that he'd never asked; with less, he'd faced more powerful enemies, and triumphed.

"Load standard missiles." For perhaps the first time during the entire campaign he settled down, deliberately putting aside his concerns.

Fifteen minutes passed. Between the temporarily use-

less *Philomela*, Captain Norman's fleet of Cruisers, and
the planet Tikhvin, protected by its Monitor belt, messages flew busily, bearing their tidings at the speed of
light. It seemed almost ridiculous: the assembled might of
two Sectors was helpless before one crippled Dreadnought.

"What else can we do?" Admiral de la Noue asked of
Commodore Steldan. Her initial delight at discovering
him to be alive had quickly faded into dismay at the turn of
events. "That ship must be stopped before it gets within
missile range of this planet. Admiral Devon has made it
clear he wants me dead, and he's not above killing everyone here to get that. Our planetary defense system isn't
fully functional yet. Nothing could stop a volley from taking out this entire base."

"I know. It just goes against my training to destroy the
Basilica, crew and all. Captain Noel can't be blamed, nor
can her officers be."

"I thought of that. Selective fire can probably cripple the
ship without killing it. Probably. And we've got time. . . ."
She trailed off, considering.

"If Captain Norman doesn't make his turnover, he'll
have fully an hour and a half to disable the *Basilica* before
it comes too close. The Monitor force would have its own
chance, with roughly eight minutes to fire before Michael
is within range of the planet. They have the firepower to
destroy the *Basilica* fairly handily. If we save them for the
final destruction—"

"You're right, of course. The issue will probably be settled by that time anyway. Two Heavy and fourteen Light
Cruisers should be able to take him out, even with selective fire."

Although Michael tried to jam all radio communications
between Tikhvin and Captain Norman, his opponents had
all the advantages. The electronic-warfare equipment both
sides used was identical; de la Noue knew of all the un-
blocked frequencies.

With respect to most operating procedures, however,
this knowledge was useless. Michael was easily able to
counter even the best Concordat radar-fooling devices,
thanks to his possessing the same devices himself.

Soon.

Now. The *Basilica*, by Michael's order, released a full

salvo of standard missiles at long range. Darting like meteors at the end of their tails of fire, the small black cylinders each carried bottled thermonuclear hell in their tips.

They flew across the narrowing space between the launching ship and the small fleet of Cruisers. Captain Norman and his group had a good twenty minutes to prepare for the onslaught.

Heavy laser beams lanced out, hunting the suddenly agile missiles, which dodged and swerved according to their on-board computers' electronic orders. As the missiles neared their targets, it appeared as if the laser fire grew more erratic, desperately and even clumsily seeking out the closing death. In truth, although the beams could be seen to swing wildly across their half-sphere of target space, the gunnery sections only at that point enjoyed a reasonable probability of striking their targets. Using the quicker lead time to their advantage, and unexpectedly switching their beams from target to target, often picking off missiles aimed for ships all the way across the formation, they knocked out over seventy percent of the incoming warheads during these few seconds of maximum fire advantage.

From blister turrets on the surfaces of the Cruisers, clusters of antimissiles leaped forth, streaking out at insane accelerations, single-mindedly bent on intersecting the enemy missiles' paths. Most of the remaining targets died under the defense.

Unheeding, the few missiles left charged headlong toward the Cruisers. At least two warheads were targeted onto each ship. They passed through the penultimate line of defense: nuclear dampers and gravitic repulsor fields, poorly focused. Eight missiles died.

Twenty-eight penetrated, either to burst at minimum range or to endeavor to contact the targets. The fireballs bloomed, casting into sharp relief the detailed surfaces of the warships even as they disfigured those surfaces, deeply etching the armor plates that were the ships' last and most trustworthy defense.

"No significant damage," reported a damage-control officer to Captain Norman.

"Range?" he asked.

"Missile range five," answered a slightly nervous radar

officer. One hundred and thirty thousand kilometers; too distant for truly devastating missile fire.

"Hold your fire. Gunnery bays prepare missiles for selective target on enemy engine rooms and drive tubes."

"Yes, sir."

All efficiency, the gunnery officer relayed these commands to the small fleet command bridge of the flag Cruiser, where they went out to the fifteen remaining ships. Soon every missile bay in the small fleet—or flotilla, depending upon nomenclature—was primed with weapons containing orders to drive itself toward the enemy's drive emanations.

"Range?" again asked Captain Norman, almost impatiently.

"Unchanged: missile five, a spot over one-twenty megameters."

"Relative acceleration?"

"Negative one half."

"We haven't got forever," he snapped. "Fleet turnover, battle formation, full dispersion, by the numbers."

"Yes, sir."

The Cruisers turned around, each heading away from the center of formation, reversing end for end. Within seconds the relative acceleration of the two enemies, the small fleet and the single ship, brought them toward each other at over seven and a half standard gravities. Less than twenty-six minutes now separated the two formations.

Two long minutes elapsed.

"We'll be left behind, sir," objected an officer.

"Not my plan," Norman said offhandedly, squinting at his station chronometer.

"Then . . . ?" began the officer.

"Fleet turnover, maintain dispersion, course as before, evasive maneuvers as judged necessary, fire all missiles in nine minutes at missile range three."

The tactic had done nothing more than to allow the pursuers a slight gaining velocity beyond that conferred upon them by their willingness to use emergency thrust.

"They still have the pursuit advantage," warily suggested an officer.

"Which remark explains why you're a Lieutenant Commander while I'm running the fleet." A trace of his normal humor returned. "Why the long face, youth? You'd think it was we being outnumbered sixteen to one. Give me a firing dispersion, smartly, *blushet,* and get it to all ships."

"Yes, sir." The young woman had no idea what a *blushet* was, and so bent to her task, her fears forgotten.

To the gunnery officer across the small command bridge, Captain Norman gave his next mysterious series of commands. "Have a series of missiles prepared for strict antimissile role from half our ships. All other bays to second-load standard birds, proximity zero, selective on drives. We've been ordered to cripple the following half of the old tub and spare the end that ain't arse."

"Why—yes, sir."

"If they aren't our friends, the command downstairs figures they aren't our enemies either. That nice little distinction may get us all killed. Don't ask me; I just work here. Why are they waiting so long?"

"I beg your—"

"Our honorable enemy. Why haven't they dropped their second load of missiles?"

"I'm not sure."

"Be prepared to fire, then, and let me know what crops up."

"Yes, sir."

"He handled that salvo with fair ease," Captain Noel noted.

"They can't think they'll beat us," Michael said, ignoring Noel's remark. He sat at the command station, perched tensely on the thick chair.

"You think they'll just keep running?"

"If they weren't stuck with de la Noue's idiotic orders, they certainly would."

Long minutes of pursuit elapsed.

"Well, I'll be damned," Michael said. Captain Norman's turnaround maneuver was the last thing he'd expected.

"Any reaction?" asked a fire-control officer.

"No. We'll save our missiles for better opportunities yet. And save a salvo for the planet's surface."

After two more minutes Norman's fleet performed its reverse turnover.

"They're not going to run away, are they?" Noel caustically remarked.

Michael ignored her. "Hold all fire until they come within missile range three, then fire all loads."

The fact that he was outnumbered sixteen to one didn't move him. "All maneuver is to be directed toward the planet. The sooner we can obliterate the surface, the better."

"That, of course, will take out the naval base, as well as our still-unproven enemy, de la Noue."

Michael failed to respond.

"That was never the original plan," Noel continued, mercilessly working at the crucial point. "You needed to capture her, and to prove your charges against her. If her saboteur was so careful not to have you killed, why do you withhold similar consideration?"

Keeping part of his attention on the display before him, Michael plainly listened to Noel.

"We have too few Marines to land, agreed," Noel persisted. "We haven't even got enough assault boats to land the ship's crew without the help of a landing grid. So, instead, you'll obliterate the naval base, the landing field, the office buildings, the barracks crammed with innocent technicians, and the computers that perhaps hold the evidence that would convict your quarry."

Her temper got the better of her. "You idiot! You're digging your own grave!" Instantly regretting her loss of control, Noel stepped back and waited for Michael's response. It was characteristic.

"Fire all missiles and reload." From the several gaping missile bays around the gigantic ship, pattern after pattern of missiles streaked, the weapons moving outward, forward along parallel paths of fire.

"Reloaded, sir," called an officer.

"Fire all missiles again. And reload."

The second salvo burst forth, with long cylinders launching themselves furiously into the void. They chased after the first group, seeking the same targets.

"Reloaded, sir."

"A third salvo. Fire all missiles. And have the beam-weapon crews stand by." Without turning, indeed without seeming in any way to acknowledge Noel's existence, he made answer to her objections.

"When the bombs went off aboard the *Philomela*, I knew that my life was lost." His voice dropped. "I was surprised to find that I was afraid. All the men and women I'd ever sent to die seemed to return, neither accusing me nor acquitting me. For a lone moment, desertion, running away, fleeing aboard this ship and making excuses later, appeared to be an option.

"That was illusion. Here and now the issue will be decided, and by my actions alone. By the time I could have alerted central Sector governments to the danger and returned, all would have been lost. It may yet be.

"My actions. I alone must decide. I'm only sorry that I have to drag you and your crew through it to your deaths. I would spare that if I could."

The pain he felt was not feigned. His voice dropped even lower. "I may yet be wrong. Do you think you could bear what I've borne? A thousand times I've reviewed the long chain of deductions; I haven't always received the same answer. Not always, but just often enough. Just often enough to convince me that the chance must be acted upon."

Noel shook her head as if to clear it. If she reflected for a decade she knew she would never find an answer to what Michael had forced himself to say.

Chapter Twenty

Three flights of missiles sped across the steadily narrowing gap between the *Basilica* and the flotilla of Light and Heavy Cruisers. Not long after they had been launched, each of the Cruisers released a salvo of its own. These groups of missiles combined and raced madly toward the looming Dreadnought.

At the point roughly midway between the two forces, the rushing weapons became aware of each other, and reacted according to their natures. Even though the Cruisers were sixteen to their enemy's one, the hurtling Dreadnought had nearly three times the firepower, concentrated in missile and laser bays. Each of its three salvos was nearly equal to the flotilla's entire launch.

Missiles that had been ordered to kill enemy missiles—just half of the Cruisers' first salvo—twisted in flight to bring the enemy weapons into their path. All the others, programmed to be reflexively wary, introduced random variations in their thrust and direction, hoping to lose the pursuing missiles. In less than a second the two flights were past each other. Reacting with electronic precision unmatched by merely human capabilities, the antimissile missiles had managed to burst in such a way as to take out almost a third of their opposing numbers.

For a long moment the bright fireballs that had been the defensive missiles glowed, coiling gently in the emptiness. From the glare sped the surviving weapons, heading in two formations toward their targets.

Captain Norman, knowing his Cruisers to be less capable of absorbing punishment, ordered two more full salvos to be launched, in a purely antimissile role. After that, the time of missiles would be past, and for a very brief time his flotilla would be within effective laser range of the on-rushing *Basilica.*

That was all he had time for. Within half a minute of that last order, the first barrage of warheads slammed into the flotilla, each seeking a helpless target. Last-minute laser fire and desperate maneuver only slightly reduced the devastating effect of the salvo.

Dead or out of action were the *Titanne, Integrity, Rectitude, Honesty, Faith,* and *Honor.* Aboard the *Titanne,* Captain Norman watched, with glazed eyes, as fleet command was transferred by computer control to the other of the two Heavy Cruisers, the *Colosse.* Satisfied that he'd done all he possibly could, he almost gratefully sagged into unconsciousness. Spinning slightly about a skewed axis, the *Titanne* drifted away from the battle that still raged, far ahead and moving farther. Its engines were stilled forever, its computer nothing more than a room-temperature lump of useless circuitry. And its Captain, with two cracked vertebrae, slept the utter, dreamless sleep from which part of him never expected to awaken.

Two flights of missiles had yet to impact.

The room's chill was bone-penetrating, soul-searing. Almost, de la Noue wished she could find an errand to take her outside into the scorching, scarred desert. Instead, she tugged her uniform tighter about her, pushed her hair back, and sat, shivering, at the communications station in her office.

"Any word from Captain Norman?"

"No, ma'am. There's a message from the *Philomela,* though."

"Put it through."

Within minutes the message cleared. On de la Noue's board, the serious image of Commodore Steldan appeared.

"We've done everything we can here." He detailed the steps taken, most of them hopeless.

"That's it, then," de la Noue had to agree. "It's up to Norman's fleet."

"You're not watching the battle?" Steldan uncomfortably asked.

She dropped her gaze. "I was. Norman's dead, isn't he?"

"We can't raise him," Steldan admitted. He glanced to

the side, listened, nodded. "Commander Joan Rogers says that the second and third flights of missiles will hit in a few minutes."

"I'll be watching."

After a long moment of silence, Steldan mentioned, almost at random, "It was Captain Douglas who planted the bombs. He'd helped prepare both Michael's fleet and mine. Originally, he was to have shipped with Michael, but missed his connection. When he got the opportunity to go with my follow-up mission, he leaped at it."

"Then it was he that opened fire on Michael?"

"Yes. That part of the story was true. I think that Douglas thought he was discovered. As he lay dying on the deck of the *Illuminator,* he confessed to me his raider allegiance. When Commander Rogers searched the *Illuminator's* computer after that battle, she found Douglas's private file. It gave the location and detonation code of every bomb in both fleets."

"She set off the bombs that disabled the *Philomela?*"

"Yes, at my urging. I'd convinced her of your innocence early in the voyage when she interviewed me at length."

"You took Michael's fleet away from him, except for the Dreadnought, which Douglas never had a chance to bomb."

"It seems that the *Vostigée,* bombed very early in the campaign, was blasted by some sort of automatic timing device, rather than by a sentient saboteur. The *Tegula's* bomb went off when someone incautiously examined one of the other bombs aboard. In every case there have been several on each ship. If there had been a person responsible, if Captain Douglas had been with Michael from the beginning, he'd have done what we ended up doing, and the raiders would have won."

"Captain Douglas. I held him back, to advise me on reorganizing the reserve fleet. That's when he planted the second series of bombs."

"He must have been incredibly frustrated at missing his main chance." Steldan smiled.

"He hid it well. He'd been with the Navy for twenty-two years. How much of that time was his loyalty with the raiders?"

"Probably he was a member of one of the raiders' parent

organizations, a sporting club or service institute. There are some likely probabilities; eventually I'll track them down. Who knows what I'll turn up?"

De la Noue made no answer. On her screen, just as on Steldan's, was the schematic of the second missile strike.

The *Virtue* skewed about, lasers madly targeting the large cluster of missiles that knew it as their target. With a final spurt of emergency thrust, applied along a transverse vector, the careening Cruiser managed to avoid the greatest cloud of the swiftly moving darts; the fringes of the group slammed into it, bursting precisely just before and beyond. Large sections of plastic-ceramic armor plate flew away, stripped from their supports by gales of thermonuclear fire.

Against the *Purity,* the missiles had managed, by sheer chance, to intersect from three disparate vectors, all simultaneously. Its defenses overwhelmed, the *Purity* died utterly, leaving behind no more than an expanding spread of scrap metal.

The *Uprightness* was more lucky. Only eight missiles came even near it. Bursting almost derisively at optimum distance, they nevertheless managed to sever the ship's engines from their control mechanisms. Without acceleration, it was quickly left behind, although not before the swiftly overtaking *Basilica* had finished the job with a flurry of precise laser firing. The two halves of what had been a Cruiser were passed by, spinning quietly, an engine room and a command section still recognizable.

The *Colosse* enjoyed its role as flagship for a very few minutes. While the direct effect of the blast from nineteen bursting warheads failed to damage it significantly, the radiation shielding was overloaded, and decayed. The ship and its crew died in less than half a second.

The *Fidelity* rang like a bell from the two missiles that contacted it, slapping all the way through. The punctures were in the fuel tankage and in the number-three laser bay. Aware that their target was inexplicably behind them, the missiles fatalistically exploded, further damaging the hapless ship. Like the *Uprightness,* it was finished off by the *Basilica*'s gunners.

With both of the Heavy Cruisers, the *Titanne* and the

Colosse, out of the fray, the fleet command passed to the Light Cruiser *Dignity.* That worthy ship didn't live long enough to acknowledge the receipt of the flag.

The *Innocence* and the *Respect* died, blown into fragments; likewise died the *Justice* and the *Loyalty.* The small reserve fleet was utterly gone.

The third and final wave of missiles, having no targets worth its time, self-destructed in glorious blossoms of nuclear flame.

All that remained was to see what effect the sixteen Cruisers' missiles would have upon the *Basilica;* almost a minute remained until that final reckoning.

"He's not a madman," Steldan said, almost apologetically. He received no answer from de la Noue; on the fleet command bridge of the drifting *Philomela,* he was unpleasantly aware that all eyes were upon him.

"We found the recording that forced his final decision," Steldan plunged forward. "He put it to tape. It's your voice saying, 'Destroy him.' "

De la Noue sighed heavily, fighting to clear her mind. "I was talking about you, to Norman." Her voice was hushed, painful. "I mentioned that I'd never given Michael orders to destroy anyone, nor had I given you any such orders. We discussed the impossibility of proving this."

"On tape, it was ambiguous enough. Michael took it as an order from you to Norman."

"Then I'm responsible?"

"By no means. Michael deluded himself. Despite that, he's not insane, not by any medical standard."

"How much difficulty will I have finding a differing opinion?"

Steldan frowned. "Any doctor that interviews him in the next few months might or might not agree with me. I don't see—"

"I don't want him to go to his trial as a man responsible for his actions. I don't think he was."

Steldan carefully gauged de la Noue's expression. "You realize that he'll fight you on that."

"In what way?"

"He'd far rather be thought of as a tragically mistaken

hero than as a madman. He'll demand responsibility for his actions."

De la Noue sighed. "I'm afraid you're right. In which case I'll have no choice as to his sentence."

From behind Steldan, Joan Rogers's voice caught his attention. "Captain Norman's missiles impact in six seconds." She indicated the display screen.

At velocities best comprehended by computers, the first flight of missiles from the now-dead Cruisers contacted the *Basilica*. From its gunnery bays, antimissile beams lanced and scissored, reducing many of the incoming warheads to incandescent vapor. Despite this effective defense fire, most of the weapons made it through.

From the *Philomela*, the nearest capital ship, high-resolution telescopes showed the stern aspect of the hard-driven Dreadnought, strobe-lit by bursting megatonnage. The bombs burst like flash lamps, growing from nothing to an intolerable brightness, then fading, the whole of the explosion moving relative to the speeding *Basilica* with the same velocity that the missiles themselves had had upon detonation.

Unwavering, the high-energy green glow of the ship's drives showed its passage through the white and gold scintillations of the warheads. It seemed incredible that any ship could survive such a pounding. Tight-focused radar showed a trail of debris drifting behind it, scrap armor sheared loose by the swift-cutting acid of atomic fire.

And when the storm cleared, the *Basilica* pressed on, its drives, at least, unharmed. Without even securing from full emergency thrust, the battered Dreadnought charged ahead.

Twice more the massive ship swam unheeding through the hellish firestorms bequeathed to it by Captain Norman's dying flotilla. Twice more all free crewmen aboard the *Philomela* and in the far-spread, drifting fleet watched on datascreens, crowding around off-duty stations to see the ship that they'd help assemble run the gauntlet of flame.

The fireballs swept past, fading rapidly in the near-vacuum of interplanetary space. Beyond them, a green-white glow showed the *Basilica* accelerating inward,

blasting at three and a half gravities toward the gray
world below.

Aboard the *Philomela,* on the command bridge, an in-
formal conference took place, revolving around two separate centers of attention. Around the open doorway to the
fleet command bridge, Captain Edwards, restored to command of the Battleship, stood with Captains Engel and
Beamish, whom Steldan had not seen fit to demote to the
former status of Commander. Inside the small passageway, Commanders Rogers and Sh'in rubbed elbows with
several technicians of the engineering staff. All were involved in the effort to put the huge ship back into full operating condition.

"You had to set off the bomb that was inside the power
plant primary coils," an engineer complained. Joan made
no response.

"Would you rather have gone through what the *Basilica*
just went through?" Sh'in asked quietly. The engineer
said nothing and applied himself to the job at hand.

Forward, in the command bridge proper, around a
screen displaying Grand Admiral de la Noue's face, Commodore Steldan and General Vai discussed the events just
past. Somewhat inhibited by the two-second transmission
delay, de la Noue strove to keep up her end of the conversation.

"There's been no contact, then?" Vai asked.

"None," de la Noue answered. "No radio contact whatever, although that's not surprising in any case."

Vai raised an eyebrow. De la Noue elucidated. "After a
savaging like that, no radio equipment known would still
be working."

"Their engines are undamaged," Vai noted with doubt
in his voice.

"Engines aren't affected by hard radiation. Delicate
electronics—and people—are."

"They're well past turnover point," Steldan observed.
"They can't match their velocity to the planet without
overshooting and returning. And it's all too possible that
no one aboard is alive." He'd said it, voicing aloud what
Vai and de la Noue had only hinted at.

"It won't come too close to the planet," said de la Noue.

"Its current path will cause it to curve just within the Monitor ring. Since there's no way to match courses with it, I'll order them to shoot out its engines. When you have the *Philomela* restored, you can chase after them and salvage whatever's left." She, too, felt that not much would be worth bringing back.

"Shall I recall the 'artful dodgers'?"

De la Noue considered. "We'll retrieve them here."

Joan Rogers wandered by at that point, evicted from her station by the repairmen who had found it necessary to disassemble her board.

"Have you analyzed their orbit?"

Steldan updated her.

She nodded, unsurprised. "All dead. Maybe." Looking up, she met Steldan's gaze. "Don't write him off yet."

De la Noue answered over her radio relay. "The Monitor system will try to put out the ship's thrust so that it can be caught and looked over."

"Instead you should destroy it." Her insistence took de la Noue by surprise.

"Why?"

"Because their orbit will cause them to pass within missile range of your base, whether or not they lose power."

This was considered.

"If they're dead anyway . . ." Steldan began.

"The ship will never be worth much," Joan added. "It's too ad hoc; too slapdash."

"Joan's been right on every point so far," Steldan admitted.

"I don't want it destroyed," de la Noue said, frowning. "Some of the crew may still be alive. Besides, I'll need all the evidence I can find on Michael and his plans. He may have kept a log."

"At least have the Monitors aim for missile bays, as well as engines. Michael is capable of this kind of ruse."

"Agreed."

Within an hour the blindly accelerating *Basilica* came within optimum missile range of the Monitor ring. The orbiting fortresses, nonmaneuverable but supplied with firepower exceeding any standard warship, were the planet's last line of defense short of the surface. Their interlocking fields of fire covered all of space around the planet for hundreds of thousands of kilometers; it was toward this haven that Captain Norman had been fleeing.

Michael, if he was still alive, had very little time in which to act.

Chapter Twenty-One

Michael was still alive.

The *Basilica* had passed through hell and emerged from the other side, battered, scorched, half its systems ruined—and yet it lived. At the remarkable velocity it had by now accumulated, it would pass through the Monitor system's optimum missile range in mere minutes. The defending missiles would be more like stationary warheads sprinkled in front of the hurtling ship than like the guided, intelligent weapons they actually were. At the relative speeds involved, the target would be through the area to be covered by a fireball in less than a fiftieth of a second; the ship's own missiles would have its 250 kilometers-per-second relative velocity imparted to them at launch.

Glad that microcircuitry and not mere human nerves would make the precise decisions, gunnery crews aboard Monitor stations Two, Six, and Seven armed, loaded, and programmed their missiles. For sheer volume of fire, the orbiting platforms were unequaled; the computer facilities were likewise impressive.

Station Six, a monumental spheroid orbiting sedately, was granted the honor of firing first. From firing-bay louvers, its first volley flashed, the missiles darting out and curving toward their predetermined bearing. Each missile bay had the capacity to launch three times the number of missiles that a corresponding bay aboard the *Basilica* had; each of the three Monitor stations now in range had four times the number of such bays as had the Dreadnought.

The fireworks were visible even against the harsh sunlight above the black Tikhvin desert. Grand Admiral de la Noue found herself clustered with a small group of officers in the observation room overlooking the landing field.

There, someone pointed, and all eyes swung to follow. Small scintillant pinpoints were discernible just to the north of the painfully brilliant sun. If an arm or a sheaf of papers was held up to shade one's eyes from the direct rays of the blazing star, the twinkling, dancing lights could be seen all the more clearly.

It occurred to de la Noue that a much better view could be had on the base's telescope projection screen. Probably the technicians there had already rigged up a viewing room where officers and crewmen could watch. She made no move to leave. This was real.

No sounds were heard in the hallways other than the rapid breathing of the two or three dozen people, and brief shuffling noises as someone edged forward for a better view. Above, the strobing flashes gave no impression of coming nearer. De la Noue was reminded of sunlight reflecting off moving water.

"No maneuver until absolutely necessary," Michael ordered; although he'd given the order before, he repeated it to stress its importance. The crew was good: well-trained, they'd faced the hellride just past without flinching. If what was to come would be worse, he knew that nevertheless he could depend upon them.

The ship in its performance had exceeded his expectations. Where most radiation shielding would have broken down under what the *Basilica*'s had been exposed to, it had instead absorbed over ninety-five percent of the incoming death. The old armor plates, battered though they were, had deflected the thermonuclear fires that splashed over them. Although deep-etched by the washing flame, the plates had held, and had kept the bursts outside.

Now, in a few minutes, the ship would be called upon to repeat its defensive success and hold back death for a time. All Michael would need would be time to arm, aim, and discharge his load of missiles. Once they were loose, he, the ship, and its crew could die, or not, as events dictated.

Behind him he heard Captain Noel, orchestrating her first combat. It was plain that she hated it, and that below the hate was a good, healthy dose of fear; like a born trooper, she forced order out of the chaos, carrying out her Admiral's orders without question. She realized, just below the level of conscious thought, that a moment's hesitation would let through the tide of doubts that only by main force of will she pushed back. Michael hoped that after the battle was over, she would be able to control her overworked emotions. More commanders by far collapsed after combat than during it; would Noel be strong? Michael thought so.

"Impact in twenty seconds," called a frightened radar operator.

"No maneuver until absolutely necessary." If he kept saying that in exactly the same tone of voice, it would at least give the bridge crew something to lean upon, something dependable. As long as the Admiral sits straight, unmoving, unmoved, the common crewman has no choice but to contain himself.

The missiles burst, timing their charges with electronic precision, aiming themselves so as to explode directly before the onrushing warship. Fireball after fireball blossomed, swelled, and slid past the Dreadnought with uncanny velocity.

"Maneuver!" Michael snapped. "Laser antimissile fire!" The time for playing dead was past. Transverse thrust altered their course, putting any extra distance possible between them and the deadly seed-pod warheads waiting ahead.

Lancing, swerving laser threads crossed and uncrossed, picking out their targets with deadly accuracy. Warheads died by the dozens, touched lightly by the swinging beams.

A cluster of four missiles burst as one just to the stern of the *Basilica*, and were left behind to burn uselessly, stepping stones to Michael's final victory.

Missiles swerving; missiles darting. Flames erupted, overlapping, incandescing away whole layers of armor plate. Radiation shielding decayed, saturated, letting the sleeting burst of deadly particles and high-energy photons through—though only in scattered places, while the rest of the ship enjoyed near-full protection.

The long seconds elapsed. Hurtling through the roiling barrage, the *Basilica* braved the stormy blast, at last to emerge, scarred, worse than scarred, beaten, savaged, living only due to the precise aim of its enemy, who only

wished it disabled, not destroyed. Its green-white engine
glow was stilled, the drive end battered beyond recovery.
All acceleration had been lost, leaving the ship to drift
along its highly eccentric hyperbolic orbit. Its velocity was
still high; unless another ship were to match courses and
take it in tow, the *Basilica* would be doomed to drift eter-
nally in a long cometary orbit around the star that was
Tikhvin's primary.

Along the ship's sides, craters and scars marked where
warheads had eaten into the armor plates. Pooling metal,
still quite warm, leaked from fissures, indicating where
the armor had failed. In three precise rows along the
wrecked flanks were the irregular hollows that had once
been gunnery and missile bays. Safety procedures had pre-
vented the ship's own missiles from detonating and adding
their energy to the general havoc. No such procedures
existed in the beam bays, where the ship's power plant directly fed power to the energy-gulping lasers. Hits in those
areas as often as not released the accumulated megawat-
tage to rampage for long milliseconds.

As the ship spun, slowly revolving around a meaningless internal axis, liquid fuel fell away from it, freezing
into ornate spirals in the vacuum. A halo of frozen atmosphere began to form: ship's air seeping from hundreds of
small crevices carved into the pressure hull.

"Are we alive?" asked Emily Young, speaking hesitantly in the total darkness that filled the command bridge
of the *Basilica*.

"Yes, Commander, we are alive." The voice could only
belong to Admiral Michael Devon.

"Are we likely to stay that way?" Young identified the
speaker as Captain Ruth Noel, and from her voice she was
somewhere on the deck. Young moved to aid her Captain.

"With the emergency power down," Commander Bolsa
said from the forward part of the bridge, "we'll have from
eight to eighteen hours to live."

"With emergency survival procedures?" Noel asked.

"We can probably extend that virtually indefinitely,"
Bolsa said, quietly yet honestly. "This is a huge ship, even
if it's taken a hell of a beating."

"On the other hand," Michael said portentously, "now it's our turn."

Noel and Young each sighed, knowing better than to say anything.

From the stern of the death-silent ship, all personnel on the command bridge heard the clanging impact of a small explosion. "What the . . . ?" exclaimed Young. The time for subsidiary explosions was far past, and with the power plant at cold shut-down, the only dangers were freezing, suffocating, and radiation exposure.

"That was probably the loading port door to the missile magazine being blown loose." Michael's voice sounded as puzzled as anyone else's, and yet he seemed to know what was happening.

Two minutes later a series of five irregular thumping impacts was discernible from astern.

"Good. Good enough." Michael's voice was subdued, but triumphant.

"Be so good as to explain," suggested Young.

"We may have no missile launchers left," Michael said, "but we do still have missiles. I left a team in the magazine with orders to push a few out an open airlock, targeted on the base below."

"Without launchers—" Young began, and cut herself off.

"Considering that we're drifting, weightless, is there any reason that a missile couldn't launch itself?"

Young had no answer.

The *Basilica* drifted, moving through three hundred kilometers every second. At that speed, its shadow would pass completely across the dark gravel face of Tikhvin in roughly fifty seconds. Already it was well within the orbiting ring of Monitor stations; as it emerged from the ring on the other side, the Monitors could, if ordered, easily destroy it. Without engines, defenses, or more of its armor, nothing could save it. Stopping it, however, was beyond the capabilities of the four orbiting stations that would pass nearest its path.

They could neither stop nor destroy the five missiles that drifted loose from it. For a long moment these weapons paralleled the orbital path of the ship, until with a flash they activated themselves and added a transverse

vector to the huge velocity bequeathed them by their
launching body. In just over seven minutes they would
place themselves in front of the planet, to smash into it at
extremely high speed.

At such speeds even the most tenuous atmosphere is
extraordinarily dense; the missiles needed to survive for
three-hundredths of a second for them to penetrate the
densest ten kilometers of air. The following multi-megaton
thermonuclear explosions would easily take out the naval
base, the landing field, and all personnel in the area.

Admiral de la Noue, Michael was sure, was doomed beyond hope of redemption.

Aboard the *Philomela* and below on the planet Tikhvin,
the launch was observed and understood. Radio messages
flashed back and forth between Steldan, de la Noue, Captain Thornton . . .

And Lieutenant Jaquish, leader of the ad hoc squadron
known as the "artful dodgers."

"Piece of cake," he reassured them, admiring his polished new rank chip. *Lieutenant Commander,* he reflected.
Not bad. Not bad at all.

"Well, gentlemen," he said into his radio mouthpiece,
addressing the nineteen members of his squadron, "it
seems that we're all that stands between the Grand Admiral and five missiles. They'll be coming in fast—how fast,
your radar should already be telling you—so you won't
have more than one shot. We'll break into five formations
of four craft each. You should know who your partners
are." From beneath his seat he pulled his jar of "brine."
"Give it your best shot, guys. Tallyho." Relaxing, he drank
deeply. *Not bad at all.*

There was no mere luck involved, of course. He himself
had proposed the idea—taking a group of volunteers in fast
Fighters and trying to get ahead of the plunging *Basilica*—in his interview with Captain Thornton of the *Later.*

"We've found the bombs, you know," he'd said, smiling
disarmingly.

Despite his frown, Captain Thornton had been contem-
plative. "We've found some bombs, agreed. Have we found
them all?"

"Why would anyone bomb a Fighter more than once?"

All wide-eyed innocence, masking his wider-eyed inso-
lence, Lieutenant Jaquish made his points sound obvious
without really trying. To him, everything *was* obvious,
whether it was true or not.

"It could be dangerous."

"No flight is without hazards. You were a pilot; you
should know."

"The risk—"

Straightening, Jaquish saluted. "I volunteer, sir." Wink-
ing, he added, "Surely you can find others."

"But—"

"Time is slipping by, sir. I think we can catch up,
though, if we really try."

Thornton forced himself to a decision. "All right. Get to
your craft. I'll make the call for volunteers immediately."

"Very good, sir."

Jaquish was amazed that nineteen others had the courage to follow.

"Didn't your mothers tell you about the military and
about volunteering?"

"You just want the glory for yourself," good-naturedly
jeered one of the pilots.

"Me? I'm as modest a person as can be found. Maybe
even more so."

"You also have a reputation for taking care of your
wingmen," the volunteer said, his voice suddenly serious.

"Only when they owe me money," Jaquish quipped.

The missiles descended at over three hundred kilometers per second. They would be in each Fighter's field of
fire for less than seven ten-thousandths of a second.

Each one was stopped substantially short of the planet's
surface.

"Watch your exhaust, Rick," Jaquish snapped over his
radio link. "You're not in an atmosphere, you know."

"I missed the missile," Rick almost wailed.

"Yeah, I know. I caught it. There's not enough left of the
cheap thing to stuff in an envelope."

"I thought—"

"The Jaquish is quicker than the eye. Remember that
when playing at dice with me."

"Yes, sir."

"How did the others do?"

Four team leaders called in their affirmative hits. Jaquish relaxed. He'd been sure of his kill, but had to depend on luck for the other four.

Finishing off his jar and tossing it carelessly over his shoulder, he signaled the recall. "Let's go home, guys, and have something to drink."

Chapter Twenty-Two

The *Philomela*, at last repaired, matched courses with the wreckage of the *Basilica* after a full day of acceleration and deceleration. With the Dreadnought secured by gravitic tow lines, it began a careful turnover that would, over the next several days, bring the two ships safely to Tikhvin.

Aboard the *Basilica*, Captain Noel met the detachment of Marines led by Commodore Steldan and General Vai. Michael stood and likewise saluted the guard.

"Michael," Steldan greeted.

"Am I an Admiral of the fleet?"

"No longer."

" 'Mr. Devon' will suffice in that case." Staff-straight he stood, his arms at his sides, hands carefully and tensely open. His face was unreadable, his pale blue eyes expressionless. His blond hair framed his square features, moving slightly to the breeze from the repaired air circulators. His bright blue and white duty uniform, straight in front, pleated in back, broad in the shoulders, gave him an almost cheerful aspect, which exactly counterpointed his grim attitude. For a moment it seemed to Steldan that it was from the uniform that Michael drew his strength, and that without it, he would be irretrievably diminished.

With an effort, Steldan read the charges; all his instincts cried out that the man be spared further pain. *Hasn't he been punished enough?*

A curt nod. A dry half-smile. "Anything else?"

The smile was sadly returned. "It will do the job."

Escorted by the grim detachment of polished Marines, Michael Devon departed.

* * *

Joan Rogers sat at her station, abstractedly preparing the final version of the after-mission report. Her fingers flew over the keyboard while her eyes flicked over the hard copy to her right. She'd read and reread the same material so many times that the words had become meaningless to her, and the events portrayed seemed more like something she'd heard of third-hand rather than something she'd participated in.

The last page slid up the datascreen, and the last line. Against her will, she sobbed, gaspingly, and slumped back in her chair.

Arbela Sh'in, to her right, turned quickly, and hesitated, unsure for the moment how to act.

Joan noticed this, and struggled for control. "I'm all right. I'll be okay. I just . . ."

"Come along, Joan. Walk with me to the lounge and have a sandwich. C'mon." Her businesslike attitude helped; the fact that she actually cared made all the difference.

"Most of the crew is below, on the planet," Sh'in mentioned offhandedly. "We'll have the lounge to ourselves."

In that she was wrong. Waiting there were Captains Edwards and Engel. Although by now Joan had regained control of her emotions, it was evident to the pair that something was amiss.

They sat together at a table, and Sh'in brought over a tray of sandwiches, soft drinks, and snacks. Taking nothing for herself, she gently insisted that Joan eat something. Joan halfheartedly tried to comply.

"You've heard?" she whispered.

"I've heard."

Edwards and Engel nodded unhappily.

"Why—why?"

"There was no other choice. He himself would have approved."

Joan looked up, shocked.

"It's true," Sh'in continued soothingly. "Who was always the first to speak of honor? Of duty? Of courage?"

"You're mocking him."

"I probably am." She lapsed into silence. *Michael, gone? Who'll hold the universe together?*

"But she's right," Engel put in. "He knew, more than any of us, that the military is run on discipline. The standards are harsh. So very harsh."

Joan looked at Edwards, as if daring him to agree. He grimaced apologetically. "It's true," he muttered, looking away. Regaining his courage, he added, "For one of his subordinates, even me, he would have moved world and stars, as long as he received unswerving loyalty. His sense of honor was of a sort we're unused to. Because we didn't offer him what he demanded, he looked down on us as less than fully loyal. But if we'd needed him, nothing would have stopped him from aiding us."

Joan stared at the table. "None of this saved him."

"He knew it could not."

"It's not fair!"

" 'Those that search for Justice: a saddened path is theirs.' "

Joan turned away. *I learned one thing from Admiral Michael Devon: that to disobey orders is right and proper sometimes. I disobeyed him, and he died for it.*

I loved him.

Not long thereafter she left, still hurting. Forgetfulness would be long in coming to her.

Captain Norman found himself reclining in the cool comfort of a hospital bed. Above him, an air outlet whispered, gently blowing cool air across the room. The antiseptic white of the small private area was broken only by the gleaming silver of various fixtures, and by the dark hair of the woman dozing in a chair to his right.

Now who might that be? he wondered, and experimentally cleared his throat.

Captain Noel raised her head, noting after a moment that Norman was awake. "Hi."

"Hello." He left unasked the several questions that sprang to mind.

"I dropped in to see how you were," Noel explained lamely. "I must have been more tired than I realized."

"Have no fears," Norman said, grinning, purposely misinterpreting her statement. "I am the perfect gentleman. Besides which, I can't move any part of me beneath my arms."

Noel smiled. "I get to be the first one to tell you, then: you'll have full use of your back and legs in only a few weeks."

"Well, now. Thank you. I hadn't even had time to become properly concerned. How about you, and have we met?"

"Captain Ruth Noel, of the *Basilica.*" Impishly, she enjoyed the mixed emotions that passed across Norman's expressive face.

"Where are we, then?"

"In the hospital at the base on Tikhvin."

"My fleet?"

She informed him. Approximately a third of the men and women that had left Triangle Sector with him were now dead.

He eyed her sourly. "I think, then, that your company has lost its charm for me. Be so good as to leave."

Noel stood, face suddenly grim. "I was as much a victim as you were. Your Cruisers killed almost as many of my crewman. If you wish, I'll leave. I'd hoped to begin afresh."

"As I have no one else to talk to, perhaps you may stay," Norman muttered ungraciously. "Speak on. Tell me what happened."

She resumed her seat. Speaking quietly, she explained the battle, telling of her part in it and emphasizing her lack of control over the tactical decisions made.

"Only acting under orders, eh? A pitiable excuse." He sighed. "I myself have none better. How did you fare?"

"I lost a kidney to blood poisoning from radiation exposure. The artifical replacement is adequate, if not ideal."

Norman was impressed. The poor woman had been through much. "What are its chief failings?" he asked, somewhat at a loss for words.

"I'm not allowed strong drink, and right now the sutures itch furiously."

"No strong drink? Never to savor the grand draft, the bottle? No grog? No *branwac?* No hooch?"

Amused, Noel shook her head.

"Ah, lass, had I but known, I never would have opened fire." His eyes flashed. "Speaking of the grog . . ." He raised his eyebrows significantly, and pretended to look around.

Noel nodded. "I'll see what I can do."

"More than that I never would dare ask."

All in all, it was a successful afternoon.

Grand Admiral de la Noue tagged Commodore Steldan in a packed corridor and took him aside. "Busy?"

He glanced at his watch. "Not really."

"Come along." She led the way to a corridor that gave onto four large auditoriums. One conference was just breaking up, letting a flood of officers loose into the hallway. She opened the doorway fifteen meters down the hall, peeked inside, and beckoned to Steldan.

The room slanted gently downward toward the front; two dozen rows of comfortable chairs faced the lectern. Except for the two, the room was deserted.

"The Praesidium finally made a decision: exoneration," de la Noue announced, smiling.

"Was it Redmond's vote, or Wallace's, that swung it?"

"Both. It was a real decision; I'm now a member again."

"Congratulations." Steldan's relief was almost as great as was his pleasure.

"One of these days," de la Noue said jokingly, "I've got to get myself a power base."

Steldan grimaced. "The biggest fleet in the history of the race, and it isn't enough?"

"Not when there are Admirals like Michael Devon—" She cut herself off. "Sorry. Not funny."

"I expect there'll be 'Admiral Devon' jokes circulating in the Navy for a good many years." Steldan's dismissal of the indelicacy hung in their minds for a long moment.

"If only . . ."

" 'If I had only known, and acted in good time . . .' "

"You're one for quotes today, aren't you?"

Steldan hung his head.

"Come along; cheer up."

"Yes, ma'am." Steldan endeavored to smile.

Over the craggy hills and badlands of Tikhvin an acrid wind blew hot. Dust rose in gritty whorls as black sand sifted between sharp rocks. Every day the air was slightly more breathable, and every day the searing heat was less.

At the base of a jagged pinnacle, the rocks were covered by a tentative patch of green.

BIO OF A SPACE TYRANT
Piers Anthony

"Brilliant...a thoroughly original thinker and storyteller with a unique ability to posit really *alien* alien life, humanize it, and make it come out alive on the page."

The Los Angeles Times

Widely celebrated science fiction novelist Piers Anthony has written a colossal new five volume space thriller—**BIO OF A SPACE TYRANT:** *The Epic Adventures and Galactic Conquests of Hope Hubris.*

VOLUME I: REFUGEE   84194-0/$2.95
Hubris and his family embark upon an ill-fated voyage through space, searching for sanctuary, after pirates blast them from their home on Callisto.

VOLUME II: MERCENARY   87221-8/$2.95
Hubris joins the Navy of Jupiter and commands a squadron loyal to the death and sworn to war against the pirate warlords of the Jupiter Ecliptic.

VOLUME III — Coming Soon

ALSO BY PIERS ANTHONY:

BATTLE CIRCLE	67009-5/$3.95
CHAINING THE LADY, CLUSTER II	61614-9/$2.95
CLUSTER, CLUSTER I	81364-5/$2.95
KIRLIAN QUEST, CLUSTER III	79764-X/$2.50
MACROSCOPE	81992-9/$3.95
MUTE	84772-8/$3.95
OMNIVORE, ORN I	82362-4/$2.95
ORN II	85324-8/$2.95
OX, ORN III	82370-5/$2.95
THOUSANDSTAR, CLUSTER IV	80259-7/$2.75
VISCOUS CIRCLE, CLUSTER V	79897-2/$2.95

AVON Paperbacks